A TASTE OF LOVE

"Nia, you're a very nice young lady and very beautiful." Pausing, he stared at her. "And somehow I feel us . . . ." Roland searched for the right word.

"Being drawn to each other?"

"Exactly."

"I feel it, too. But it can't be."

His expression said why not, even if he didn't express it verbally.

"Roland, look, I don't want a man like you."

Highly offended, he reared his head back. "Oh, you don't." He liked her honesty, but not that much.

"You're everything a woman could dream of," Nia elaborated. "Sweet, hardworking . . . and you're sexy. But I want a simple man. Simple. Not a rich man, but a man who won't leave me."

He couldn't help frowning. "Who said that a rich man would leave you?"

"You'll be with a lady like me for fun for a while, but when you realize you need something serious, you'll choose to be with someone like yourself, the one with the education, the status, the one who came from a well known family."

"That's not true, Nia. I had a woman who had all that, *all that*—but it didn't work out. But it's interesting to know you think so little of me. Goodnight, Nia."

He hurried up the stairs, leaving Nia standing in the center of the room. She hadn't meant to say what she did. She was simply trying to save herself. Roland had weakened her. With his lips brushing across hers, teasing her about all the lusciousness that could come, she had almost forgotten her vow— her vow to seek a man who was the opposite of the ones who broke her mother's heart.

Reviews About Louré Bussey's Novels

Love So True

Love So True is a fantastic can't-put-down romance filled with depth, emotion, conflict, drama and love ... Don't miss this one ladies, or you'll miss the treat of a lifetime.

—Romantic Times Magazine

Twist Of Fate

A moving story. You can feel the character's passion and pain, cherish their loyalties and hate their deceit.

—Rendezvous Magazine

Most Of All

Most Of All is a beautiful, tender love story set on the beautiful island of the Bahamas.

—Affaire de Coeur Magazine

Nightfall

Nightfall is packed with the passion, thrills and excitement that every woman craves for

—M. Mahan, Black Romance Magazine

A TASTE OF LOVE

LOURÉ BUSSEY

ARABESQUE
BOOKS

BET Publications, LLC
www.msbet.com
www.arabesquebooks.com

To My Angel, There are no words to thank a real, live angel when he comes along; there is only the love I hope you feel from me.

ARABESQUE BOOKS are published by

BET Publications, LLC
c/o BET BOOKS
One BET Plaza
1900 W Place NE
Washington, D.C. 20018-1211

First Printing: August, 1999
10 9 8 7 6 5 4 3 2 1

Printed in the United States of America

CHAPTER ONE

Nia Lashon stared into the unforgettable face of a woman who clearly had hated her for years, when both of them knew it should have been the other way around. Standing in front of Suzanne Greer was such a shock, Nia's heart harshly jerked her chest up and down as if she had been running and then suddenly stopped. Perspiration dotted the baby-hair that waved around her forehead, despite the crisp night air. And that queasy feeling creeping through her stomach hadn't bothered her since the last time she faced Suzanne.

Stepping out of the club at midnight, Nia anticipated her typical routine. She was grateful that twelve hours of serving cocktails was over, and had planned to go home, soak in a bubble bath and close her eyes. That's when she would wonder like she did every night, wondering how to change her life for the better. Having a job she loved always came to mind, along with an extravagant salary. There were other thoughts too during those moments of pampering, when after wondering, hoping, and planning, she drifted into fantasy.

Warm thoughts, womanly thoughts, thoughts that made her feel achingly alive, always further relaxed her. They were fantasies that she tried to convince herself weren't important to her happiness.

But now peering into Suzanne's embittered eyes, Nia knew as she drenched herself within her favorite raspberry-scented bubbles later, she wouldn't imagine dreams that rendered her breathless with longing for them. No. When she was alone tonight, bittersweet memories would be right with her. Facing Suzanne, Nia didn't understand why this person still made her so uneasy. One might have believed that just the day-today intricacies of striving to get ahead in life and find happiness would have pushed the past so far in the back of her mind that nothing could ever immerse her in any of its emotion again. How wrong she was.

"How are you?" Nia asked, trying to soften her old friend's expression with a little smile. She knew it wasn't healthy for either of them to hold a grudge.

Suzanne's mauve glossed lips did curl amusedly to one side, even if her gaze remained cold on the eyes whose unusual shape she considered strange, rather than *sensuously exotic* as someone had alluded to them in the past.

"I'm absolutely wonderful," she replied. "I have all sorts of successful business ventures taking place, and I have a man in my life who is crazy about me." Pausing, her eyes glided slyly from Nia's head to her toes. "Too bad about what happened though . . . you know? But I guess things happen for a reason." French manicured fingers tugged up a fur collar nearer to Suzanne's neck. "Don't you think so?"

Unsure if Suzanne was touching on a sensitive subject to humiliate her, Nia avoided the question. They needed to steer this conversation into another direction.

Her eyes drifting over Suzanne's squared face, framed by short, flawlessly layered tresses, she remarked, "You look good." Her full lips swirled up in an affirming grin. "And it's good to hear your life is going well."

"And you?" Suzanne glimpsed up behind Nia. The Big Boys International Club glowed in white lights on the marquee. To her astonishment, she had spotted Nia exiting the swanky establishment as she was about to enter it. Instantly Suzanne assessed the plain style of the wool coat Nia was wearing, along with the lack of jewelry, and concluded that Nia definitely wasn't a patron entertaining with a member of the aristocratic men's club. Whatever she was doing with her life, she was still poor. Fond of that possibility, Suzanne intended to make her feel horrible about it. "Out on the town tonight?"

"No," Nia said, fixing a loose clip on the side of her hair. "I work here actually. I'm a—"

"Don't tell me you're trying that singing thing again?" Suzanne cut her off. Suzanne's lip quivered like she wanted to laugh. "I know some people who can really—I mean really sing and even they say it's a hard field to get into."

Nia couldn't smile anymore. "I'm a waitress actually."

"A waitress?" Suzanne's penciled brows flew up.

Nia was offended by the look on her face. "It's a honest, decent profession."

It's just the low wages and crap I have to put up with in there that makes it unbearable.

"A waitress, *here?*" With her nose squiggled up, Suzanne glanced at the entrance. Shifting her deep-set eyes back to Nia, she was smirking. "Don't they make you wear skimpy uniforms? Classy as Big Boys' reputation may be for all the sports and business consorting, that's what I heard about this place."

"It's true." Nia slid her purse high on her shoulder. "We wear seductive uniforms."

Suzanne's lip quavered again. "I see." However, another thought that wasn't so funny swiftly sapped her amusement away.

Strained silence lingered in the February air as Nia realized that Suzanne hadn't lost her touch in skillfully insulting her. Nothing cordial on Nia's part had softened her old friend toward her. Mystifying to Nia was that something in her old pal's face was more malicious. She never understood the reason for the hatred, jealousy, or whatever it was that Suzanne harbored for her. If anything, Suzanne should have pitied her. Pitied her cursed luck in life. And Nia knew it was a petty, immature wish, but there were those days once in a while. Days when she couldn't help envisioning that she ran into her pretend-friend from junior high and high school, and amid their exchange of catching up on their lives, Nia would share with Suzanne that her life was incredibly blissful. That everything she envisioned for her glorious future had come true. Reality was far away from those dreams.

The club had its moments of excitement and fun. It was paradise to many of the hard-working women employed there because they encountered fascinating, powerful, and wealthy men. Nia couldn't deny its thrill when she first started working there three years ago. Nonetheless, after some interesting episodes, her definition of excitement had changed.

"I chit chat with Monell and Jackie from time to time," Suzanne's voice lurked into the quiet.

"I talked to them last week," Nia said.

"Too bad they had to marry those twins," Suzanne added with a sour twist of her lips. "And they should never have left New York." She mingled her nails within the mink stroking her jawline.

Nia tugged her bag strap even higher on her shoulder. "They sounded really happy when I talked to them. Monell is even trying to get pregnant."

Suzanne shook her head. "They come from two different worlds than those losers. And don't believe that happily ever after image." With a sigh, her eyes rolled heavenward. "People put on airs. Don't you know that? But what I want to know is, are you *really* happy, Nia? Working *here?*"

Two thirty-something men leaving Big Boys' entrance distracted Suzanne, tempting Nia to turn around. Each guy innocently smiled at the two women.

Only Nia returned the smile, before focusing back on Suzanne. "That is how I make my living right now. But it's not what I plan to do with the rest of my life."

"It isn't?" Suzanne scratched the corner of her thin mouth, where a tiny mole was. "At this age a person's life is usually set. What they're doing then is probably what they're going to be doing forever.''

"I don't believe that. I'm only thirty-two, a year younger than you, Suzanne. And my life's work is not over by a long shot." She didn't know why her heart hadn't stopped racing since standing there. "I hope yours isn't either. That would mean there's nothing left for you to accomplish or to strive for."

To that, Suzanne hushed a minute, then glancing at another patron exiting the club, she commented, "I guess they give you good tips in those barely-there outfits?" In light of who was supposed to be in Big Boys that notion bothered her more than she showed.

"We aren't allowed to accept tips."

"That's too bad. Can't make much money on waitressing alone, can you?"

Not about to discuss her finances with Suzanne, Nia thought of an excuse to get away from her. "Were you going inside to meet someone?"

"Yes, that fine man of mine." Pride curled her lips. "But I assure you he's not there for ogling tacky costumes. I'm sure that's what he would call them too. No, his business associates brought him in as a member, and all in the matter of doing business, he accepted. They belong here, you see. He's extremely successful."

"That's nice." Nia started fumbling through her suede hand-bag for car keys.

"I only associate with successful men. Besides that, he's a looker too. He has this body that's out of this world, and sexy, dark eyes that look like they're seeing right through you, and this thick, curly, black hair that matches his mustache, and this adorable, little earring in his ear too. Think you might have seen anyone fitting that description?"

Nia reached her keys, but lost them as she stiffened. There was no way she could have missed him. Three weeks ago he had accompanied some regular members of the club. Nia wasn't assigned to their table that night. Regardless, at every location in the room where she worked, upon glancing up, sexy, dark eyes were beckoning her. Eyes blazing with undeniable attraction and boasting excruciating bedroom pleasures. In no time, Kal Hunter introduced himself and asked her name. Thereafter, he was begging Nia to go out with him, or at least give him her home phone number. Super fine as she found him, Nia resisted. There was something about Kal that didn't feel right to her. It cautioned her to keep a distance. He was too slick, too anxious, too confident and bragged too much about his wealth. It was as if he presumed all women were gold diggers, and in his pursuit of her he was relying on that perception.

Despite his undesirable qualities, Nia was always pleasant to Kal, even in the way she expressed that she was unavailable. Nevertheless, Kal was relentless. The only reason he wasn't escorting Nia to her car tonight was because three gentlemen had practically nailed him to the table during a business meeting. She knew as much because he whispered in her ear upon serving them cocktails. Added to it, he asked if she could wait around for him. Never had he mentioned a girlfriend.

"No, I haven't seen anyone like that," Nia lied, and made a step away from Suzanne. "It's really late. I better get going." She shuffled several more steps away. "Take care."

"So long," Suzanne told her. She watched Nia closely until she faded from sight.

Letting the car engine warm up, Nia was too entrenched in her mind to drive away immediately. Gently she leaned her head on the side of the window and pictured herself standing before the entrance of Big Boys with Suzanne. Why did Suzanne hate her? Every look, every sly comment, every gesture assured that she did. God knows, it should have been the opposite way around. Rather than despising Suzanne however, for the unforgettable in their past, Nia was always aggravated by her whenever their paths crossed. Just aggravated. That is until tonight. Now there was another brew mixed with her feelings.

In all sincerity Nia was glad Suzanne was doing well. She was always inspired and uplifted by anyone's success. With all the negativity in the world, to her it was a torch of light and hope among the darkness. It made her feel good to see someone doing well. It nourished her spirit for her own achievement. That being as it may, tonight she felt odd. Odd because she couldn't stop comparing herself to her old chum. Nia felt she worked as hard as Suzanne probably did, and tried as best she could to do the right things. So why then whenever she trudged on that uphill road to success, something was always sneaking out from the side, snatching her back down to the bottom again? Even finding true love was an impossible dream. All that kept her going was her faith, that voice inside, God's voice inside speaking to her, strengthening her with *"Keep on, Nia. Just keep on and I'll show you heaven on earth."*

Opening the glove compartment, Nia removed an orange candy, unwrapped it and was about to plop it on her tongue when a pecking presence at the window startled her. She jumped aside before looking at the glass.

"Hello, beautiful." Kal Hunter's smooth baritone voice was a seductive mixture of sophistication and urban cool.

Pressing a button that rolled the glass down, Nia returned with "Hello." Subtly she looked around to see if Suzanne was nearby.

Kal leaned over in the window. "Heading home?"

Champagne breath blew over at her. "Yes. Can't wait to get there and get cozy."

"Can I come?" He flashed a wide, frisky smile.

Playfully Nia twisted her mouth. "Sorry."

His gaze strayed sideways with his disappointment, then roamed back over to the alluring heart-shaped face surrounded by glistening, relaxed hair.

"I couldn't keep my eyes off you in the club," he admitted. "Up close, this view is even better." Baring how much he wanted her with his look, his longing lingered in his eyes. Like the outer corners of Nia's eyes were pulled upward in play to reveal a seductress, their natural exoticness turned him on from the instant he saw her. There was also that shapely rest of her body. Kal hadn't stopped thinking about her since that night, and it was no secret why Big Boys was suddenly his favorite place to be. "You are so damn fine," he uttered, his lustful fascination dropping to her full mouth. Colored with a lipstick that appeared raspberry to him, he ached to discover if it tasted like it looked: delicious. "You look good enough to eat."

"Are you always full of such provocative compliments?"

"For a sweet, sexy creature like you, I am."

"How do you know I'm sweet?" She was having fun with him. "I can be mean and evil when I want to."

"Naw, you're not mean and evil. I'm very observant. Kal Hunter Jr. doesn't miss a thing. I see how you interact with people in the club. And everybody likes you. Especially me." His voice grew raspy. His heated gaze plunged below her neck and wound back up to slowly savor each exotic feature.

Getting nervous from his scrutiny, Nia moved the gear in drive. "I have to go now." She looked ahead, clutching the steering wheel.

Kal touched her chin, curving her face toward him. "Not now." Dark, sensual eyes skidded over her. They did seem to see through her like Suzanne had said. "Don't go now."

"I have to go now." She swerved her head out of his fingers, but couldn't thwart the force of his stare.

"I heard you last night."

"Heard me?"

"Singing."

Surprised, Nia swung back a bit. She quickly thought back. The previous night she had worked the late shift, ending up alone, except for a security guard stationed outside for the later AM. hours. Waiting around to punch out, she tidied the place, straightened napkin holders, candles and all else that was out of the club's posh order. As she did this, a slow jam attached with succulent memories simply flowed from her. Strange as it was, it was the first time she'd sung in a long time. And did she sing. Sang her heart out, believing that no one was listening. Now knowing that someone had eavesdropped on her, she was embarrassed.

"Where were you? I didn't know anyone else was in the club." She switched the gear back in the park position.

"I wasn't in it . . . not really in it. You see, I was at a party yesterday, and after it was over I swung over to Big Boys . . . to check you out of course." He dabbed at his mustache. "But it was closing, and I tried to slip past the guard outside. But he wouldn't let me any farther than the foyer. That's when we heard you. Both of us were knocked out by your voice. I was going to wait around for you to tell you how much I liked it, but unfortunately I was beeped. A supposed emergency." He paused, recalling how that crazy Suzanne had made him rush to her condo by lying about having an accident. Too bad she really hadn't tumbled down the stairs, he had joked with himself afterward. "Anyway, the important thing is that I know you can sing your pretty little . . ." Naughtily, he grinned. "Well, I'll just say you can sing *it* off. And that's all the more reason I know we have to get together. It's fate that I heard you."

"Why is that?" She was hiding how good the compliment made her feel.

"Don't you remember what I told you?"

Barely, thought Nia. He might have mentioned something about writing a song, but she heard so much during the unfolding of a night, hardly anything stuck with her. Guys were endlessly telling her spectacular tales to try to get her in bed. "I remember you telling me something about writing songs."

"*Something?* Baby, if you go to any record store in this country—any one—you'll find my name on the backs of the albums and CDs. I've written songs for many popular artists. I've arranged, produced, played keyboards. You name it, I've done it. Done it for years. Started when I was twenty and have been doing it for almost eighteen years."

"How come I've never heard of you?"

"Because lots of times you never hear about the behind the

scenes people who are the real ones making stuff happen. But the name Kal Hunter is going to be out there real soon. Recently I've been in business negotiations for my own label. *Mine.* There's a major record company who'll be the parent of the venture, ensuring generous financing and worldwide distribution. Those are the guys I've been meeting with at Big Boys. And when I have the deal sealed, you're the first artist I want to sign."

"No thank you."

His mouth dropped open. "Girl, are you mad? I mean out of your mind?" He shifted his feet while still leaning in the car's window.

"Not at all. Your so-called label isn't a sure thing."

"It's about as sure as I am about wanting to get next to you." He stared at her so hard, Nia had to look away. "And if you just give me a chance I'll show you how *amazing* I can be in *every way.*" His hand slipped in the car, finding hers.

She wiggled out of his grip. "I know you have a girlfriend, Kal."

"What?"

She watched a frown seep over his handsome features. "Matter of fact, I know her."

"You know her?" Now looking somewhat angry, he reared back. "How could you know someone that doesn't exist?"

"Her name is Suzanne."

"Oh, brother." He clutched the side of his head. "How do you know about that nut?"

The snub to Suzanne stunned Nia. According to Suzanne, they were so in love. "We . . . ah . . . so—you do know her?"

"Suzanne and I used to date a few months back," he explained with annoyance. "Had to cut that loose though. Yeah, had to do that." He sighed, shaking his head. "Whooh, talk about possessive. Plus, she's just not my type."

Nia wondered which one was lying. "I know Suzanne from junior high and high school days. Growing up, we also lived a few blocks from each other. And tonight we ran into each other as she was about to go inside the club tonight—*to see you.*"

"And I told her to stop following me when she found me," he stressed irritably. "Are you two best friends or something?"

"We used to hang out with the same group of girls." Her heart always warmed, thinking of Jackie and Monell. "I would consider *them* my best friends."

"But not Suzanne?"

There was a flicker of the past, of how Suzanne treated her years back, of the way she hurt her most. "No. We're not best friends."

"Forget her then!" Kal looked relieved.

"I had. So much stuff has gone on in my life, she rarely crossed my mind. But if she's your girlfriend I'm not getting involved with you. And even if she isn't, I'm still not. As I told you before, Kal, I'm unavailable. And it's interesting when I tell you that—that you never even asked if I have someone, a husband, a boyfriend, or mostly a reason for not going out with you."

"Reasons can be kicked to the curb. As for boyfriends and husbands, they can too. I don't give a damn about them. What do they have to do with me?" His nostrils flared with his hardening expression. "Nobody is going to get in my way when I want a woman. And I want you, Nia. That's all there is to it."

"Didn't your mother ever tell you, you can't have everything you want?"

In response, Kal merely studied her. While he did, Nia hoped he now understood she wasn't for sale pending the right price. Based on his apprising her of his bank figures, she was certain that's what he assumed. And sure, like most women, Nia would be thrilled when the right man came along and lavished her with presents. She imagined that a man who was in love with a woman, and who showered her with gifts of affection, was extremely wonderful. But a man who wanted to buy her reminded her too much of her childhood. Her mother always received presents, but never love. Nia knew she deserved better than that.

"You're saying all that now," Kal told her with a thick raised brow. "But you'll change your mind about me." He paused as an idea formed in his mind. "I'm going to show you something. Yeah. You'll see what I can do for you. I can change your life!" The words rang like a commercial. "What shift do you work tomorrow? This time, or the later one?"

She hesitated, even if his conviction did pique her interest. "The later one."

"Perfect. If you just tell that security guard to let me in, we can be alone so I can show you something you'll find very exciting."

"Something that has to do with music?" She observed the little ball earring in his ear sparkling.

"Instead of answering that, I could show it to you now if you let me. Come to my place."

"No way."

"Have coffee with me then and I'll explain it? Let's go to that café around the corner, the one with the little jukeboxes in the booth seats. Maybe they'll have one of my songs on their boxes."

"No."

"I gave you my number before and you never called. Let me call you then? Give me your number?"

"That's not a good idea."

Ignoring her rebuff, Kal scribbled her name on the back of his business card. He thrust the paper toward her with a pen. "Put your number on there. That's all you have to do and the world will look so different in the morning."

Nia glanced at the paper, then Kal, before shifting the lever to drive. "Have a good night, Kal."

The Toyota drove off, blending into the four lane avenue and between two yellow cabs.

"Damn!" Kal cursed, shoving the card down in his overcoat pocket. After a minute of reflection, a smile eased onto his face. "I don't care what you say, I'll impress you all right. Tomorrow, you just wait."

Stepping beyond the marble doors of the skyscraper that housed his penthouse, Kal was greeted by the doorman, then stirred aimlessly before three elevators. Soon riding one up, bypassing towering lobby trees that were viewed from its glass cylinder cast, he recreated Nia's gorgeous features in his mind and reflected about things she said to him.

As much as she rejected him, he still yearned desperately for her body. That was surprising to him. Women were a subject he always received an A for. On the infrequent chance that one was playing hard to get, Kal wasted no time in moving on to the next object of his desire.

As a poor teenager living in Harlem, the opposite sex succumbed to him because of his striking looks and honeyed words. When he became an adult, achieving wealth via his musical brilliance, ladies that he desired more often than not were charmed straight into his jumbo-sized waterbed because of the same combination, but also the money.

Getting off the elevator, swaggering with his urban style along a lush, green carpeted hallway, he was imagining how awestruck Nia would be tomorrow, when thumps behind him halted his tracks and whirled him around. With her thin lips tilted flirtatiously to one side, Suzanne was coming towards him.

"I missed you," she confessed, strolling so close to Kal she could practically taste the champagne on his breath.

"Didn't I tell you earlier to stop following me?" Shaking his head, he turned his back to her, walking ahead to his door. "What the hell do you want?"

She followed, nearly bumping into him when he stopped. "I want you."

He spun around. "Why can't you process what I've been telling you? I know you're smart."

Gazing up at him, her deep-set eyes hid none of her longing.

And as she stepped closer, the spicy musk oil scent exuding from his collarbone, wafting about her senses, awakened titillating memories of her once massaging the warm oil all over his bare, muscular body.

"I'm not in the mood for this, Suzanne. I'm tired. I want to go to bed. *Alone.*" He turned toward the door.

She grabbed him by his coat sleeve. "We need to talk about us."

Peering at her over his shoulder, he yanked himself out of her grasp. "We did all our talking at the club and before that too. I don't want to see you anymore. That's all there is to it."

"You're just mad because I did a few things."

"You did *a lot* of things!" he said, facing her again. "Correcting my English. Trying to tell me what fork to use at a restaurant. Telling me what to wear. Pushing me to take my earring out of my ear. But it's even more than those little silly things." He eased back a step. "It's like you think you're better than everybody else. But most of all, you're too damn possessive."

"I'll change my ways, Kal." Suzanne brought her body nearer, so near her soft breasts grazed his iron-hard chest.

Yet instead of Kal being aroused, which would have happened to him so easily before, he didn't have the slightest physical reaction to her. Attractive as Suzanne was to him, her desperation turned him off. Wanting nothing greater at that moment than for her to disappear, he realized she had to be handled another way.

"Look, baby," he said, softening his expression, but mostly his tone, "all that crap you do gets on my nerves. And I don't feel I have to put up with it right now. You know I'm starting my business, my empire, and that's where I need to concentrate. A lot of money is riding on it. So let's give each other some time and space, and maybe things will be different. But right now, I'm not looking for a relationship. So take care of yourself, okay? And maybe in a few months things will change. You never know what might happen with us."

Swiftly Kal reached in his overcoat pocket, carelessly and

hurriedly fumbling to reach his door key. Within moments, Suzanne faced a door that shut as softly as he had spoke to her upon their parting. But as she was about to walk away, she spotted something intriguing on the carpet, which made her kneel down to pick up. It was a business card. Kal's business card. On the blank side three letters were written: *Nia*.

CHAPTER TWO

A blue-green Caribbean sea. Nia sprawled by its shore while a blurry faced man held her, his warm, probing mouth brushing her ear, whispering erotic words of his fantasies to pleasure her body with intolerably sweet ecstasy. This was a dream Nia wished to cling to when Saturday's sunshine spilled through her pink venetian blinds, nudging her awake.

It was a strain to see the clock through the bright rays. Nia did so anyway, while dragging herself back into a sitting position against the headboard. She read that the time was a quarter past noon. Knowing there were thousands of things she had to do today, she hoisted up a body that craved a massage. Stretching, yawning and sticking her feet in her slippers, she was awakened more by the lively sounds filtering in from outside her window.

Looking down from her apartment's fourth floor view, there were cars soaring down the Manhattan avenue. People were strolling about. And her neighbor was waxing his Jeep. The soulfulness of the Ojay's classic tune "Stairway To Heaven" streamed from his radio.

Swaying her curvy hips slowly, and gliding her head to the

torpid rhythm, Nia found herself singing along, her lyric soprano voice blending like a duet with the phenomenal lead vocalist. She felt like singing a lot lately.

After returning a call to a guy named Daryl, who she had gone on a date with the previous Saturday, Nia's stride lagged a bit when she mentally replayed their conversation and simply reviewed her love life. Cross-legged on the love seat with the receiver still warm in her hands, she plopped back into the flowery cushions, wondering why she let him get on her nerves with countless stories about his ex girlfriends and all the things that were wrong with them, their families, and their friends. That was his main rap during the date too.

Nia knew she didn't talk about her ex that much even if they did cross her mind from time to time. Aside from the one love that destroyed her in high school, there had been only two serious relationships in her life. One was with an accountant named Guy, who became crazily jealous and possessive. One strike across her cheek was all it took to let him know he needed to be by himself. The other involvement was with a struggling writer, who claimed to have loved Nia. In an obsessed pursuit of his dream, he just never had any time to spend with her. Nia loved both men, but neither as deeply as the one who had changed her entire view of love, and the world.

Forcing her thoughts away from her love life, Nia wrote checks for her two brothers college fees, for her own student loan payments and for other expenses. On the wind-up of those tasks, she caught a sale at a new mall, and attended to chores she neglected during the flurry of the week. Time swept by. As it did, there was a strange sensation she started to feel. Every stir she made, anything she did, it seemed to hang around, almost moaning over her.

Nia didn't know whether it had to do with running into Suzanne, or waking up several times throughout the night to contemplate Kal's proposition. Whatever the reason, the weird sensation endured into the later hours of the day and far into the night. Even as Nia dressed for her late shift at Big Boys, the feeling didn't go away. Most bizarre to her was that it was familiar. It was the same strange way she felt one day long ago.

A memorable day it was when Nia discovered that her mother wasn't merely the person who loved and nurtured her; she was a flesh and blood woman. One who longed to be desired and in love with a man. One who ached to feel the magic of a man being in love with her in return. Reflecting back, the sensation was warning her about what was to come.

On a freezing December morning so many years ago, a few weeks shy of Christmas, Nia woke up feeling *funny*. There was no other way to describe what it was like. Never had she felt that way before or since. As the day progressed, it tormented her by lingering on.

That night her mother Lauren went on a date with her boyfriend, Mr. Falcon. From the window, Nia giddily watched the sleekly dressed couple laughing themselves into his white sedan. Before long, the car blended into the ever-exuberant nightlife of New York City. When her mother returned home shortly after leaving, she arrived there by taxi. More peculiar was when Lauren Lashon made her first footstep in the house, somehow she didn't look like her mother to Nia. A dazed stranger gazed at Nia and her two brothers.

"We're not going to have presents this Christmas," her mother announced, sounding as unlike herself as she looked. "We're not going to have a lot of things any more. We may even get evicted if I can't get the money to pay this high rent." With the last prediction she let out a quick laugh that could have been mistaken for a cry.

Alarmed, devastated and not understanding anything about what her mother was saying, Nia asked, "Why?"

Not having Christmas presents didn't matter all that much. What did unsettle her was leaving the cozy brownstone home they'd been accustomed to and all the friends they had made in the neighborhood. The tiny boys echoed their sister's question, "Why?"

"Because your mama was a fool," their mother answered

calmly. Moving like an elderly woman, she pushed the door to her bedroom, letting it close gently behind her.

Nia and her brothers were frightened by the way their mother was acting and looking. They felt like parents concerned about their sick child. One of Nia's brothers went inside his mother's bedroom. Sleeping so soon after laying down, she was unable to be wakened. An empty bottle of sleeping pills was on the night table near her bedside.

Hours after her stomach was pumped at the hospital and her consciousness was completely regained, Lauren begged to speak to her daughter alone. Powerless to the tears flowing down her cheeks, Nia sat silent by her mother's bedside.

"Mr. Falcon broke up with me," she told Nia, her large, hazel eyes glazed with tears. "I was just trying to ease my pain taking the pills. Wasn't trying to kill myself. No, I wasn't trying to do *that*. I have too much to live for in you and your brothers. Just wanted to sleep a long time. And then when I woke up, maybe it wouldn't hurt so bad. Guess my taking too many pills shows I just wasn't thinking the right way. But I'm clearer right now than I've ever been.

"Darling, Mr. Falcon was paying for the rent on our house, for our clothes, our food, our furniture, even your school bills. He paid for everything. And since he did, I let him tell me what I could or couldn't do. That's why I didn't work. Didn't have a career or go to school. Because he didn't want me to. He controlled me. But so foolish I was, I thought I was controlling him by having him buy me everything and do everything for me. I even believed I had my heart out of the way.

"How wrong I was! When he wanted to break up with me, I didn't even think about the money. I thought about him not wanting me. Not loving me. Not anymore would he love me. No matter what I did. No matter how beautiful I am, or how good I treat him, he doesn't desire me anymore."

Lauren paused, picking up a handkerchief that lay on the covers and blotted it over her heart-shaped face that was identical to Nia's. Nia couldn't understand why someone wouldn't love her beautiful, sweet mother. So breathtaking she was, no one could keep count of all the men who wanted her. But even more alluring than that, she was warmhearted. It all made Nia yearn for her father. He died in the army just after her youngest brother was born. If only they were together, her mother wouldn't have even known Mr. Falcon. Her mother wouldn't have known the heartbreak the other men filled her with either.

"I'm telling you about this Nia, for a reason," her mother went on. "Don't let a man buy you for the right price. You might think you're getting over, but you're not. Always want more for yourself than that. Be with a man because you're his friend, because you're the woman he loves and respects.

"It doesn't matter how pretty you are when it comes to love. And my daughter, you are so beautiful. But beauty is not going to make a man love you forever. Catering to his desires won't keep him either. So don't depend on that to keep a man like I did.

"Do something with your life, child. Yes, you can't help being beautiful as you are, but with it build character, and make your dreams come true. *Dreams.* Have something you can do that's all yours. That way if someone ever tells you they don't love you anymore—you can always stand tall and go on— because you love yourself. *You love yourself!* Because your soul and your life is full of good things without them—and excitement and success waits in the future without him. And if you love yourself . . . one of these days you're going to be blessed with someone who can really love you too.

"He won't be like Mr. Falcon, who has a wife and who had me too. He won't be like those other men who made me their mistress. No. This man is already in your heart. God just has to steer him to you from out in that big old world, and when you meet you'll know—and he'll know that inside your heart is where he is supposed to be. I pray that he comes to you soon. I pray that he gives you what I've ached for. I pray that you experience a taste of love."

* * *

"I want to show you something."

With dawn moments away, Kal stood in Big Boys clutching a jumbo-sized portfolio, and peering at Nia. He was glad they were the sole two occupants in the club. She had been arranging the chairs around a table when his surprising appearance stopped her.

"How did you get in here?"

"I told you last night I had something to show you."

"Cornelius wouldn't have just let you in like that."

"Pretty lady, that so-called security guard would do anything I wanted him to after I slapped that crisp hundred dollar bill in his palm." Kal strode further into the club and nearer to Nia. "He was real happy too. Real happy. Said he was going to that twenty-four hour store down the block. The one that sells those fine spirits." He laid the portfolio on the table, all the while winding his eyes up Nia's legs. A student of hosiery, he was certain she was wearing french coffee.

"You think money is everything, don't you, Kal?"

"I'm in here, aren't I?"

Shaking her head, Nia had a sudden pain on the ball of her foot. Knowing it had to be caused by her spiked pumps, she plopped onto the velour cushions of the nearest chair. Slipping each shoe off, her eyes caught the bulging portfolio sprawled in front of her.

"So what do you have to show me so bad in there? Open it up then."

Delighted to oblige, Kal made himself comfortable in a chair opposite her. "I knew you would change your mind about singing on my label."

"I'm not changing my mind. I'm just curious about what's in there."

"Your curiosity shall be satisfied."

When the mystery bag was finally unzipped, Nia saw that it was stuffed with an assortment of interesting items: gold and platinum records, CDs, a few press clippings and awards. All were adorned with the name Kal Hunter.

"All this is very nice," Nia complimented him, repressing how impressed she was. Since Kal was already full of himself, she refused to give him any more for his arsenal. "You're very talented, Kal. You've wrote and produced some of my favorite songs."

She wasn't reacting the way Kal anticipated. Most women were extremely excited by his accomplishments. Nia was supposed to be all over him too, like he was God or gold.

"So?" he asked.

"So, what?"

"So are you going to sign with my label?" An arrogance tinged his tone. "You see what I can do for you. Superior production, songs, arranging and musicians. The best for that voice of yours."

Nia wasn't about to get involved with Kal in business. Obviously he would use it to his advantage for pleasure. She had too many responsibilities to waste time, create headaches and take chances. Besides, he couldn't guarantee anything.

"You don't even have a label yet," she told him. "And even if you did, it wouldn't be a good idea."

"You're wrong."

"No, I'm right. It's not like you just heard me singing and thought I was a terrific singer and wanted to sign me."

"It is like that."

"No, it isn't. Yes, you wanted to sign me. But all the weeks before you knew I could sing, you've been trying to get me in bed."

Amen, Kal thought with a grin.

"You're a beautiful woman, who I happen to be attracted to. What do you expect? I'm a healthy, hot-blooded man."

"See, that's a problem. Mixing business and pleasure." She shook her head. "It won't work."

"It could work. And what's so bad about us making love and creating music? It's not a bad combination."

"See, I knew that's what you wanted."

"I can give you anything, Nia. Anything you want. Money, a singing career, and . . ." He allowed his gaze to indulge freely in what he starved for the entire time sitting there—wandering over her entire healthy body. Returning to her eyes, he burned his into them. "And I can give you the meaning of *joy*. If you just give me a chance, you won't ever have to do a job that doesn't pay you enough or not appreciate you again."

"Your label isn't real yet, Kal. Plus, I just don't think—"

"Ssh," he cut her off. He placed his two middle fingers where his lips ached to be: an inch from hers. "Think about it overnight. I'll be back tomorrow night."

Moments after, Nia heard Kal laughing with Cornelius as he exited the club. Loud as Cornelius sounded, Nia was positive he had purchased some spirits and had sampled them too. The nerve of him doing that while on duty, Nia thought. *While guarding me.* Nevertheless, her tipsy security was quickly forgotten, faded by larger reflections of Kal. Throughout the silence that swiftly permeated the room, she pondered on the positives and negatives of his offer.

A hard thump in the rear of the club yanked her attention in that direction. Trying to remain calm, promptly Nia stood and scanned the room. No one was there. Nothing was unusual. Nia hurried out to Cornelius to inform him of the noise. If there was any investigating to be done, he was the one getting paid to do it.

Poking her head out of the admission door, she didn't see Cornelius standing guard in front of it. Much to the contrary, she saw him bouncing a little too much down the street toward his beloved store.

"I can't believe this man," she murmured to herself.

Now unconcerned about punching out at her appointed time, Nia hurriedly clocked out and gathered her coat and purse. She was more than happy to leave Big Boys, then she stopped and inhaled. She smelled smoke.

Surveying her surroundings, she detected that it was coming from the back, where the thud came from. Trailing the increasing fumes was the sound of crackling, which soon became unmistakably, fire. Her heart racing, Nia didn't know whether to try and put it out, call the fire department, or just flee and phone for help outside.

The smoke burgeoned, clouding the room she was in, burning into her throat, making her cough, taunting her with advancing baby yellow and red flames. Scrambling to get out the door, she screamed when the knob wouldn't turn. The door wouldn't move. Harder she wrenched the knob, yanked it, kicked the door, all the while glancing back. Tenaciously, an inferno was working its way to the front.

His eyes bloodshot, Cornelius wallowed on the ground outside of where he used to work. He was in the midpoint of an enormous crowd that had gathered. Astonishment over every face, they had watched Big Boys burn completely down. It amazed him that the firemen were unsuccessful in salvaging the ritzy establishment. For nine months he had been employed there.

His heart felt lighter knowing they had rescued the girl. Deeply he regretted straying from his post. Perhaps Nia wouldn't have been trapped in there if he hadn't left. Furthermore, if a probe revealed that an arsonist set the fire, he could possibly face more woes for negligence. More disheartening, after the commotion of Nia's rescue, the police called Cornelius aside from the mass of people. For nearly a hour they questioned him. When they finished, he went to check on Nia in the ambulance. A medic informed him she had insisted on removing the oxygen mask and removing herself. According to them, she strolled off in a daze.

Coughing repeatedly and nearly breathless, Nia had passed her Toyota three times before realizing how disoriented she was. After sliding onto the cloth seats, attempting to absorb her close brush with death, and wondering who or what had

caused the fire, she had to confront another tragic factor: she
didn't have a job.

In the heat of her panic, she reached in her purse for Kal's
business card. Perhaps she could find a way to work with him
without doing the unthinkable and without putting him in a
great position of power over her. Anything was possible and
she was desperate. Yet upon taking the card out, staring at his
name written so boldly across it, Nia knew that calling Kal
wasn't the right thing to do. After all, his record label wasn't
a sure thing yet, and she needed something real and tangible
to survive on: money. Doing anything for it was out of the
question. If she did the right things, the money would come.
Success would come. If she was really blessed . . . one day
love would too.

Cruising down the avenue in a month old Jaguar, listening
to his favorite R&B radio station, Kal rocked his head and sang
very off-key with the music. All that enticed him away from
the seduction of the sexy ballad was the fire engine and police
cars racing by in the opposing lane. Some time earlier, he had
seen another fire engine and police cars racing by. Curious
about what was happening, Kal changed the dial on the radio
to a news station. Several stories were reported before they
arrived at one that made him turn the volume up louder.

*"A young woman was rescued from a raging fire at the
luxurious club, Big Boys International, this morning. She
received minor smoke inhalation injury. As for the club, it was
completely destroyed. Officials don't know the cause of the fire
yet and are investigating."*

Within a breath, Kal was headed in the direction of Big
Boys. He hoped with every beat of his maddeningly pounding
heart that Nia was fine, but also hoped for someone else—
Suzanne. "No, *she* wouldn't do *that,*" he tried to convince
himself. "Not *that.*"

CHAPTER THREE

Christiansted, St. Croix

The dark master bedroom, illuminated by myriad candles, scented with coconut incense and romanticized with a low volume of Gerald Levert's latest CD made it seem like it was midnight, the lover's hour, rather than a sun-blinding island afternoon, shut out by drawn blinds and curtains. Roland Davenport, who had just finished loving his lady senseless, now snuggled with her beneath royal blue silken sheets. He knew that any time was the right time for making love if you were with the right person.

In affairs of the heart, he understood that if you loved someone, you made love to them all the time—even when you weren't engaged in the physical act of making love—even when you were outside the bedroom. That's what he did with Cameron, his girlfriend of two years.

Roland made love to her by showing her that it was a privilege to be in her presence each time he saw her. He made love to her by being supportive of her dreams, by being considerate, respectful, loyal, honest, and by always letting her know that

she was the only woman in the world for him. He made love
to her by talking straight from his heart, letting her know that
she was the only woman in the world who could make him feel
the magic he felt with her. He made love to her by showering her
with any gift his millionaire status could provide, by calling
her when they were apart, by hugging and kissing her for no
reason at all, by giving of his heart and soul unconditionally.

Making love to her in these ways, it was easy to manifest
that depth of love through his physical expression of love for
her when they were alone. Their intimate moments were always
so spectacularly erotic for both to them, neither of them could
speak immediately after. That love-drugged look in Roland's
naturally intense eyes conveyed everything she needed to hear.
The tears continuously rolling from the corners of Cameron's
eyes, down her temples and on to his chest, spoke for her.

With her mid-length, coiled hair sprawled against his hairy
chest, Cameron could only catch her breath and caress her
cheekbone on his skin. With his mink-hued eyes and the I-
can-kiss-you-into-madness lushness of his lips, Roland was an
extremely erotic, passionate, tender and powerful lover. She'd
always heard about the really good-looking guys being lousy
in the bedroom. Far from true in this case. What Roland could
do to her body, she'd never even heard of before and didn't
know any word for it.

Cameron wasn't interested in lovemaking before meeting
Roland. She was always wondering what was the big deal
everyone was making over sex. Sure, she had lost her virginity
in her early twenties. Now she was thirty. However, no one—
not one single man—had ever made her experience the rapture
that Roland did. At times, his wholesomely muscular body
could perform such sorcery on hers, she questioned if Roland
was human. The addictive joy was often so awesome, she would
have spasms long after their encounter was over.

They met when her modern dance troupe traveled to the
island to perform at Destiny Resorts. Performing her lithe ener-
getic and graceful moves, Cameron was immediately attracted
to the owner of the resort chain. When she asked him to dinner

later, they had a fabulous time, talking until dawn. She learned he was from a lower middle class background, the son of a carpenter and a school teacher. Quite the contrary, Cameron had a wealthy upbringing. She was a Washington senator's daughter.

Roland's magnificent prowess in bed aside, Cameron would have loved him even if he was an awful lover. Above all, he was a good man, a man with integrity. No man she'd ever been with had treated her better. Roland always showed how much he appreciated her, unlike someone else in her life—her father.

A widower with two children, Marshall Carrington always seemed to adore her older brother. A lawyer and an aspiring senator, Spencer was following in her father's political footsteps. A dancer from the heart, Cameron felt she had to pursue her own passion, performing all over the world. Nonetheless, no matter how much she was praised by adoring fans, it seemed her father never thought it was enough.

Now Cameron had a surprise for him. Mizelle Winthrop, head of the world renowned Parisian Gales Dance Troupe had approached her, dangling a most tempting carrot: to be the lead dancer in its new production. It started in three weeks. There would be only one cost.

"Roland, honey, there is something I want to talk to you about." Her long, slender fingers dug into the mattress, supporting her as she sat up.

Emulating her position, Roland fluffed a pillow behind her back. "Comfortable?"

"Very."

"Good. What is it, doll face?"

Cameron loved when he called her that. Her father always had pet names for her brother. But never Cameron.

"Mizelle Winthrop is on the island, vacationing. He's renting a villa here in Christiansted."

"Mizelle Winthrop?" Roland repeated, squinting his eyes in wonder of why that name sounded annoyingly familiar. Suddenly realizing why, he looked at Cameron. "Isn't that that elderly guy who attended your performance when I went with

you to France? Isn't he the one who I thought was hugging
you a little too long in congratulating you on your show there?
And wasn't he looking a little too hard at that sweet thing you
have there?'' He pinched her bottom.

"Ouch," she squealed, wincing. "He's just an old man who
loves the arts."

Roland raised a brow. "The arts isn't the only thing he loves.
That man loves some booty. *Yours.*"

Cameron slammed him with her pillow. "Stop it."

Ducking, he grasped the pillow. "No, really," he said,
fluffing it behind her back, "I don't trust that guy. And you
know I'm not insecure. I just don't trust him."

"Oh, I can handle him," she said, her fingers toying with
the sheets.

"I don't know about that. Older cats like him these days are
armed with Viagra. They have women running for their lives."

Both of them laughed.

Cameron settled down. "No, I'm being serious now, Roland.
I ran into him yesterday when I was headed out snorkeling.
And it must have been fate that both of our dance troupes are
on hiatus, and we're resting on this island, because as soon as
I spoke to him, he told me he's pondering a new production
in three weeks. And he wants me to be in it."

He raised her hand and kissed it. "That's a wonderful opportunity."

"Being a lead dancer in the Parisian Gales Dance Company is
a tremendous opportunity. Do you know what it would mean?"

"I have some idea."

"Roland, my whole life would change. My father would
even be proud."

The mention of her father made Roland take a deep, aggravated breath. She was obsessed with gaining her father's
approval. Haplessly, after seeing the father and daughter interact
on many occasions, Roland doubted Cameron would ever
receive what she desired so desperately.

"Why did you react like that?" she asked.

"Because it's all about your father again."

"What do you mean?"

"I mean you don't just want to be the lead dancer in the Parisian Gales because that would make you happy. You're mostly doing it because you believe your father would finally take notice of what you're doing. Take notice of you."

"That's not true. Of course, I want him to feel proud, but I want to do it for me."

"You sure, Cameron?"

"Certainly."

For a moment, Roland searched hard in her small, plain eyes. He loved this woman and he wanted her to be happy. He was happy. Most likely because he never sought anyone's approval. Proof of that was being in a relationship with Cameron. When his friends first met her, they were always remarking that she didn't seem like his type. Though he knew what they really meant.

With her unadorned features and lanky body, she wasn't a beauty by their conventional standards. His friends had seen the types of women Roland dated in the past: the ones with the cover girl faces and centerfold bodies. In any case, he wasn't about to let anyone's opinion dictate who he shared his life with. Cameron and he were in their own beautiful world. His friends could never conceive how incredible it was to live there.

"Cameron, I hope you're telling me the truth," he told her, "because I hate to see you constantly trying to prove yourself to him when he always slights you. When I first met you, and you told me your dad treated you that way, I didn't believe it. I thought you were exaggerating. But after witnessing his behavior over and over, I know you're telling the truth. But what I want to say to you is . . ." Swerving to face her more, he picked up her hand. "You don't have to do anything to get anyone's acceptance or their love. Your father should accept you the way you are. You don't have to join the top dance troupe in the world to get his acceptance or attention. Don't put that kind of pressure on yourself."

"I'm not putting pressure on myself because of him. I really want to join the dance troupe for myself."

"You sure?"

"I'm sure."

"Because you don't have to prove anything to anyone, but you."

"I know. And guess what?"

"What?"

"Mizelle Winthrop wants to meet with me for lunch to talk it over."

"When?"

"Today."

"Today? Aw baby, I thought we'd spend the day in bed and every other freak-rousing place in the house." Burning his eyes into hers, he rolled his tongue across his lips.

She giggled. "You are so fresh."

"And you like me that way."

She giggled again, then glanced at the clock. "I better get going." She slung the covers off of her and sat on the side of the bed.

Her back was facing him. He rubbed it. "I think I should come with you."

"Not necessary." She stood and groped her fingers through her tousled hair. "I like to handle my own business."

He sighed disappointedly. "All right."

"I better get going. We have plenty of time for you-know-what when I come back." She strode to the dresser, removing a lacy red camisole with matching panties, then took a dress from the closet. All the garments were tossed on the bed. Afterward, she went to the vanity, picking up a Red Door perfumed body moisturizer and some peach-scented bath beads.

"Where are you meeting him, anyway?" Roland asked, his back against the headboard.

With his muscular legs imprinting the sheets that covered him and with his bare chest shimmering in the room's candlelight, Cameron really hated to leave him. "We're meeting at Ana-belle's Tea Room," she said. "You know I love those Cuban dishes they serve there."

After blowing him a kiss, she gathered her belongings and headed to the bathroom.

Roland was still lounging in bed when she returned to the room minutes later. Smelling her fragrance and checking her out fully dressed, Roland sat up even straighter against the headboard. A red, super mini knit dress clung to her willowy form. Black high heel ankle strap shoes, and a matching black leather purse completed the outfit.

"You're looking . . ." Inspecting her from head to toe, he was at a loss for words. "You're looking like you're out to reel somebody in." Forcing a smile, he tried to hide the fact that he disliked her wearing such a provocative outfit. "Do you think you should be wearing that around *him?*"

Cameron threw a lean hand at him as she walked toward the door. "You're being silly. I'll be back soon."

"You made it, Angel."

A yellow smile with eyes to match, greeted Cameron when Mizelle Winthrop opened the door to his villa. Striving not to show the disgust she felt in meeting him in his home, Cameron forced herself to make a pleasant expression. "How are you, Mr. Winthrop?" Nervously, her eyes scattered over the antique-styled room.

"Fine, thank you, Angel." He sauntered up behind her.

Feeling him getting too close, she pivoted around. "I really want to get the part in your production. It would mean the world to me."

"I'm sure it would. Otherwise, you wouldn't be here." A wicked witch laugh drifted from his parched lips.

"So would you like to see some of the African steps I did at the last show with my dance company?"

"All in due time. All in due time." Conspicuously, his watery gray eyes trailed the length of her body. "Are you ready, Angel?"

Disgusted, Cameron closed her eyes and opened them. "Ready for what?"

She heard the wicked witch laugh again.

Curtly, it stopped. With it, his countenance appeared stern. "You know why you're here, Angel. Don't play games."

"Mr. Winthrop, all I want is that lead part."

"And you can have it if you truly, *truly* want it."

Disbelieving that she had put herself in this position, Cameron pleaded, "Please don't do this to me, Mr. Winthrop."

"What am I doing? You're the one who came here willingly. You're the one who wants the lead part. What are you willing to do for it?"

Cameron didn't respond, but shifted her eyes frantically to each side as if each direction bared the answer. Though she loved Roland with her whole heart and soul, she knew this opportunity could probably garner her the love of someone else she loved. If she could just have the starring role in a production with the most famous dance company in the world, it could make all the difference in the world.

"Come to me, Angel?"

Cameron aimed her eyes ahead to behold Mizelle sitting in a recliner chair across the room.

He patted his lap. "Come, I'll make sure we enjoy each other."

Three long hours had passed before Roland started picturing scenarios of the old guy getting fresh with Cameron. Other scenarios of her getting hurt in an accident or even getting attacked because of that outfit prompted him to get dressed and hop into his Jeep.

Coasting down the highway, he questioned if he was overreacting by tracking her down. What if when he arrived at the restaurant, she saw him and became mad because he didn't let her handle her business on her own? Would he seem insecure, possessive or jealous of a man old enough to be his great grandfather?

On arriving at Anabelle's *Tea Room*, Roland was shocked

to learn that the hostess hadn't seen Cameron. One of their regular customers, they knew her well.

Stepping back into his Jeep, Roland debated what other restaurants Cameron and Mizelle might have wound up at. The Bombay Club? The Royal Garden? Or The Comanche Restaurant? When he visited each, no one had seen her.

Driving down the highway, Roland started hearing conversations in his head, not with Cameron, but about her.

"As long as you're happy, son, we're happy," was his parent's standard statement on the subject of Cameron. No other comments were made about her.

Much the opposite, his sister, Keisha, had much to say. "She's rich and spoiled and only cares about herself."

Those observations were the result of Cameron wanting Roland to take a six-month leave of absence from Destiny Resorts and travel with her dance troupe across Europe. Roland agreed, taking a lengthy leave and traveling with the dance company. To his misfortune, his business suffered because of it.

The idea of an engagement ring had been circling his mind lately. It didn't matter that his sister didn't approve or that he didn't feel quite right about Cameron's obsession to please her father. He was in love. Love made a man do anything. Even search desperately for his girlfriend's car. Roland spotted her Jeep parked in front of the new villas. They were the ones that elderly vacationers were renting.

Roland had returned home and was laying awake in bed when Cameron sashayed into the master bedroom. Assessing her from head to toe, Roland thought she appeared as neat as when she left.

"How was your meeting with Winthrop?" he asked.

The mattress jiggled as she plopped down on the side of it. "It was a good meeting." Lifting her feet, she began removing her shoes. "I got the part."

"Great. That's beautiful."

"Yes, it is." But she didn't sound happy. She stood, wiggling out of her dress. "I can't believe it."

"Believe it. You get what you deserve."

The dress was off. Rolling off her black stockings was next. "I can't wait to hear what Daddy says about me pulling this one off."

"He'll probably be pleased," Roland responded.

"Probably," she said, pulling back the covers and swinging herself into bed. "He'll be ecstatic. The Parisian Gales are the supreme dance company in the world." Snuggling up to Roland, she brushed her lips across his ear. "Ready for more love?"

"For more?" he echoed.

"Lots more," she teased. "I sure am."

"Is that right?"

Something in his tone and even in the rigidity of his body made her feel odd. Must be imagination, she told herself. She snuggled up to his warm body more. "How about you giving me that whipped cream treat you gave me the other night? You drove me mad."

"Later," he answered, drawing back. He wanted to really look in her eyes. "How was the restaurant?"

"Out of this world! The food was scrumptious as usual. I had my favorites palomilla and asopao."

"Is that right?"

It was the second time he had made that remark. It made her feel strange. "Why do you keep saying that?" she asked.

He shrugged his shoulders. "Just saying it."

"Is something bothering you? Are you mad because I met the old goat?"

"Met him? No, I'm not sorry you met him. Not that." Pausing, he grabbed her by the shoulders and his eyes grew triple their size. "I'M SORRY BECAUSE YOU SCREWED HIM!"

"I didn't."

"Get out of my bed!"

Her hand eased toward him, touching his rib first. "I didn't do anything."

"Get out of my bed!" He jerked her off.

Seeing his thriving rage, she complied. "Were you following me? How dare you!"

"How dare I!" He jumped out of bed. "How dare I care about you so much that I go out looking for you to make sure that pervert doesn't do anything to bother you! Then I see your car parked at the new villas."

"You don't understand!" Burying her face in her palms with her back facing him, she shuffled toward the center of the room. "You don't understand." She began to cry.

By the shoulder, Roland swung her around. "What don't I understand, Cameron? I don't understand how much you wanted the part. How much you wanted to please *your father*. So much that you'd sleep with a man old enough to be your great grandfather."

"Roland, you don't know how it is for your parent to always ignore you, to always put you down, to never show you love or affection. You would do anything to get it."

"You're wrong there, Cameron. I wouldn't do anything for it." Sighing, he stared hard at her. "I don't even know who I'm looking at right now. I thought I knew you. I know we all have our faults, but I really thought I knew you. You were the girl who would hear that another woman slept with someone for a job and you would say she was disgusting. And now look at you. Look at you! And this is all about impressing your father."

"Roland, I love you. It had nothing—nothing at all to do with you. It was just my bad judgement. My desperation to please my father. I won't even take the role. I'd rather have you."

"Really?"

"Oh, yes. Please don't end what we have. I need you. I've never loved anyone like you. Please, please give me another chance. I'll never do it again. I love you so much I would die without you, Roland. So will you? Will you give me another chance?"

CHAPTER FOUR

Three months later . . .

"Enough is enough!" Nia swore under her breath, visualizing the nightmare that was probably awaiting her. Pushing the linen cart down the hallway's jade carpeting, much too soon she arrived before the red numbers on the white door, which read 939. She raised her fist to knock, but hesitated. With a passion, she hated the patron who occupied this suite. Pawing her body, stroking her hair, trying to kiss her and once even tossing her on the bed, she wasn't standing for it a second longer. Yes, she was the maid, but did that mean she attended to everything?

It all made Nia tug at the stiff, cotton dress the hotel required its female employees to wear and wish for the millionth time for all that seemed so impossible: that someone would consider her fifty college credits in hiring her for a job, allowing her to do something she had studied for, that she wasn't trapped in a paycheck to paycheck existence, that a legitimate music executive had heard her singing instead of Kal. Oh, how she wished that.

As a child discovering that she was blessed with an exceptional singing voice, and witnessing how much it pleased others, she longed to be a singer. Life, nonetheless, stole her heart's desire long ago, chipping it away with its harsh realities. Nia hadn't been strong enough then, or knew how important it was to fight for your dream. Only now, as she arose every morning to a life that didn't feel like it was supposed to be hers, she understood why one should hold on for dear life to their dreams.

So happy and fulfilled she would have been if she could have merely shared what was overflowing inside her. Having a purpose would have even made up for something nonexistent in her life: a man's love. The right man's love. Not those rich men who wanted to buy her. She wanted a regular man with a regular job, who she felt comfortable with. That way he would never leave her because she wasn't educated enough, or wasn't from the right type of family or upbringing. He would simply adore her, love her to no end. If she could have had merely that gift, her every breath would have seemed so alive.

Facing suite 939, Nia willed herself back to more reality. Finally knocking, she predicted Jason Cantrell's famous line upon her entering the door. "You look just like a beauty queen."

The compliment would have been wonderful coming from anyone else. Yet when Jason's puny pea eyes landed on Nia, she wished to be anything but physically appealing. Repeatedly she went as far as asking to be assigned to another suite. Her employer was made well aware the middle-aged patron was getting much too fresh. To her misfortune, Beatrice Brightwater dismissed Nia's complaints as frivolous.

"Do your job or else!" she always warned.

That being as it may, this time Nia refused to endure any more harassment. If subjected to the beastly behavior once more, she was grabbing those few long hairs that were faithfully whisked over his bald spot, and she was yanking 'til the cows came home. With his scalp on fire, he wouldn't feel too sexy.

Taking deep breaths to calm her scurrying nerves, once again Nia knocked on the door. Seconds passed. The door didn't swing open. Neither did the dreadful, puffy face appear. Nia knocked again and again, then again, louder. No answer. A long, winded breath escaped and her muscles relaxed. Among the numerous keys dangling from the chain attached to her uniform, Nia located his.

Stepping inside his room, it was apparent that Jason wasn't a messy person. The sole things out of order were butterscotch candies spilled over one of the tables. So she didn't have too much to do. Most of all, she planned to do everything fast. By the time he returned, the fragrance of her raspberry body lotion would be all that remained of her.

Nia removed the old sheets, slipped on new ones, emptied ash trays and dusted night stands, all the while humming her gladness to be alone. Although, bending over to lift the waste-basket, she suddenly felt a presence behind her that straightened her posture and whirled her around. Jason Cantrell was across the room.

Oversized false teeth gleamed at her. "Hello, foxy. Hope I didn't scare you? I was in the rest room."

"You were in here all along!" Her anger hid the fright that made her heart pound wildly. "You were mighty quiet. Too quiet, actually."

"That's because I wanted to surprise you." Grinning, he moved a step toward her.

A black loafer made a step backward. "I don't like surprises."

"Ah, you're too young to be so stuffy. You know . . ." He paused, scratching a sagging cheek. "You look just like a beauty queen."

"Mr. Cantrell, I can come back later. Seems like you need to be alone."

"No, no, no. I want you here. I want a private moment with you."

"No thanks."

Nia made fast tracks to the door. By the time she gripped the knob, a clammy hand covered hers. "I want you," Jason professed.

Glowering, Nia swung around. "But I don't want you! Now let me out!"

"Not until I show you why we're meant to be together."

All Nia saw were those jumbo teeth coming toward her. Prune lips kissing at her, she noticed too. Repulsion shivered over her as she imagined their stickiness meeting the skin on her face and neck. Unfortunately, she had felt them before when he tried to kiss her. Vowing *never again,* Nia reached for those long hairs covering his bald spot. Too much grease made them too slippery to grip. He laughed when she did it. She assumed her fingertips were probably tickling his head. Nevertheless, his I-haven't-brushed-my-teeth-in-ages breath blowing on her cheek while he bent his head for a kiss, meant all decency was off. Pushing him away with one hand, Nia grabbed the iron off the night stand with the other.

"Oh!" Jason yelled. He clutched his forehead as the cold metal whacked it. "Oh, God, you hit me!"

"You deserved it!" Finally free, Nia backed away, wiping his poisonous prints off her arm. "You need to keep your filthy hands to yourself."

His nostrils flared. "You've done it! You've done it now!" His withered lips tightened. And when he raised his hand off the lump on his head, Jason leaped.

He wrestled Nia, rather than striking her. His strength was magnified by his rage. Fighting with all the brawn she could muster, Nia threw a few solid licks. Regardless, there was no way she could beat a man. Nothing she did prevented him from tossing her on the bed. Hollers filled the air.

Out in the hallway, Roland Davenport heard the ruckus next door to his room. He was just returning from a business meeting, fumbling through his pocket for his suite's key. Soon realizing this wasn't a couple having some afternoon fun, but a woman screeching for help, Roland pushed the partially opened door, charging inside.

Being caught weakened Jason Cantrell. It befuddled him so, Roland pulled him off the maid and flung him across the room with no effort. Impacting like concrete smashing, Jason's back bashed against the wall.

Squiggling his face from the pain, he leered at Roland. "You won't get away with this!" His fury shifted to Nia. "And neither will you."

Roland ignored him. He was too occupied assisting the maid up from the bed. After staying at the hotel for two weeks, he had seen her several times. Each time they passed in the hallway, there were smiles, hellos and on Roland's part lots of looking. Big, unusually-shaped hazel eyes, and full lips curled up in the corners, along with a body that he believed was every man's fantasy, made her unforgettable. Now seeing her up close, by far she was one of the most beautiful sights he had seen since his arrival in his old home, New York.

Alone in his suite, Roland often wondered about her too. He wondered if she was nice as she seemed, or if she liked to go out a lot, or if she had a boyfriend or a husband. Despite all the questions, he knew better than to pursue assuaging his curiosity. There was too much at stake to stray off his path. Promises that had to be fulfilled were made to many.

"Are you okay?" he asked.

"I'm fine," she answered, and was so busy looking down, tidying her dress, she didn't see how closely the near stranger was looking at her. When Nia did look up at him, she was lured inside familiar eyes, mink-brown, intense and warm. He was the man whose room she always wished she was assigned to. Whenever their paths crossed, he seemed friendly and charming. On top of that, in her opinion he was one of the most gorgeous men Nia had ever seen. Even in her state of upset, she couldn't help being entranced by his scintillating brown eyes, which enhanced lush lips, both perching seductively beneath an oval of wavy hair, and all this atop a muscular build that made her hungry—and food wouldn't do.

"Thank you for helping me," she said, but felt not even thank you was enough.

"I was glad to help."

Help would be needed again. A fifty-something woman, clad

in a linear gray suit, sauntered in the room, clearly unhappy. Immediately Beatrice Brightwater looked alarmed at Jason Cantrell clutching his head and back.

As she hurried toward him, the woman who many thought favored Mr. Magoo with hair and high heels, couldn't talk fast enough. "A call came to my office that some type of commotion was taking place in here."

"There was," Jason confirmed. He grimaced as if in terrible pain, then glowered at Roland and Nia. "Those two attacked me."

"What!" Nia's brows flew up as her bottom lip fell down. "How could you lie like that?"

"Because he's an idiot!" Roland answered.

"No, because it's true!" Jason lied. "And I want to press charges, and I want her fired! You see my head?" He pointed to the steadily growing lump. "And oh, my aching back."

Beatrice examined the lump, saw how much agony Jason's back was giving him, then glared at Nia. "How could you do this? For years we've provided excellent service to Mr. Cantrell when he was in New York on business. Then you come and now this! How could you?"

"Because he was attacking me. That's how."

Emphatically Roland was nodding his head. "Yes, he was all over her. If I wouldn't have stopped him, he might have raped her."

"Raped!" Jason appeared outraged. "Do I look that desperate?"

"Yes!" Nia retorted.

Roland snickered, but quickly straightened his face, seeing how upset the maid was.

"He did attack her," he pointed out. "And I'm a witness to seeing him do it."

"Do you know who this man is?" Beatrice grilled. She was harshly frowning. "Do you have any idea?"

Nia couldn't believe what she was hearing. This woman still wasn't heeding her warning about this man. Obviously she didn't care. The hotel's success was her bottom line.

"Yes, I know who he is," Nia spat. "He's a sex fiend. That's who he is!"

"Wrong!" Hands on her hips, Beatrice lowered her head and narrowed her eyes, making them resemble slits. "Mr. Cantrell is a shareholder in this hotel chain. A *major* shareholder."

"Big deal," Roland remarked.

"Yes, so what," Nia joined him.

"So nothing!" Beatrice snarled. "If he wants me to fire you, you're fired!"

Roland was waving his hand. "No way. He was attacking her. I saw it and I'll give the police a statement to that effect."

Jason swallowed. Venomous words on the edge of his tongue fell back inside his throat. Much the opposite, Beatrice was full of defiance. Folding her arms, she raised an uneven brow and stared Roland down. "Oh you will, will you? Well, I'll tell the police a different story. I'll tell them that Ms. America here was after some money."

"You liar!" Nia shouted.

"And she planned to seduce Mr. Cantrell to get it. I'll—"

"You're a liar!"

"And I'll swear this was about consensual sex. I'll even say Nia told me what she planned to do."

Jason grinned now. An eerie laugh escaped.

"LIAR!"

"You can't do that!" Roland argued. "She can fight this in court."

"Can she now?" Smirking, Beatrice lifted a lopsided brow again. "With what money? She's as poor as a church mouse. Poverty equals powerless."

A line of water rolling down Nia's cheek distracted Roland from telling Beatrice off. God knows he hadn't planned on getting involved in all this, getting all worked up about someone's sticky affairs. After all, there were important matters of his own to take care of. Even so, somehow he found himself ushering the beautiful maid to his room. Once there, he handed her tissues. Both were sitting on the side of his bed.

"I really needed the job," Nia admitted, between wipes and

sniffles. "It's hard out here without finishing college and having solid job skills."

"I can imagine." He blotted wet spots she missed.

"Thank you," she said, feeling comforted by the delicate grazing of his fingertips beneath the tissue. "And I appreciate your speaking up for me too."

"It was no problem. But you don't have to stand for what happened." Staring in her soft, hazel eyes, he also lightly held her arms. "You can press charges and take him to court."

"I would love to do that," she said, loving the way he was looking at her.

"You can!"

"But while I'm doing that, whose going to put a roof over my head and food in my stomach, and I have others depending on me. I can't afford to put my energy there. I need a job and I need one fast."

Roland thought for a moment. He knew there was something he needed all his energy and focus for too. But when he looked at her, there was something about her that affected him. It made him speak instead of think.

"Look, I can get you a great attorney. All fees on me. It will be a gift, not a loan." *Now what am I getting myself into?*

Nia's eyes widened. She was shocked and flattered. Equally, she knew that few things in this world were free. Kind as this stranger was, someone like him would never make such an offer without expecting something of significance in return. Everything about him reeked of class and wealth, from his Italian suit to the educated inflections in his voice.

"Thank you. That's very kind, Mr. . . . ."

"It's Roland. And you?"

"Nia." *Now those are some lips I wouldn't mind kissing me . . . all over.*

"Nia, it's no trouble, really."

"But it would trouble me. I can't take your money for a lawyer."

"Are you sure? It's no problem." *Eyes like those make a man feel like he's making love by just looking in them.*

"I'm sure. But maybe you could tell some of your friends about me. I'm a good maid." She removed a paper from her pocket. As she scribbled her name and number on it, Roland watched her, and could have went on watching her.

She looked up. "I can be reached here." Long, ringless fingers handed him the paper.

So she isn't married. He accepted it, then reached in his pocket, handing her a business card.

Capturing her attention first was: *Roland Davenport, CEO, Destiny Resorts International.* Reading further and learning that he was the owner of the Caribbean resort chain, Nia looked up at him, her lips curled in admiration. "I'm impressed. But now I better get going. Have to get on that job hunt."

"What are you going to do about Mr. Hands over there?" He threw his head toward the next room.

Nia inched toward the door. "I'm going to tell him I won't press charges if he won't." She placed her hand on the knob. "He'll probably go for it, considering you saw what he was doing. But I know Beatrice won't give me my job back. She hated me from day one. She always said I thought I was Ms. America."

Seeing that she was as striking as any beauty queen, he was drawn to her moist full lips. "You could be Ms. America. You have a very beautiful, exotic look. You're very attractive. *Very.*" His eyes blended with hers.

Standing there, staring at this stranger, Nia felt unlike herself. A little warm, even, in spite of her troubles. Warm like when she first had a boyfriend. Warm like when she first discovered how aroused a man could make a woman feel.

"Goodbye, and thanks a lot . . . Roland."

"Goodbye," he said with a smile. "It was very nice meeting you. And I will ask about some positions with my friends."

Her lips curled up, enhancing their natural tilt. They seemed to tease him. "Thanks."

From the doorway Roland watched her. He watched and watched until he couldn't watch any more. He had to do something. Who was he kidding? He needed a maid. His maid of seven years had retired two months ago, and he hadn't found a replacement yet. One was needed fast too, particularly since he recently closed a business deal with his best friend Wade and his buddy's cousin, Suzanne Greer. He invited them to be guests at his home in St. Croix, while they all worked on redeeming his company.

And yes, this sultry creature would be a distraction. And no, he hadn't intended to hire someone who could easily take his mind off what he had to do. Though all he had to do was keep things in perspective, Roland reasoned. Above all, he could never forget what his father did for him. There was nothing Roland wouldn't sacrifice to set things right. Not even this woman would get in his way.

Nia was a few feet away when he called, "Nia?"

"Yes?" She turned around. Dark, shimmering hair framed the heart shape of her face, making him want to capture her looking exactly like that in a portrait frame.

"I know someone who needs a maid."

Nia lit up. "You do?" Sprightly, she stepped toward him.

"Yes, he has a fairly large home in St. Croix. He can't cook and doesn't have time to clean. And he's just a lousy housekeeper. His maid recently retired. And if you wouldn't mind relocating to that island paradise, I'm sure he could work out satisfactory salary arrangements."

She was glowing. "I have nothing to leave behind here." Her excitement raised her voice octaves. "It seems like a dream job. Give me his address and number so I can call him. Who is he?"

"Me."

CHAPTER FIVE

After a lengthy meeting, Suzanne sat in the midst of a noisy board room, drumming her fingers against the cherrywood table. Her all-male colleagues team who used to hang on her every word swarmed the newest addition to Brayward & Boyce Consulting. Her name was Bianca Harris.

Suzanne had been out sick when they hired the latest Senior Consultant. Otherwise, she would have never picked a near twin to her old school chum Nia Lashon. Scrutinizing the young woman standing with the men around her, Suzanne observed she was the same Indian-brown hue as Nia, too. Then there were those other detailed attributes, like those eyes Suzanne thought looked funny. Like Nia's eyes, Bianca's were hazel and had an upward slant at the outer corner.

Suzanne pushed herself up from her chair as the men and Bianca began to vacate the room. She pulled the arm of the co-worker she was closest with, Justin, before he left the room.

Suzanne didn't look happily into the green eyes of her faithful ally at the consulting firm. A notorious gambler, and a senior manager like Suzanne, Justin was constantly losing his six figure salary in debt. So in exchange for being her flunky, on several occasions he'd borrowed money from her.

"I want her fired," Suzanne declared and threw her head toward the door. Chatting with the men, Bianca had just strode out of it.

Justin was taken aback. "Who? You don't mean, Bianca, do you?"

Suzanne blinked as if to say *dummy*. "Did you see any other *she* in the room?"

Justin still looked surprised. "She's doing a great job. And she's real nice too."

"Don't give me that sappy mess. What do you have on her?" Suzanne leaned her bottom against the table edge, propping her hands near the sides of her hips. "She has to be doing something wrong."

Suddenly Justin couldn't meet Suzanne's gaze. "She hasn't."

Attuned to him as she was to her own breathing, she grabbed the sides of his face, holding them sternly in front of her. "You're lying, Justin."

He wiggled out of her grasp. "I'm not."

"You are!" She raised up from the table, standing inches above and in front of him. "What do you have on her? No one does everything perfect at a job. Hell, she's been here for nearly a year. She couldn't have been perfect all the time."

Turning his back to her, Justin simply took a deep breath.

"Tell me," she pressed, "or no more of that good old stuff you need for your bookies—money. I guess you'll never win those millions because you don't have anything to play with."

Justin swerved back around, meeting the squared face, which he had loved at first sight. Now he hated it since he knew the monster that lay behind it. "She's late."

Suzanne brightened. "Late coming to work?"

"No," Justin corrected. "She's late coming back from lunch."

"Wonderful. Just wonderful." Suzanne beamed. She now had a reason to fire Bianca.

"But she hasn't done anything," Justin pointed out. "I mean to you."

"I don't like her."

"But why?"

"I just don't! And that's reason enough."

"Well, whatever your ridiculous reason is, you should know that she has a good reason for being late."

"What's that?"

"Her kid is in the hospital. He was hit by a car and is mostly recovered. But she still needs to see him on her lunch hour."

"That's tough about the kid. But it's not my problem."

"You wanted to see me, Suzanne?" Bianca asked.

Popping up at Suzanne's doorway with a smile, Suzanne could hardly acknowledge her verbally for gawking at her. Bianca's resemblance to Nia was uncanny.

"Uh, yes," Suzanne answered, pulling her chair forward to her desk. "Sit down, Bianca."

Pleasant-faced, Bianca did as she was invited to. "Is it my work?"

Suzanne's thin lips spread contently. "No, it's not your work."

"Whooh," Bianca blew out, getting more comfortable in her chair. "I thought I had done something wrong."

"You did."

Bianca's expression went blank. "I did?"

"You were late," Suzanne announced.

"But Justin and the others told me it would be okay."

"But I'm the senior manager that has been here the longest, and as you know, in this company that has rank. So I say that coming back from lunch late is *not okay.*"

Bianca looked like she wanted to cry. "But it's only because my son is in the hospital. He was hit by a car." The tears vying to release from her eyes were already skittering through her voice.

"Visiting a relative is no excuse for lateness."

"He's not just a relative. He's my child." Her chest was heaving. "I'll never be late again."

"You're right you won't. Because you're fired! See yourself out."

"But—"

"Don't but me."

Bianca wiped the water sliding down the middle of her cheek. "I need this job so bad. I'm a single parent and the insurance helps with my son's hospitalization. Otherwise—"

"I don't care! Get out of my sight. You should have thought of that before taking liberties."

Blotting her fingers against the corners of her wet eyes, Bianca closed the door behind her. Immediately standing, Suzanne brushed the sitting-wrinkles out of her brown charmeuse dress. Seconds later, she posed before the window.

Her fingers playing with her ear lobe and the ruby earring on it, she felt very satisfied in getting rid of Nia's lost twin. She couldn't bear her showing off her boobs to all the guys around the office anymore. They were acting like her intelligence was connected to those things. Suzanne couldn't remember the last time any of them really listened to her.

But turning back to her desk and all the work piled on it, she knew a way to get them all back. Suzanne wouldn't tell anyone she was taking a leave of absence until a week before she requested it. The partners would divide her tons of work among her colleagues. They would be miserable. And she would be happy. Happy because she would be on to an exciting adventure in St. Croix. Assisting Roland Davenport in resurrecting his company was going to be pure enjoyment for her.

On meeting Roland, Suzanne was truly impressed with how he'd built a near empire. How could she say no to helping him increase profits after the resorts had suffered a decline? An exciting opportunity it was to use her sharpest business expertise. Being on a tropical island was another benefit.

The biggest advantage however, would simply be seeing Roland Davenport again. Ever since that day of meeting him, Suzanne couldn't stop thinking about him. One of the finest creatures she'd ever seen, he was also so passionate about his business, she wondered what else could he be so passionate about.

She couldn't wait to find out. Because as sure as she was standing there, she would. She even debated crashing his and Wade's yearly fraternity bash.

With her plump, copper-colored legs draped in taupe hued hosiery, the cocktail waitress at the rebuilt Big Boys International Club sashayed toward Roland's table. After setting two champagne glasses on the table, she began to dance uninhibitedly in front of Roland. A new song by Montell Jordan was playing.

All of Roland's sweaty-faced, grinning-faced fraternity brothers, who rented out the club for their yearly event, gave a mighty roar of cat-calls as the woman slung her shapely hips in front of Roland. He laughed with the fellows and occasionally made eye contact upward at the doe-eyed waitress.

When the number was over, and another song started, the waitress grabbed Roland's hand, pulling him onto the floor. Entertaining his fraternity brothers, Roland was playing Mr. Cool at first, moving almost stiffly. For everybody in the room knew the way he truly danced. In college, that was as well known about him as his magnetism with the ladies.

"What, Roll, you're scared of all that woman?" his best friend Wade shouted, bearing two tiny dimples. To get a better look, Wade took off his foggy glasses and began wiping a handkerchief across them. Placing them back over his eyes, he saw Roland balling up his fist at him.

"Do I look scared?" Roland yelled at Wade.

"Yes!" several of the guys answered with laughter.

Feeling more and more of the champagne he was drinking all night, Roland concentrated on his dance partner's hips, moving his accordingly. Every move she made, he simulated, but with agility, masculinity and style. Before long, the waitress was perspiring more than Roland was. More than that, she was really checking him out.

When they finished their dance, his fraternity brothers clapped for them. Afterward, everyone continued conversing in their individual groups.

Smiling, Roland gently held the woman's hand. "That was fun. Thanks for making our night special."

"I loved it," she admitted with a deep, feminine voice.

Roland granted her a smile again before making a step toward his table. Her grabbing him by the arm swung him around.

"If you want to see me after tonight I'm available." Staring firmly into his eyes, she was still holding his arm.

"Other than being a great waitress, you're a great dancer. Give me your card. I might have some friends who want to hire a lovely waitress/dancer for one of their parties."

"But I'm not looking for work," she said, admiring all of him again. She loved the way the black silk shirt molded over his broad shoulders, unbuttoning at the top to reveal a triangle of dark hair. She loved the way his black pants covered his bottom. She loved him period. "I'm looking for a man, baby. A man as fine and sweet as you. And fine as you are, I don't even care if you're broke. I make my own money. Not that much, but it's mine. But I just want me a good man—a fine one that's all mine, and I do believe you could be the one. I'm looking for something serious."

A feeling of awkwardness led Roland's attention across to Wade, as he thought of his response to her. Undoubtedly, he was flattered that this woman found him attractive, but she was seeking something he was not.

"You're a very attractive young lady. And the fact that you work in an environment that is surely to attract many men to you doesn't even bother me. But the thing is, I'm not looking for a serious relationship right now. I just date. Go out to dinner from time to time. Catch a movie, a play, a club, things like that. But I don't want a serious relationship. I'm trying to focus on my career at this point in my life."

Disappointment bloomed in her brown eyes, even though her girlish smile tried to hide it. He didn't want to hurt her. Although, he felt better being honest. After Cameron devastated him, he took a look at his life and he didn't like what he saw. Because he ran around with her in Europe for six months, his company revenues reached a dangerously low level. His depression after their breakup dropped them even lower. This was particularly bad since he had investors, his father's friends as investors. Everyone was counting on him and he couldn't let anyone down, especially himself.

Now that Wade and his cousin Suzanne were temporarily hired to help him reclaim his company, Roland wasn't going to do anything to risk its success. Hence, he'd decided not to get into a committed relationship. He needed all of his time and energy for rebuilding his life.

Moments later, Roland sat at the table.

Wade was grinning and shaking his head. "You're crazy. Turning down that honey like that. I would have devoured her like she was that lobster I just ate."

Roland picked up his champagne glass, clutching it before taking a sip. "That's you. I had to be honest." He took a swig, smacked his tongue, then set the drink back down. "That young lady straight-out told me she's looking for something serious. And I'm not. Besides that, I don't jump on every woman I see."

"You mean you *didn't* jump on every woman you saw because you were with Cameron. You're free now, Roll. If I were you I would play the field. You know you can't do without it long." Wade lowered his head, giving Roland a knowing look over his glasses.

"Don't worry about me. I'll be all right." He took another swig of champagne. "But like I've been telling you, my focus is on my business."

"But what if a woman you really want wants something serious?" After a glimpse around the room, he leaned closer to the table. "You won't get your groove on unless you tell her what she wants to hear."

Roland chuckled. "And you won't get your groove on unless you get some new clothes." He was noticing Wade had worn the same suit for three days. A millionaire and entrepreneur of various enterprises, Wade was the cheapest person Roland knew. "What do you do, get that suit cleaned every day?"

Wade laughed at himself. "I'm not wasting all my money on suits."

"What do you spend it on then? Women?"

"Not them either. They're not going to take everything I have and break my heart."

Like my heart was broken, Roland thought.

"Roll," Wade said, seeing a sadness coming over his friend's face. "Do you miss her? Cameron?"

Roland did miss her, missed hearing her voice, missed her laugh, missed her talking about her dancing, missed making love with her. Even so, he couldn't forget the pain she caused him. That he could have done without. On the more positive side though, he had been feeling more like himself lately. That was proven when he met Nia. For the first time since he broke up with Cameron, he was very, very attracted to someone.

"I miss her," Roland confessed, hating the somber look suddenly on Wade's face. "But I'm moving forward." Silent a moment, he cleared his throat. "Enough about that mushy stuff. I want to know what you think about my chances of recovering the profits for the resorts."

Wade nodded. "I think everything is going to work out. You were smart enough to try to save the company just when the profits were low, but not when you were actually losing money. And you brought in the geniuses to help you." A devilish grin tipped his broad lips. "Mwa and Ms. Genius herself, Suzanne."

Roland's finger toyed with the rim of his glass. "So she's still in?"

"Of course. She's looking forward to coming down there and working her magic on your company. Think she has a crush on you. She'd probably fly back to St. Croix with you if she could."

"I already have some company flying back." He tried not to smile. His lip quivered anyway.

"Who?"

"A young lady who is going to be my maid. I met her at my hotel. She'd lost her job."

Wade saw an excitement in his friend's expression that he hadn't seen the entire night.

"She's *bad,* isn't she?"

Roland started shaking his leg. "Why do you say that?"

"I can tell. It's all over you."

Roland visualized her. "Yes, she's fine. Very beautiful. And she seems *sooooo* nice, at least from what I can see."

Wade started smiling. It was a huge smile.

He looked outright silly to Roland. "What? What are you looking like Howdy Doody for?"

Folding his arms, Wade reclined back. "Just looking at you, that's all. Just looking."

"Ooh, yes," Nia purred, laying back in the pedicurist's chair at Marvell's Beauty Spa. Her hair was already styled in sensual ringlets with golden highlights that framed her face and skimmed her shoulders. As well, her nails were painted raspberry and a glorious massage had gave her the ultimate sensation in pampering.

"Why do you always like raspberry?" the pedicurist, Alma, asked as she finished moisturizing Nia's feet. She was also one of Nia's dearest friends. They didn't see each other all the time, or even phone all the time, but even through lack of contact, the love was always there.

With her lengthy, peppermint-hued nails, Alma picked up a bottle of Raspberry Crush nail polish. She put it beside her pedicure kit.

"It reminds me of my mother," Nia said, looking up into Alma's round, beige face. "She loved to eat raspberries. I remember the scent always around the house."

Alma picked up the little toe first. She sniffed as if something smelled. "Something smells kind of stinky in here. *Funnnnkkky!*"

Nia snatched her foot back. "I know my feet don't stink."

She bent her head, tempted to smell it herself, until Alma threw her head back laughing.

Settling down, she grabbed Nia's foot. Positioning it between her knees, she said, "I was just kidding, girl."

"I know you were. Shucks, I would have you know I had to pull some men off of these babies because they smelled and tasted so good. They couldn't get enough."

Almas raised her softly arched brows. "Are you going to let *him* sample?"

"Him who?" Nia was intoxicated by how delicately Alma always handled the pedicure. She was a wonder with every instrument and every step of the beauty ritual. Nia's eyes fluttered closed. "Who are you talking about?"

"The man you're getting all dolled up for. The big shot guy you're going to leave me to be with."

Nia's eyes opened. "Who said I was getting fixed up for him?"

"You did by your actions."

"How?"

Alma shook the file. "Now you know good and well Marvell has been begging you to come in here and get a full day of beauty for years. But you always just get your toes done and that's because I'm your friend. And now today, you get the works. I know you went to the bank on this one." Alma took the file to the middle toe.

Nia's eyes closed again. "So I decided to get the works. I went to the bank and practically depleted my little funds. So what? I deserved all this treatment. I work real hard. And also, I'm going to live on an island. It's a new start and I want to look fresh."

"You want to look good for him. When you first called me up and said you were going to work as this guy's maid in St. Croix, I knew something was up. Your voice had this sound in it."

"What sound?"

"Like a little kid—like a little kid whose calling his friends up on Christmas day and telling them he got just what he wanted."

Alma teased Nia during the remainder of the pedicure. It was the way they were with each other. Nonetheless, as Nia was about to leave, tears clouded each woman's eyes. Nia was leaving tomorrow. She even gave Alma and another friend most of her home furnishings. When would they see each other again? Each promised to write, call and visit on vacations.

Missing Alma already, Nia left the salon, striding down 34th Street, browsing in the boutique windows. She didn't have that much money, but she wanted something cute to take with her to St. Croix. She couldn't wait to start working and getting that fantastic salary Roland Davenport agreed to pay her.

Although, as she browsed throughout the stores, she became less interested in buying something. In each window she looked in, in every step she made down the street, an image drowned out all else, and she had to admit the truth to herself. Alma was right. She was excited about working with Roland Davenport, and for some reason, she had a keen interest in looking extra good.

She knew she couldn't get involved with a rich man like that—a man who was educated, rich, had status, and whose family probably wanted him to marry a woman that reflected him. Despite that, it hadn't stopped Nia from thinking about him, wondering about him from the moment they met. Just looking at him and being around his positive spirit would have to be enough for her. She would fight to the death not to entertain anything romantic between them. No way she would end up like her mother. And no way would she go through what she went through before.

All in all, the man gave her a job. Just looking at him and being around him would be enough. Nia couldn't wait to see him tomorrow. Not since laying eyes on that gorgeous devil, Kal Hunter, had she seen a man so handsome.

* * *

With seven of his buddies crowded around him in the dusty pool hall, Boggys, Kal leaned over a pool table, aiming his stick at a ball, which aimed at a right corner pocket. He hit the ball in the pocket exactly when a short, slender woman wearing Senegalese braids grabbed his buttocks roughly. Kal nearly shot up to the roof, making some of his buddies laugh uproariously.

Turning around, he greeted a smile complete with one of the sexiest gap teeth he had ever seen. "Felicia, what you trying to do to me, girl?" He grabbed her hand, kissing it.

"I've been looking for you. I had to find you through the people on the street."

"Glad you found me." He leaned the pool stick in the corner.

Her eyes shifting from his butt to his eyes, Felicia was tickled. "You're sensitive in that area, ain't you? I have to check that out."

The men that weren't jealous of Kal snickered. To them it seemed that women were either with Kal, looking for him, or coming on to him. Kal smiled back at the men, then looked at her. "So you're saying I need to take you home?"

"Yep. And after that I want to sing and audition for you. I want you to give me a record contract. I'm ready. I've been practicing."

Kal liked the idea of her going home with him. He didn't like the idea of her singing. Kal had heard Felicia sing before. It was the night he introduced himself to her at the rib joint, when she was sitting and laughing with her girlfriends. He couldn't get over the way she ate her ribs. It sure did make him think of things.

After convincing her to join him on a boat ride that night of their meeting, he took her home. Making love came easily after. During their after-play he told her about his label. Enthusiastically, she informed him that she could sing. Kal never forgot being subjected to such an experience, and prayed that he could. It was like mooses and bulls and elephants and pigs and dogs and everything in hell crying out at the same time.

"You sure you been practicing enough?" he asked tonight. She was clueless that he disliked her singing. "Oh, a whole lot. But first let me just go to the ladies' room. Where is it?"

Kal motioned toward an oblong hallway, covered with brown, scuffed tiles. "That way."

"Be right back."

Kal and the other men watched Felicia's round bottom wiggle down the hall until she disappeared into the ladies room. Her buttocks were the biggest, most well-shaped part of her. Kal loved them. Every other part of her was slim.

"You're going to wax it tonight?" one of his buddies asked.

Kal nudged him on the arm. "A gentleman doesn't tell."

Playing with her braids as she entered Kal's lobby, Felicia loved that Kal was from around the way like her, but was so rich the doorman always tipped his hat at him. Riding up the elevator, she kissed him on the neck. He rubbed her back.

"Won't be long," he assured her, his breath catching in his throat. He couldn't wait until they were upstairs.

"I'm going to tear you up," she promised, nibbling his ear.

Entering his penthouse, she kicked off her thick bottom sandals and plopped on a black, velvet chaise. Relaxing there as he went over to the bar to prepare their drinks, she closed her eyes, finding another something she loved about Kal: he was rich.

Soon sipping on her Mai Tai, and watching him at the other end of the chaise sipping his, Felicia took a long, good look at Kal from head to toe. There was something else Felicia loved about Kal: he was fine. She loved that bad boy smile of his and that thick, curly hair the most. She liked him wearing that tiny ball earring too.

Before long, Felicia couldn't resist crawling to his side, leveling her face with his, letting all her softness cling to his hard, muscular body. Her insides grew warm and her womanhood moist as her drink. Still, she had a higher purpose tonight.

Kal was going to give her a record contract before any fun. She moved off of him suddenly.

Kal raised up. "Hey, I thought you wanted some good loving."

Felicia sassily propped her hands on her hips. "I do. And I want a record contract, too."

Sitting up straighter, Kal took a long breath. Maybe she had gotten better. "Okay, let's here what you got?"

Felicia's dazzling gap nearly blinded him. "Okay, I'm ready." But she didn't sing right away. She began taking deep breaths. Kal understood. Breath control was essential to good singing. Except by the tenth breath, he was tired of wasting time and she was looking like she could be so freaky, he wanted to make some love.

"Felicia, you've did your breathing exercise enough. Sing."

Sing she did. In her same way. Whoever told her she could sing, Kal wanted them shot and feathered a thousand times. It didn't take long for him to hear enough and think of a way to rescue himself at the same time. At once, he jumped up, lightly shoving Felicia back down on a recliner chair. She was still singing when his mouth hungrily covered hers and his hand went underneath her skirt, quickly freeing her of everything beneath it. Seconds passing, he was still kissing Felicia, and when he released both of them for air, she was no longer singing. Silenced, her eyes fluttered close as if she were drugged.

"Oh," she cried of the powerful thrusts that soon filled her body with maddening pleasure. "Oh, I can't take it. I'm about to . . ."

Three hours later, Kal sat on the edge of the bed, his narrow hips indenting into the gray satin sheets. After sliding his red briefs up his golden, muscled thighs, he pulled his pants up his legs. Once standing with them on fully, he glanced back at Felicia sleeping. Long braids were sprawled all over the plump pillows, and her breathing was steady as her body curled tightly in one spot. Seeing that she was really knocked out, he walked into the living room where his piano was.

Aimlessly pecking the keys, he grinned about the cool time he'd just had. He always enjoyed women sexually. Precisely as with his music, sex was an area where he knew he was king. Being practically raised in the streets of Harlem, he had learned from the masters at how to please a woman from the slightest detail to the most obvious pleasuring technique. When he was a little younger, he prided himself on his expertise.

It was just that lately . . . lately sex always left him empty afterward. Empty like he was now. Shouldn't he have been happy? He had just gotten laid. And *good,* too.

But why did it seem that sex wasn't enough for him now? Especially when he went to family get-togethers and saw his sisters and cousins with their mates and children. Sometimes he would even pass lovers in the street and wonder about them. Was their relationship just about sex, or were they really *in love?*

Kal was certain he hadn't been in love since he was a teenager. And even that didn't last because he fell out of love very quickly. Undeniably, since he had been an adult he'd been *in lust.* But never could he say *in love.* Music was what he'd fallen in love with.

It saved him, too. It was a deliverer from his days as a teenage drug dealer, leading him to prosperity beyond what he could have ever imagined as a child growing up in the projects. And he was damn appreciative for what he was now accomplishing. For his label, he had signed two male groups, one solo male artist, and one female group. All spectacularly talented. Now he was looking for a female singer whose voice would make thirteen songs he wrote come alive.

God knows that voice wasn't Felicia's. But he did have a voice in mind. The one he'd heard months ago. Nia Lashon's vocal prowess was what he envisioned for those songs. In fact, after meeting her, he wrote three ballads with her unique soprano in mind. Signing with his label was all up to her now. Often he wondered what had became of her after that fire. She knew how to reach him. Maybe one day she would call. Or one day their paths would cross.

CHAPTER SIX

From the moment Nia took one last look at her empty apartment and stepped outside of her building to behold the white stretch limousine that Roland Davenport had sent for her trip to his private jet, she could feel herself leaving one world and entering an entirely different one. Excitement mixed with jitters and fear skittered through her while she slid herself on white, leather cushions inside the car. Part of the emotions derived from all the change that was taking place in her life. What's more, she always wanted to go to the Virgin Islands, particularly St. Croix. The other part had to do with Roland Davenport.

Days ago, at the hotel, she had accepted the position of his maid, acquiesced to the generous salary he offered, then listened as he made travel arrangements with his private pilot for their trip to St. Croix. That day Nia went home wondering if she was dreaming all of this happening to her in one afternoon, the good and the bad. She especially wondered about Roland. Was he for real? Was he a psycho who was planning to kill her when they were alone? Or was he a *dog* just trying to seduce her and move on to his next conquest? Researching him and his business at the library did answer her questions that he was legitimate. There were several newspaper and magazine articles, which featured his handsome photograph. Women's intuition also assured her that Roland Davenport was simply a nice businessman, who needed a maid. He was also so fine she went to bed that night with his image closing her eyes.

The driver escorted Nia to an asphalt landing strip. Roland's enormous jet stood in the distance. With his hands in his pockets, Roland stood nearby it at the bottom of the plane's stairwell. Once more Nia wondered if she was dreaming. The jet was incredible. The vision of the man standing by it was something she couldn't describe.

Watching Nia approaching him, Roland did a "Lord have mercy," under his breath. With those eyes and that body, she had already made his day. Somehow to him she appeared even more sensuous than the first day they met. Perhaps it had to do with that form-fitting red dress she was wearing. It sure accentuated her cinnamon complexion. It accentuated everything.

"So you made it?" he said, feeling an urge to greet her with a hug. He restrained himself.

"Yes, I'm ready to go." Looking up at him, merely inches from his face, she had to remind herself not to stare in his eyes too long. There was something about them that were almost hypnotic. Seeking something tamer to look at, she sneaked a glance downward at his white, silk shirt and beige pants. But with the wide width of his chest, along with his brawny arms and the pants fitting across his pelvis so neatly, Nia knew it wasn't safe to gaze at those attributes either.

She looked beyond him to the plane. "This jet is really something, so big. I'm excited about riding it. I'm excited about everything. Thank you for this opportunity. I really appreciate it." She switched her eyes from the plane and back into the intense eyes she avoided.

They were looking in hers a little too hard. "I'm excited too, Nia. Very excited."

* * *

Striding into the jet's interior, Nia's expression complimented Roland on the lavish interior even before her words did. Thickly cushioned, deep purple seats were enhanced by lush, black carpeting. The walls, couches and bar were mauve colored. Further accents were a state-of-the-art giant screened television, CD player and a buffet table with every type of hors d'oeurves imaginable.

On take-off they had to remain in their seat belts until reaching the standard flying altitude. Nia wanted a seat away from the window because looking out of plane windows always frightened her. Roland thought that was funny. However, after they reached their peak flying altitude and he'd brought some hors d'oeurves over to her, he could tell she was changing her mind. She was constantly glancing out the window at the clouds.

They were sampling crispy butterfly shrimp when he nodded toward the window. "Want to sit over here now? Come on and switch places with me."

"No, that's okay." She bit on the shrimp.

He smiled, watching her. *She even eats sexy.* "You sure? I see you keep looking over here. There's nothing to be afraid of. It's beautiful out there."

"It is beautiful," she thought aloud, the sight of a cloud shaped similar to a heart capturing her attention. She leaned closer toward the window and slightly over him to get a better look.

Roland joined her in savoring the view. That is until he realized that her not paying him attention gave him an opportunity to look at something more appealing. So as Nia watched the cloud, he watched her. Up close her features were even more beautiful. The skin on her face was so smooth and pretty, and altogether her features blended together softly and exotically. Far better, he liked her nearly brushing against him like this, even though he knew he couldn't get used to it.

When she raised back to her former position, and accidentally brushed him in moving, their eyes met uneasily. "I'm sorry," she apologized.

"There's nothing to apologize for." He picked up a glass of Monet that he'd ignored and took several sips.

They were quiet after that. Roland lay back against the headrest, closing his eyes and thinking he must have been crazy to bring this woman back home with him to work as his maid. He didn't even think he was this attracted to Cameron.

Resting back on the headrest also, Nia didn't feel as restful inside. In fact, she was debating whether she had made a mistake. Something was different about Roland now. For some reason, he seemed ill at ease with her. Nia had anticipated that they would get to know each other a little during the flight— nothing personal of course, just small talk and general getting-acquainted conversation. But now somehow it seemed almost as if he'd closed his spirit off to her. Was something pressing on his mind? Was he shy? Was he regretting his choice in a maid? Or was he the type of person that one had to initiate conversation with?

"So you own a chain of resorts?" Nia said. "What's the difference between those and regular hotels?" She tasted another shrimp.

Roland opened his eyes and rolled his head toward her, just in time to see her savoring the delicacy. The way her mouth moved was so sexy to him, but he dared not show how much. "Ah . . . the difference is basically the service. At a regular hotel, they provide rooms and suites. At a resort, we provide those services of course, but also sports activities, entertainment, card games, gambling and things of that nature." He raised his drink to his lips.

"Sounds nice." She thought he had the sexiest eyes she had ever seen. The color reminded her of fur. But it was their intense expression that was the real turn on.

"It is nice." Gripping the armrests, Roland sat up straighter in his seat. "The business is a whole lot of fun. Lot of work too. Hard work." He glanced out the window, remembering all the financial troubles he had as of late. To cut costs he had originally decided he wouldn't even ride his private jet on trips. Nevertheless, since Nia was his guest accompanying him to St. Croix, he felt she deserved to be pampered.

"My friend, Alma, heard about your company Destiny Resorts," Nia added. "A couple she knows went to a resort in St. Thomas on their honeymoon. She said they had a great time." She tasted another shrimp.

"That's what I like to hear. Maybe I can show you around one night." He didn't mean for it to sound like he was asking her on a date. But why did it sound like that anyway?

Nia responded only with an awkward smile. *Is he asking me out?*

Both of them were quiet once more.

Roland lightly shook his drink, letting the remainder swish from side to side. "So ah . . . have you lived in New York your whole life?"

"Yes," she said. "What about you? Is St. Croix your native home? I don't detect an accent."

He grinned. "Because the only accent I would have would be from New York. I grew up in Crown Heights in Brooklyn. After that I moved to midtown Manhattan to go to New York University. Lived there even after graduating, and then moved here. That was seven years ago."

Nia was looking surprised. "I lived in Queens in Jamaica Estates, but I was in Crown Heights a lot as a kid. One of my cousins lived there. I used to play stick ball all over those streets."

Roland raised a finger at her, bringing to her notice that there was only a graduation ring on it. Yet she already knew he was single from reading a clipping about him and his company in the library.

"I knew you looked familiar," he said. "You were that ashy-kneed little girl I used to beat up."

Nia laughed. "Yeah, right."

"Now fate has brought us together." He watched her curling plump lips, then found his way up to her eyes. "Together to work I mean."

He looked out the plane's window, as if pondering something deeply. Since he wasn't looking at her, Nia felt safe in looking at him. She loved his firm, squared jaw, his strong cheekbones and the way his narrow, shimmering black mustache lined his sexy top lip. Her eyes were about to probe lower, when he faced her with a serious expression.

"So ah . . . did you leave any family behind in New York?"

"My family, my brothers, aren't in New York anymore. One is in Texas, the other in Florida. They're both in college."

"Really?" His question was answered. He was really inquiring about *man* family.

"Yes, but we call, write and see each other when we can."

"Same with my family. They left New York and moved to Atlanta. We call, write and see each other when we can too." Roland sipped more champagne until the glass was empty and they both were so quiet the atmosphere seemed strained. Roland wanted to talk to her, was bursting to ask so many things about her. At the same time, he knew the less he knew about Nia Lashon the better. Hence, again he laid his head back against the headrest, closed his eyes and attempted to contemplate what he could do to get his business on track. Too bad he only wondered about one thing: the woman sitting next to him.

Sitting beside him, having finished her meal, Nia pushed her tray aside and laid her head back also. Repeatedly she looked over at Roland sitting there with his eyes closed and wondered what he was thinking. Was it work? Or was he thinking about a woman in his life? As much as she caught him sneaking looks at her figure during the ride, she knew he couldn't have been thinking the same thing she was: how am I going to work with someone I'm so attracted to?

After all, he didn't even want to talk to her. Evidence of that was his preferring to close his eyes and go to sleep. Deep down though, Nia knew it was all for the best. A man like that would not be *seriously* interested in her. They lived in different worlds. A man like that could do the same things those men did to her mother. It all prompted Nia to close her eyes and try to sleep also. Tired as she was, she was unsuccessful.

* * *

Seven hours later, as the jet began to land in St. Croix, meeting with pitch blackness, Nia took a deep, exasperated breath. It had been the longest trip she'd ever had, and it was the longest because it was so unpleasant. During the duration of the flight, Roland slept, did paperwork, listened to his Walkman, read books, magazines and did just about everything except talk to her. Several times she attempted to make conversation. In spite of her attempts, they all ended up the same way: brief answers with long periods of silence afterward.

During the ride to his home in an area of the island called Christiansted, he did open up a bit, promising Nia that she would get a tour of the island in daylight the next day.

"I really want you to feel and experience this magical place," he further promised, opening the door to his home and extending his arm for her, welcoming her inside.

Slowly pivoting around and around at the stylish decoration of his home, she could see that the jet's décor was tame compared to this house. Lush and luxurious was the only way to describe it. Antiques mixed with modern pieces. Pastels mixed with vibrant hues. Everything shouldn't have blended together visually. Exquisitely, it did. A quick tour of the house displayed the same appealing design.

"And this is your room," he said, escorting Nia into a room decorated mostly in pink and complete with a waterbed. "I can change the bed if you like."

"Oh, no." She dropped on it, watching her body wave and bounce. "I always wanted one."

"I love them too," he divulged. "Thought you might like one. But if you don't I'll be glad to have another put in here."

"Don't you dare." Nia purposely bounced a little more on the waterbed with Roland looking on and smiling. Catching sight of the wall to wall closet, she then decided to check it out. Not only did it look lengthy, but a partial opening indicated it was deep also. Nia stood from the bed, poked her head inside the closet and turned back around to tell Roland a joke about sleeping in there.

As if he couldn't wait to get away from her, Roland was hurrying to the door.

Nia had had enough. "If you don't like to associate with the help all you have to do is say so!"

Noting that her tone didn't sound like she was clowning around, Roland spun around. A tightened mouth, accompanied by the biggest, prettiest, angriest hazel eyes he'd ever seen confronted him.

"Something wrong?" he asked. Seeing how incensed she was drew a scowl on his face.

"Something's wrong my butt!" Nia hurried to the phone and snatched it up. "You heard what I said."

"What are you so mad about?"

"What's the airport number? Or information? Either one will do."

"Why?"

"I'm getting a flight out of here! If you now feel like you don't want me here, I will gladly leave! I won't be anywhere where I'm not wanted!"

Roland cursed himself for taking the distance he tried to create between them too far. He felt the less he knew about her, the better. The less he opened up to her the better. He had taken it too far.

He came toward her, gently removing the phone from her hand. After placing it in the cradle, Roland gazed down at her. Hurt blazed in her eyes and he sorely regretted putting it there. "I don't want you to go, Nia. Really, I don't."

"Yes you do, Mr. Davenport. And believe me, it's no problem. I'm accustomed to disappointments—disappointments in people, disappointments in life. When knocked down, I get up and dust myself off and keep on stepping. So Mr. Davenport, I will do fine thank you."

"Why are you calling me Mr. Davenport?"

"Okay, is Mr. Snob better?" But she had no time to be

insulted further. He was blocking her path. She reached around him for the phone.

Roland blocked her again, causing her to inadvertently stumble against him. Automatically, she grasped his shoulders, while reflexively he gripped the sides of her tiny waist. At contact, their eyes met just as spontaneously. Nia was overwhelmed not only by the rock hardness of his chest against hers, and the stirrings in her lower belly that his touch on her waist incited, but the intensity in his eyes. Impossible as it seemed, they were more intense than they naturally were.

Roland beheld intensity too. Emanating from her eyes was some type of recognition, an unspoken revelation that each was suddenly aware of. With the softness of her pressing against him, he found it somewhat frightening feeling her, feeling that her heart was beating as rapidly as his. It all roused a fullness below his waist, which reminded him that he hadn't been this close with a woman in a while. For that matter, he hadn't *been with* a woman in a while—and so God help him if he ever had the chance to be with this one.

Spellbound by her gaze, and captivated by the sensations, he was still holding on when she let go of his shoulders.

"Are you okay, Nia?" He gazed down at her bare legs revealed from the short dress. They glistened as if they'd been sprayed with a mist of baby oil. "Your ankle isn't twisted or anything, is it?"

"Yes, I'm okay." But why was her heart still racing so that her chest was writhing? And why did the simple gesture of his hands on her waist feel so arousing?

Hesitantly, Roland released his hold on her waist. In turn, Nia backed away to elude being so close to him. "No, I'm fine physically."

"But emotionally you feel you've been treated badly," he completed her thought.

"Yes," she acknowledged, uncomfortable with the fact that her heart was still racing.

"Nia, I really didn't mean to make you feel unwelcome."

She thrust her hand forward. "Save it. I know how you are now."

"No, you don't." Taking a walloping breath, he lowered his head, while placing his hands in his pockets. Raising his head, he looked at her gently. "I have some problems. Some financial problems. My business has lost a substantial amount of money because of my negligence. I'm indebted not only to my father, but to investors that he enlisted for me. You see, he's a carpenter, a very simple man too, a man with a good heart, and he worked for all these rich people over the years. When I had an idea about my resorts, I drew up a business plan and begged him to see if these people would invest. He had developed real good relationships with them. So this carpenter, this very simple man, convinced these millionaires, even a billionaire, to believe in what I was doing—to invest their hard-earned money with Destiny Resorts. And I . . . I failed."

Nia would have never imagined this, and somehow she felt rather honored that he shared something so personal with her. "So how can you afford to give me such a fantastic salary?"

"I have financial difficulties, but they are not so bad that I can't afford to pay for excellent service. My profits are much lower than normal. I haven't lost any money yet."

She half smiled. "How do you know I'll give you excellent service?"

He returned her amusement. "I know. Some things you just know without reason."

Nia looked off, absorbing all this. Finally she lent him her attention again. "I'm sorry about your difficulties."

"I'm sorry too. And I'm sorry if I made you feel like I didn't want you around. That's not true at all. I wasn't talking that much because I . . . I was just so absorbed in my business situation."

Nia could understand that. "I bet you worked hard to accomplish all you have."

A sadness crept in the curve of his smile. "I just about gave my blood to see this dream through. And almost lost it because . . . well it doesn't matter now. The constructive thing to do now is get the company back on track. And now I have two business geniuses to help me. One is a friend of mine that I've known since college, and the other is his cousin. He's a very successful entrepreneur with various projects. And she also has various projects, along with being a business consultant at one of the top firms in the country. She's spent a major part of her career rebuilding fledgling companies.''

"Good. I hope everything works out for you, Roland.''

"I hope the man upstairs hears you. But enough about my problems. I'll leave you to get settled in. And I'm just down the hall. So are you and I all right?''

"We're more than all right.''

"Great. If you need anything, just call. And I'll give you a tour tomorrow too.''

"Wonderful.''

Roland walked outside the door, closing it behind him. Thinking, he held the knob for a moment. He didn't mean to tell her all that. He didn't have to. So why did he? If Nia tugged that information out of him, what else could she weaken him into doing? To think about her, he answered himself. To think about how it felt to be close against her like he just was. Closing his eyes, he bit his bottom lip. He was turned on. So turned on.

Though opening his eyes, Roland knew he wouldn't allow himself to be that way anymore. Being around her all the time would cure him of that. He would get used to her, like he had his other maid. They would be friends. Nothing more. And from what she said, it seemed like she needed a friend. What did she mean by life and people disappointing her? Who had disappointed her and why? It all gave her a toughness he didn't expect—a fire that was masked by her ultra-feminine appearance. Oh, yes, he imagined there was much fire beneath her surface.

Unable to sleep, Nia cut on the lamplight and shifted her eyes to the clock. It read 3:15 AM. Perhaps she needed to get used to this room, this bed, this home, this island. Pulling the covers off of her and sliding her legs over the side of the bed, she was soon standing, beckoned by the many stars brightening the sky outside the window.

Looking out, Nia inhaled the fresh air and looked out over the land shadowed by night. She couldn't wait until day to see how the island looked beneath the sunlight. The only thing she could see was the pool. A lone light highlighted it. She loved to swim. And since Roland's bedroom was situated at another end of the house, and Nia knew she wouldn't disturb him, she thought swimming at that moment was a fabulous idea.

I'm going to be out here as often as I can. Nia stood outside, surveying the considerable length of the pool. Taking off her nightgown, her bra, then panties, she thought nothing would be more relaxing than a skinny dip. Certainly Roland was sleeping. She was the only fool who couldn't get to sleep at 3:15 in the morning.

Closing her eyes, Nia took three steps, then did a jackknife dive off the diving board, her body splashing into the water. She did several laps before she swam down to the inmost part of the pool, then came back up. Feeling exhausted now and ready to head in the house for some sleep, she realized she didn't have a towel. She went into the bathhouse at the left edge of the pool. After looking around and finding none in there, she came back out. Except she wasn't expecting to see what she saw. It was the back of a naked man. It was the back of Roland.

He turned around, equally startled by Nia—a naked Nia.

CHAPTER SEVEN

Will you please, please, please give me some of that! If Nia could have read Roland's mind at that moment, those are the words he would have pleaded. So floored he was by the sight of her nudeness exposed to him, he couldn't speak, couldn't move to reach for something to cover himself and couldn't stop looking.

From the vulnerability in her eyes, to the tremble of her full lips and on down to what he imagined about her, she left him breathless, and knowing undoubtedly that his imagination could never create how blessed she was. *Lord, Lord, Lord have mercy,* he thought, swallowing the rush of desire in his throat.

He had been restless from all the travel and all the commiserating about his business, but mostly from all the wondering about Nia. That stumbling incident in her bedroom didn't help matters. So he decided to take a dip in the pool. He loved swimming and once was even considered good enough to make the Olympic trials. Nonetheless, college won over his athletic career. Now he settled for expending his athletic energy either at his other loves, scuba diving and basketball, or in his pool, often late at night after a grueling day of work. Always during those times he enjoyed swimming nude.

Roland had no idea Nia was even awake. He wouldn't have taken a chance on embarrassing himself like this. And God knows he had never predicted her to be outside and looking like she was. Relaxation is what he sought by going to the pool. But as he saw Nia's eyes slinking up and down his bare form, and lingering below his hip and above his thigh, it was obvious to both of them that he wasn't relaxed. He was excited. He was ready. He had never been more ready in his life.

Standing across from Roland, neither could Nia speak, or move to get her clothes, which weren't far away. What's more, she couldn't stop being fascinated by the image of Roland completely exposed before her. From the sexy way he looked in his clothes, she had suspected he looked good out of them. But never, never ever, had she expected what she was seeing. Everything God had blessed him with put the capital S into sexy. And who had caused *all that* in that place where her eyes stuck to most? *What* had caused *all that?* But no one else was around, and the earth was still steady beneath her feet. Did this mean he found her as awesome as she found him? What she was beholding was the most delicious surprise she'd had in a long time. "Thank you, God," she whispered under her breath.

It all made Nia acutely aware that it had been a long time since she'd been with a man. Holding on to her bottom lip to keep it from trembling, Nia wished she could have controlled the other motion inside her. It was like warm liquid was rushing down between her legs—a rush that ached to be satiated. It brought an explosive urgency of erotic need for him.

"Oh, I want him," she cried inside, loving what she was seeing, loving the way he was seeing her. It was almost as if his eyes were beckoning her to come to him, to make love to him until the ache was soothed with sweet love. Except some revelations came to Nia suddenly. They barely knew each other. More importantly, there was no love between them. Therefore, they couldn't *make love*. Roland was her employer, a wealthy, gorgeous man, the kind who married and stayed married to someone in his own social class.

"I—I'm sorry," she said, gathering her clothes from the ground. Straightaway, she slid her nightgown over her head and wiggled her limbs into the neck and armholes. "I didn't know you would come out here." She fought for her eyes to remain up at his head.

"Don't apologize, Nia." Roland picked up a towel that he'd brought from the house and wrapped it around his hips. "You were here first. I should have taken into consideration that I'm not alone here anymore at night. My other maid used to go home to her family after 6:00 in the evenings. And I had no idea you liked . . . you liked skinny dipping too."

"I won't do it again," she promised, her admiration drifting across his broad, hairy chest, then winding back to his eyes. There was something exuding from them that turned her on as much as his unclad body did. She began looking at everything but at them. "It's your house. And you have the right to come out here and skinny dip."

"And so do you." The more he looked at her, the more beautiful she appeared. What had he gotten himself into? Especially having seen what that nightgown hid? "My home is your home now. Really. We'll just let each other know when we're going to do it. Swim, I mean."

Trying to hide how awkward this all felt, Nia's lips curled into a smile. "Whatever you say, Roland. Anyway, I want to get an early start tomorrow."

"So do I. I want to show you around the island before heading to the office."

"You don't have to do that you, you know. I can find my way around."

"I want to," he admitted. *And I wish I could do a whole lot more for you.*

"If you insist."

"I do."

"All right." She strode off, stepping beyond the glass patio doors.

* * *

The next day, sunshine splashed over the blade-like palm tree leaves waving in the clement island breeze as Roland drove Nia throughout St. Croix's laid back capital, Christiansted. Acting as a tour guide for the various attractions, Roland was furtive in admiring how beautiful she looked today. She was equally elusive in stealing glances at him.

Multicolored orchids, morning glories as well as tropical flowers and trees decorated the immaculate lawns of colonial buildings and Victorian houses. Intriguing castle ruins, forts built by pirates, sugar mills, tree-lined courtyards, cobblestoned alleys, large galleries, chic boutiques and swanky restaurants were competitive attractions for any tourist. Stretches of sugar sand beaches sprinkled with ocean lovers swept by the Jeep's window much too fleetingly for Nia to get a real good look at one location. Although, it really made no difference. She hadn't been concentrating on the picturesque scenery of the island anyway. What she had beheld at the poolside last night was foremost in her mind.

Over an hour into the ride, Roland parked his Pathfinder along the southern shore at Grapetree Beach. Nia was the first to swing her legs out the door and stand a few feet from it, reveling at the ravishing sky and the water. Watching her, Roland leaned against his car with his hands in his pockets.

Nia turned around toward Roland. The top of his white shirt was opened just enough to expose what she'd been treated to last night. "This is a beautiful beach."

"I come here often."

She swung back toward the dazzling water. "Real nice. And this weather is so perfect."

"And you're so nice for pretending."

"Pretending?" Swirling toward him, she looked baffled.

The combination of sky and water bestowed on her already luscious skin an even more sensual glow. It just made Roland yearn to see more of what he saw last night. "Pretending that last night didn't bother you. Embarrass you, I mean."

Nervous laughter sifted from her. "Roland, didn't we get all that stuff straight last night. No big deal." *Liar!*

Folding his arms, his head tilted a little to one side. Roland shifted his weight on the other leg. "If you're not embarrassed by us seeing each other like that, then why did you seem so distracted in the car?"

"I wasn't distracted. I was just listening to you."

"Really? I was thinking you were uncomfortable with me now. I was hoping you didn't feel *strange.*"

"No, I don't feel strange," she lied.

"Me either."

Nervously, she laughed again. "We'll just act like it never happened."

He nodded. "I'm with you. I'll act like it never happened."

"I'll forget what I saw. And you forget what you saw."

"Right," he agreed. *Just tell me how? How? How?*

"We can act like today is the first time we met and you can tell me all the things you didn't on your jet."

He smiled. "All right. Ask away."

With her hands folded behind her back, she strolled over to him, making deep prints in the sand. "The first thing I want to know is, what in the world gave you the motivation to become an owner of a chain of resorts? I truly admire that."

Roland shrugged his shoulders like he had done nothing spectacular, but Nia could see from the sparkle in his eyes that he was proud of his accomplishments. "I guess I just always believed I could do and be anything I wanted in this world. And fortunately for me, my parents reinforced that belief in my siblings and me. But believe me, it wasn't easy. I struggled to prove myself to people, worked real hard and sacrificed a lot. Sometimes I had to eat tuna fish ever night of the week, because I couldn't afford anything else. Everything was put into the business. Do you know how it is to eat tuna fish every night? Every night?"

Nia laughed.

His eyes lingered on her lips. She had one of the prettiest mouths he'd ever seen. She had so many things that were pretty to him. "And what about you, Nia? Tell me about yourself. Like where you went to school and tell me all the things you dreamed of being."

Nia scanned the ocean. She tried to smile, but thinking back over her life made it impossible to do so. "I went to some private schools. In junior high and high school."

"Oh, you did?"

"Yes. Then I went to college. Pace University. But I didn't finish."

"Why is that?"

There was a long pause. "My mom was sick with cancer. While she was, I easily received a credit card because I was a student. So I took her on a wonderful, expensive cruise to the Hawaiian islands. She died right after. There were crazy debts from that. Plus, I had to take care of my younger brothers and wanted them to go to college. So I took care of them and put things off for myself. I have college credits, but no degree."

"I'm sorry about your mom." Now he understood why she said there were disappointments. "And I'm sorry about everything that was put on your shoulders. I want to help."

She faced him. "You are helping. You gave me a job."

"No, I mean help with your dreams. Being a maid is not what you want to do with your life." He could tell by the way she spoke, by what he now saw in her eyes—a broken spirit. Tell me what you really want to do."

Smiling, she placed a hand on her hip. "Are you trying to get rid of me? Did you change your mind?"

"No way. I have two guests coming to stay a few months. I'm not sloppy, but not the greatest housekeeper either. I can do enough to get by. And I can cook too. I can. I just don't know if anyone can keep what I cook down their stomach."

She was tickled.

So was he. "No, but seriously, I'm talking about a dream that you might want to pursue in your spare time, in hopes that it can be something full time one day. I'm all for people being all they can be. Although, there's nothing wrong with being a maid. It's a respectable position like any other. But there is something wrong with being one if that isn't what you want to do with your life."

She wondered if he really cared as much as he sounded like he did. "I . . . I used to want to be a singer."

"A singer?" He grinned. "Aw shucks. Hit me a few notes?" Getting comfortable, he sat on the sand near her feet, and looked up.

Feeling silly, she giggled. "I just can't sing to you like that."

"Why not?"

"Because."

"Because what?"

"Because I stopped singing. I don't sing anymore. Not really."

"When was the last time you sang?"

Since that night when Kal heard her, she had sung often. "Let me clarify myself. It's not true that I don't sing at all. I do sing sometimes . . . well, lately I've been doing it. But for a long time I just stopped."

"I want to hear what you sound like."

"Nope."

"And you call yourself a singer." He sucked his tooth at her. "No, you're not a singer." Playful as he sounded, she couldn't tell if he was being serious. "You're not passionate about it. If you were a singer, you'd want to do it all the time and sing for anyone. You would even do it for free because it feels so good to you."

Chuckles escaped from her after hearing the truth. "That's funny what you said. I used to be like that before I stopped singing. Used to sing anytime and for anyone. I just wanted to sing. Just had to sing. I was so, so passionate about it." Feeling like facing the shore again, she did, and spotted a yacht passing in the distance. Somehow it reminded her that time had passed too. Precious time she couldn't get back. Time in which she'd let her dream die. It was like that yacht heading farther and farther out to sea, until it was no longer in sight.

"So why did you stop singing?" Still sitting in the sand, gazing up at her, he wanted her to turn around. Not just to see her face again, but because he detected a quiver in her voice, and soon saw her hand go up by the side of her eye.

"Something happened to me and all the songs I'd sung just went away."

"You mean your mother's death?"

"No, my mother encouraged me to sing before she died. Told me she'd be watching me and that I should never stop. It was something else that took my music away from me. Couldn't sing anymore after that. I didn't feel like singing. Just felt like . . ." Her hand went up by her eye again.

Roland stood, positioning himself directly behind her. He knew whatever the memory was, it was making her cry, and all he could think about was taking her pain away. He wouldn't ask her anymore. He merely raised his hands to reach for her shoulders. Although just as he was about to touch them, he stopped himself. As attracted as he was to her, it was better for him not to cross any lines. He knew if he touched her just once, comforted her just once, he would want to touch her again, comfort her again if she ever needed it. He would want to do as much as possible to see that no tears ever came to her eyes.

Nia turned around and faced him. With her cheeks dry, she smiled. Even so, Roland could see that the luster in her eyes was gone. A faint redness lined the rims.

"Shouldn't you be heading to work now? You've given me a wonderful tour, but all good things must come to an end."

Raising his wrist, Roland glimpsed at his watch. "You're right. Let me drop you home first, and after that I'll head to my office. I have to get some papers ready to overnight to my friend Wade and his cousin. Hopefully, they'll be here in a few days. Wade won't give you much trouble at the house either. He's easygoing like myself. But I don't know much about his cousin."

On the terrace of Suzanne's Park Avenue penthouse, Wade sat basking at the sundown shading the Manhattan skyline from a yellow, oblong patio table. Sitting across from him, Suzanne placed her elbow on the table, laced her fingers through her short, layered locks and aimed her concentration downward to examine the contents of a package Roland had FedExed them earlier in the day.

For a moment, Wade switched his fascination away from the scenery, took a sip of his neglected glass of lemonade, then perused the squared angular face of his cousin. Suzanne made him smile. She was the smartest woman he'd ever met. She was the owner of five small successful businesses. In addition, she had garnered countless accolades in the corporate world as a consultant. He knew she was the perfect person to assist his best friend in resurrecting his business. And, when Roland's opportunity presented itself, she was ready for a change.

Finally, Suzanne met her cousin's gaze. "Things do look bad for the resorts. But not so bad that they can't turn a substantial profit again. You see, from what I see, most of the problem lies with neglect. How did he let things get like this anyway?"

Wade pulled himself up straighter in his chair. "He wasn't thinking." *Not with the head on his shoulders.* "He was distracted by personal matters."

Suzanne peered down, scanning over numerous other documents. "Well at least the losses didn't occur because the company itself wasn't drawing tourists. Destiny Resorts was making major profits at one time." With a content expression, she raised her head. "And they will again with your expertise and mine. I think we should start revamping the marketing strategy first."

"From what I've read, I agree."

"We'll see what cutie pie says."

Grinning at her pet name for his closest friend, Wade tugged his glasses up by the middle. "I saw how you checked Roland out at the meeting."

Suzanne twisted her lips with her amusement. "Like I said he's a cutie. No, I take that back." She put both elbows on the table, lacing her hands together in front of her mouth. "The man can take any woman's breath away."

"Aren't you curious if he's available?"

"Doesn't matter to me. You know that. If I want him, I want him."

"That's wrong, Suzanne. But luckily for you he is unattached. His girlfriend and he broke up three months ago."

"I don't care if they were screwing every night like they breathed off the stuff. If I want him, I want him. And what I want, I get."

"Not always." He spoke between sips of lemonade. "I distinctly remember a Kal somebody who was out of the picture pretty quickly, and not because you wanted him out."

Promptly, Suzanne smiled. Kal, Kal, Kal. Thinking of Kal always made her think of Nia. If only Nia knew they had more than Kal in common, more than the other man in their past, more than Nia could ever imagine. What would she say if she knew *everything?*

In answering Wade, Suzanne shrugged her shoulders. "Oh, Kal was nothing. I didn't really want him. If I did, he'd be right here with me."

Wade's two tiny dimples appeared. "I guess confidence is good."

"Good my foot! It's not confidence that's going to get Roland's company to where it should be, and it's not confidence that's going to get Roland in my bed. If I decide that's where I want him. It's simply me."

Knowing he really wanted to call her conceited as hell, Wade shook his head. "If you say so." Despite her obnoxiousness he loved her anyway.

Their fathers were brothers. Her father was an affluent New York cardiologist. Having a father in the armed services, Wade was an army brat. Even though they always talked on the phone, it was only occasionally that he saw Suzanne in person as children. Yet, even during those times, instead of her clinging to her girl cousins, Suzanne always clung to him. Though she swore she never needed a protector, Wade always tossed himself into that role. More than that, their bond was likened to a brother and sister. Being an only child, and one that was perpetually attempting to prove he wasn't a nerd, he was proud of that role. As adults they were thrown into each other's lives more regularly. What's more, lately with the new venture with Roland, they were together often. And now after always talking about his best friend from college, Roland, Wade had finally introduced the two.

"I really don't know if you're Roland's type," Wade pointed out. He tugged his glasses up by the middle.

"What do you mean?" she snapped, leaning forward.

Wade thrust his hand forward. "Hold on now. Of course, you're attractive and successful enough. You know you're bad, girl."

"You bet I do."

"It's just that Roland likes a . . . a certain kind of woman."

Steely-eyed, Suzanne leaned across the table even more. "And what kind is that?"

He wanted to say "A nice one." "A quiet one," he uttered instead.

"I can be quiet."

"Be who you are, Suzanne. Don't deny your spirited nature. Just be *the best* of who you are. But enough about that. Are you taking the flight with me to St. Croix on Tuesday afternoon?"

Hours later, Wade had fallen asleep on the couch with the remote control in his hand. His mouth was open. His tongue hung southward out of it. "A sorry sight," Suzanne muttered, her gaze dropping to the same suit he'd worn for the last few days. She hated that her cousin was so cheap, but she loved him anyway.

After removing his glasses, she laid them on the coffee table. Following that, she tucked a blanket around him. Taking a moment to look at how innocent he looked while sleeping, she then grabbed her shoulder bag and headed out the door. It was well past midnight. Wade looked too tired to wake him up and have him walk with her. She wasn't afraid. Suzanne wasn't scared of New York in the wee hours, wasn't scared of getting mugged, raped or killed. If anything, her attitude was that the muggers better be afraid of her. Not only did she carry a little razor in her bag, but she once scared off a would-be attacker by honoring him with a sailor's dictionary of curses.

Ice cream was the reason she strode out of her lobby door minutes later. The corner store always had her favorite, Haagan Daas, Macadamia Brittle. She loved to crunch, especially when she was mad. That was often.

Sauntering down to the corner store, lots of people were enjoying the warm, yet comfortable night air. Particularly lovers. They sickened Suzanne the way they held hands, locked each other's waists and kissed so brazenly. In her opinion, they just wanted to show off being in love, which was childish to her. What did being in love really mean anyway, she asked herself. It would never last. Her parent's thirty-seven year marriage ended in divorce. Furthermore, none of her relationships ever lasted. She always became bored with someone, or they couldn't deal with her *spirited nature,* as Wade put it. Therefore, she usually broke things off, or there was a mutual break up. Only Kal and the man Nia knew all too well had left her. But what if . . . what if Roland could be the star in her next romantic show? Drop-dead gorgeous as he was, he sure looked good enough to keep around.

Unfortunate for Suzanne though, that Nia lookalike, Bianca, had decided to fight her firing by filing a complaint with the Equal Employment Opportunity Commission. There was going to be an investigation on Monday. Because of that, Suzanne wouldn't find out until late in the day if she could take off to St. Croix with Wade on Tuesday and greet Roland with every flirtatious teeth in her mouth.

After settling for Vanilla Swiss Almond because they didn't have her favorite flavor, and buying Wade a carton too, Suzanne stepped out of the store onto the avenue, strolling back toward the penthouse. When a car slowed up next to her, she didn't pay any attention to the driver, who was rolling down the window. She thought it was just the average lonely guy trying to pick up someone for the night.

But when she heard "Suzanne, Suzanne," the double pronouncing of her name, like *he* usually had greeted her when they were friendly, she knew it was only one person calling her.

When Suzanne looked over to the street, Kal was double-parking his Jaguar.

He hurried out toward her with the cynical words he was about to express practically written on his face. "Suzanne, Suzanne," he repeated.

She didn't slow up or stop. "It is *not* good to see you, Kal. So I won't lie to you saying that it is."

He caught up to her. "Oh, wow, and I thought we meant something to each other once. That's too bad. But still, I have something to ask you."

"Get lost." Her fingers were getting cold from the bag of ice cream. She switched it to the other hand. "I'm over that disorder that made me want you."

"Ah, baby. I'm not trying to ask you out, if that's what you're thinking."

"What do you want?" She stopped.

Ceasing his footsteps too, Kal faced her. "Did you set that fire?"

Suzanne dropped the bag of ice cream. Promptly, she knelt to pick it up. His eyes never leaving hers, Kal beat her to it.

"Did you?" He handed the bag to her.

She yanked it from his hands. "What the hell are you talking about?"

"I'm talking about that fire at Big Boys months ago. You're the only one who is crazy enough to do something like that."

"Get out of my face." She started walking again, much faster than before.

Kal kept up with her pace. "Mighty defensive, Suzanne. You had been following me all night the night before. You probably saw something you didn't like."

"Like what? What reason would I have to set a fire?"

"You might have seen me talking with Nia Lashon."

"Who is she?"

Kal found her funny. "Girl, now I know you're hiding something. You know, Nia. She said you did."

"So what? I know the slut."

"Uh huh, now we're getting somewhere. You clearly don't like her."

"I don't like you either. That doesn't mean I'm going to set fire to your house."

"You knew that I was trying to get with her."

"I could have cared less."

"Oh, you care. You cared enough to want to hurt her."

She slung her hand at him. "Please don't make me laugh."

"You know you had something to do with it."

"Because of you?" She stopped and glared at him. "I'd have to have much more than *you* to make me want to kill that slut. A whole lot more."

She was approaching her building. Before entering it, she merely leered at Kal for a moment. "You can't bother me, Kal. Unlike you, I have an exciting life to live. I have no time for lowlifes. You know, deep down I never did think you were good enough for me. Too much street in you. All the money in the world couldn't buy you class."

Kal thought that was funny too. "Say what you want about me, baby. I may be from the streets and the streets may still be in me. And I have done things that I'm not proud of. But none of them is as bad as trying to murder someone."

"Keep spouting that lie and I'll sue you for slander. Goodnight, Kal."

She sashayed into the building. Kal stood watching her. What did he ever see in her besides her looks? He never liked snobby women no matter how fine they were. Along with snobbishness, this woman was crazy too. Had she set the fire? If she did, was her jealousy about him the only reason she did it? Nia had expressed that they weren't true friends. Suzanne verified that by calling Nia a slut.

In any case, Kal merely wanted to mess with her. He wanted

to let her know that if she had attempted to harm Nia, she hadn't gotten away with it. He sure hated that Nia had vanished when Big Boys burned down. He really needed her for his label. How could he get in touch with her? Easy, he then thought, and wondered why he hadn't thought of it before. He would hire an investigator. He would have Nia Lashon signed to his label if it was the last thing he did. Just as enticing, he would have her in his bed, too.

CHAPTER EIGHT

With the delicious scents of bacon, eggs, biscuits and grits encircling the kitchen, Nia was standing by the stove when Roland came down the steps and sat at the table.

He looked like he'd won the lottery. "How are you on this wonderful, sunny morning, Ms. Nia Lashon?"

"I'm fine." Nia carried his plate over to the table, unable to stop looking at that big, beautiful smile formed on those I-can-kiss-you-into-madness lips. "Are you always this happy in the morning?" She set the food in front of him.

"Of course. I'm alive another day."

"I hear that. Maybe some of your good temperament will rub off on me." She pointed to the juice and the milk. "Which one?"

"I'm a juice man. Can't you tell?"

You're a healthy man. That's for sure.

She poured him a tall glass of juice, placed the carton and milk back in the refrigerator, then headed toward the stairs. "You have a good day at work."

"Wait a minute." He hopped up and pulled out the chair opposite his. "Aren't you going to join me for breakfast?"

"I thought you might want to be alone."

"No, I'd like to have some company. Yours." His eyes deepened into hers.

The look made her so warm, Nia knew she couldn't sit comfortably across from him. It would just feed the attraction she was already feeling toward him. "I do have some things I want to do upstairs." She began to mount the stairs, turning around as she talked. "I want to get this house in perfect shape before your guests arrive for their stay. But you have a nice day."

"You too, Nia."

She had only walked up a step when she heard him call, "Nia?"

She backtracked that step to see him. "Yes?"

"Do you mind not cooking for tonight? I'm going to bring home some Chinese food. We both can relax. It's Friday. On Fridays I don't want you to cook. The weekend is always special to me. It should be to everybody."

She thought that was thoughtful of him. "All right."

"What do you like?"

"General Tso's Chicken."

"Good choice. I like that too. I'll get each of us a large one."

For the first time in a long time, it felt like Friday night when Roland headed up to his doorway after a long day of work. He didn't know if it had to do with him knowing that he was getting some help with the business, or how much he was enjoying Nia, or even if it was the music she was playing. He heard it from the window. The Prince classic Purple Rain hit him full force when he opened the door.

"Now that brings back memories," he said, closing the door.

Wearing a brown sweat suit and sneakers, Nia was relaxing on the floor with piles of CDs, 45s and albums surrounding her. "I hope you don't mind my disturbing your record collection. But it looked a bit messy."

"Of course I don't mind." He laid the bag of Chinese food on a crocheted server on the coffee table. Joining her on the floor, he agreed. "The collection was messy."

She began stacking the albums. "What does this song make you remember?"

The memory made him chuckle. "Being so young. Thinking I was *so in love.*"

"How do you know you weren't?" She stopped stacking and looked at him.

His smile faded. "Because when I really fell in love, it didn't feel like it did then. And when it was over, it hurt like hell." He continued smiling, but his eyes didn't match.

Nia observed him a moment before she started arranging the 45s. "I guess songs do remind you of certain times in your life. This song makes me remember going to basketball games, and then going to a party after, and then slow dancing with this cute guy that I liked. Purple Rain brings back good memories."

Just then, the bell rang. Roland went over to the door, looked through the peephole and opened the door. A stocky repairman, whose lean face didn't match his body, stood looking at him.

"Can I help you?" Roland asked.

Nia stood. "I called him. The dishwasher isn't working properly."

The man's fleshy eyes took a slow, head to foot look at Nia. Roland missed none of the staring, not even his continued gawking as Nia escorted the repairman into the kitchen.

When she returned, Roland was once again relaxing on the floor. Nia resumed her place too.

She noticed that something was funny to him. "Something tickling your funny bone?"

"Somebody was checking you out."

"So." Nia knew the man was staring at her.

"Would you go out with him if he asked?"

Surprised, Nia widened her eyes. "What is that supposed to mean?"

"I'm just curious."

"Why?"

"You're a nice young lady. Maybe I just want to make sure you meet someone nice."

She didn't know how to take that. On one hand, she knew they couldn't be involved. On the other, it gave her a slight thrill that he could be interested in her romantically. Was he telling her not to get any ideas about him?

"How do you know I haven't met someone already?" she asked.

"I don't know."

"Well I haven't." She began stacking the CDs. "Have you met somebody?" She hadn't seen any women coming around.

He couldn't tell her how much he'd been thinking about her, thinking about her in ways that he shouldn't. He had to be committed to his goals like he promised himself he would. "I'm not looking to get in a relationship right now. I'm trying to remain focused on my career."

That statement shouldn't have disheartened her, but it did.

"So are you hoping to find love here on the island?" he asked. "Are you looking for love as they say?"

"I wouldn't say that I'm looking, but I am open. When God sends me the right person, my soul mate, my passion mate, my best friend forever, I'll know it."

"How?" Frowning, he positioned his legs more comfortably.

"Because each time I look into his eyes, I'll know."

"What will you know?"

"I'll just know." She glanced up at him, then looked downward at the CDs. She was still stacking them. There were so many she had three piles already. "My mom used to say that when we meet we'll know it and he'll know that inside my heart is where he belongs." She carried her eyes back up to Roland's. He was staring hard in her eyes. Uncomfortable, she looked back down at the records. He looked over at the stereo. Purple Rain had finished. Roland stood and searched through a pile of CDs. He found one he liked and put it on.

"What are you playing?" Nia asked, looking up at him.

"This collection of 70s, 80s and 90s slow jams I ordered from Cable."

"I heard that advertising before. Those are some nice songs."

Always and Forever by Heatwave began to play.

"They're even nicer to dance to."

Gazing down at her beautiful face, her sultry body covered simply in sweats, Roland knew he shouldn't have been inviting temptation, but emotion won over sense. He extended his hand.

Hesitantly, Nia placed her palm in his and raised herself directly in front of him. Looking in each other's eyes, their bodies drew close together, his arm sealing her small waist, her arms slowly embracing his never-ending shoulders. Closing her eyes, Nia began to feel her heart. It was raging like a machine out of control. But as he drew her even nearer to him, making her thoroughly aware of the hardness of his chest, she realized it wasn't just her heart she was feeling. It was both of their hearts beating as one.

"Is this all right?" she heard him ask as if breath were catching in his throat. He was gazing down at her. "The way I'm holding you?"

Looking back up at him, her eyes dividing between his eyes and lips, she nodded. "Fine." More than fine, she told herself. It had been a while since she had slow danced, especially with a man she found so incredibly sexy.

"Beautiful song," he said, his hips mildly swaying to the rhythm.

"Very beautiful," she agreed, her movements matching his. *Ooh, this feels so good*, she heard her body moan as he drew her even nearer. Her head nestled near his neck, titillating her with a scent that reminded her of citrus and woods.

"So what does this song remind you of?" His fingers began to gently caress into her waist as he held it.

"Always and Forever?" she said, feeling his fingertips gentle prodding. It was like a trigger to her arousal. Tremors of desire began to awaken below her belly. "It reminds me of basement parties where people were dancing . . ."

"Like we are." He was whispering into her hair and his movements were no longer mild. With each second, they were growing more and more provocative.

Nia could feel his hold on her becoming more intense too. More than that, she could feel *him*.

Unable to resist succumbing to the sweet feeling of it all, Nia locked her arms tighter around his shoulders, gliding her hips with the rhythm of that stirring ocean of arousal she felt surging down inside her. When was the last time she had been this turned on?

"Oh," she heard him whimper as he bent slightly, curving his tall body deeper into hers. "This feels so nice dancing with you." She felt him hold her tighter and tighter.

"I like it too," her voice slurred above the maddening feeling overwhelming her, and her lips found themselves brushing against his ear.

The song ended, but their feverish rhythm didn't halt. Like there was music in the silence, they continued, and continued again with the next song, the classic, The Closer I Get To You by Roberta Flack and Donny Hathaway.

"This used to be my jam," Roland whispered, his cheek caressing hers, his eyes shut tight as his embrace of her body.

"Oh, this song really reminds me of something," Nia said, feeling his lips inching dangerously close to hers.

"What happened?" He sounded out of breath. His hand raised. His finger ran torpidly along her cheek.

It felt so good to Nia to have him touch her that way. He was so gentle. "There was someone I loved so much and he hurt me." His finger continued gliding along her cheek. His lips were getting closer.

"Was he the reason why you stopped singing?"

"Yes, he hurt me so bad. I loved him." She felt the sweet breath from his mouth blowing against her lips. "He . . . he was my high school sweetheart. He was the first one . . ."

"Go ahead," he rasped. "You can say it. He was the first one who made love to you."

"Yes." His increasingly erotic body fluctuations, combined with his lips getting closer and closer to hers, was driving her mad with longing for him. What was he doing to her? It was wrong, but it was too pleasurable to stop. When finally their lips pressed together, she simply savored the taste and each froze at that delicious place.

"And how did he hurt you, Nia?" he spoke, the combination of his lips and tongue faintly meeting hers through a tiny opening of her mouth.

"He asked me to marry him," she revealed, tasting the honeyed tip of his tongue. But at the same time, tears began to stroll down her cheeks. She didn't know what was making her feel more emotional, his lips against hers, or the memory. "We made wedding plans." Tenderly his lips blotted away the water. The warmth of his mouth ignited a spasm of heat in her lower body. It rushed downward, beckoning him to place his excited love inside her. If he could have just touched her intimate place, felt how ready she was, he would have known how attracted she was to him. But now it was even starting to feel like more than attraction. It was as if holding him and dancing with him like this was as natural as their breathing. Being this close to him felt like heaven, like magic, like she never wanted to be apart from this amazingly seductive creature. "We even set a date and sent out invitations. But then . . ."

Roland was still patting her tears with his lips. "If you don't want to talk about it we don't have to. I know how it is to be betrayed. I know, Nia."

"You do?" Her lips trembled with wanting as his found their way back to the heated entrance of hers. "Do you know how it is for a guy's mother to tell you her child is too good for you, and that he'll marry a more suitable young lady? And he made some choice in the young lady." Cynically, Nia laughed.

Roland was abhorred that some snob had treated Nia so horribly. "I'm so sorry." Now holding the sensual masterpiece of her face in his hands, he drew back and stared at her. Tears persisted in strolling down her soft cheeks, and her expression was one of such emotion. There was sadness, but he wondered if perhaps there was also desire.

He regretted prying enough to draw out a part of her past that solicited her tears. He ached to comfort her, to end her tears, to make her forget what was still embedded in her broken heart. And looking down at her body, then gazing back in her eyes, Roland knew that he could. Not just because she was beautiful outside, but inside too. She was sweet and honest. At the same time, she was filled with fire and strength. And he admired the way she'd survived. He admired the way she had unselfishly taken care of everyone else to make their lives wonderful, and forgot about her own. It was time she knew what joy was.

"But through it all, I never understood something," Nia went on. *"He* kept telling me there was something I should know. That there was a secret—a secret about me that he knew, but I didn't."

Roland didn't care about secrets, didn't care about anything right then but making Nia feel better. Bending his face closer to hers, he parted his lips, preparing to taste nectar beyond her lips. Except just as he was about to, he heard a clearing of someone's throat.

Nia and Roland swerved around, and moved a considerable distance back from each other.

The repairman was standing across the room. "Dishwashers fixed."

"Thank you," Roland said, escorting him to the door.

The man was continuously looking back at Nia. "You have a nice evening, Ma'am."

He looked at Roland as the door opened. A frisky smile crept over his uneven lips. "You're a lucky man." He winked.

Roland closed the door. Looking at Nia, he didn't know whether to be embarrassed or to continue. Didn't people's lives depend on him? On him staying focused? Aside from that, how would his behavior toward her seem when she awakened from her emotional haze? Caught up in the moment, it was like he had no reasoning.

He noticed that her demeanor was different after the interruption.

"Roland, I'm sorry to unburden all that stuff on you."

"No, it's quite all right," he said, maintaining his distance.

"And I'm sorry that our lips touched. I don't want to scare you off from your position by your thinking that I'll always be coming on to you and expecting sex."

"I don't think that."

"I'm glad. It's just that you're a very nice young lady and very beautiful." Pausing, he stared at her. "And somehow I feel us . . ." He searched for the right word.

"Being drawn to each other?"

"Exactly."

"I feel it too. But it can't be."

His expression said why not, even if he didn't express it verbally.

"Roland, look, I don't want a man like you."

Highly offended, he reared his head back. "Oh, you don't." He liked her honesty, but not that much. If she didn't want something of his, what was all the tension when they were dancing about? She felt the heat like he did.

"You're everything a woman could dream of," Nia elaborated. "So far you seem sweet, hard working and you're sexy. But I want a simple man. Simple. Not a rich man, but a man who won't leave me."

He couldn't help frowning. What she said made no sense to him. "Who said that a rich man would leave you?"

"I've known men like you when I was a child—well, they were somewhat like you. You'll be with a lady like me for fun for a while, but when you realize you need something serious, you'll choose to be with someone like yourself, the one with the education, the status, the one who came from a well known family."

He couldn't believe Nia was saying something so ludicrous. "That's not true, Nia. First of all, I am not looking for a serious relationship like I told you. And if I was, status, education and social standing wouldn't be my criteria for marrying someone and making a lifelong commitment with them. I had a woman who had all that, *all that*—but it didn't work out. But it's real interesting to know you think so little of me. Goodnight, Nia."

He hurried up the stairs, leaving Nia standing in the center of the room. She hadn't meant to say what she did, even if she was thinking it. She was simply trying to save herself. Roland had weakened her. With those lips of his brushing across hers, teasing her about all the lusciousness that could come, and with his hardened body rubbing hers, stirring her desire so powerfully, she had almost forgot her vow—her vow to seek a man who was the opposite of the ones who broke her mother's heart.

Trudging up the stairs to her bedroom, Nia knew she had to always remind herself of what she wanted in a man, in what was best for her. Even as she laid down, and threw the covers over her still warm body, she continued trying to convince herself. Try that she did, it was the feeling of Roland's lips and body that followed her off to sleep hours later.

En route downstairs the next morning with a tightened jaw, Roland was about to bypass Nia's room. Except hearing the most beautiful voice he'd ever heard halted him in his tracks. The record was one he'd never heard before, and he would have gone into Nia's room and asked her what song was that, and who was the artist, when he realized something. The record had no music. It wasn't a record. The awesome voice belonged to Nia. He shook his head at the prowess of it. She wasn't exaggerating when she claimed to be a singer. She definitely had the goods to back it up. He started toward the door to tell her how fabulous she sounded. Then he was reminded of the previous evening. Not the sweet part when they were dancing. He had thought of that too much last night in bed. He was reminded of the other part. Her insulting him, calling him shallow. He continued downstairs.

When Nia came down the steps to prepare Roland's breakfast, she saw that he had already eaten, and was going back and forth through the open door, putting some packed bags out into his Jeep. Not acknowledging her with the slightest look, but concentrating on the rest of his bags, he came back inside.

"Going on a trip?" she asked.

"No, just packing my scuba diving gear."

"Oh, wow. That sounds like fun. I've read brochures about all the things to do on the island."

"There are lots of fun things to do." He was zipping a bag that was stubborn in closing. "And I hope you get out and enjoy this Saturday too."

"I have work to do."

Finally, he looked at her. "Not on the weekend you don't. You're off on Saturday and Sunday."

She smiled. "Thanks."

Roland remained stern-faced. "No problem." He headed toward the door, but stopped before going out. He looked back at her. "Nia, you're not the type of woman I want either."

"Oh, no?" She tried not to look as insulted as she felt.

"I'm not looking for anything serious like you are. I want to stay focused on my goals, and I want a woman who can handle that."

"You mean you want a woman who'll give you sex without commitments?"

He didn't like the way that sounded, but he guessed that was what he wanted. "Yes," he said, nodding slowly.

"Good for you, Roland."

"Have fun today," he said dryly, then closed the door.

Roland was halfway down the highway when he realized how childish he had behaved. He turned his Jeep back around. Looking bored, Nia was sitting at the kitchen table when he opened the front door.

"Look," Roland said, shuffling toward her with his hands in his pockets. "I'm sorry about what I just said to you about you not being my type. It was silly."

The apology made her feel a little better. "And I shouldn't

have said what I said last night. We both want what we want, and we shouldn't want each other anyway."

"Exactly." He nodded. "Ours is a working relationship."

"Right. A friendly working one. Sort of like a brother and sister friend thing."

"Exactly." He nodded again. "So that being out of the way, would you like to go scuba diving with me?"

She looked like an excited little girl. "I'd love to."

"And by the way, I heard you singing."

"You did?" She hoped it wasn't when she hit a sour note.

"When I passed your room this morning. I thought I was hearing a record. You have all the right in the world to state that you're a singer. Many of those on the radio can't hold a candle to you."

She blushed. "You're just being nice."

"No, I'm laying it down to you. Pursue your dream, Nia. If you do, I promise it'll lead you to experiences so incredible you would have never imagined they were possible."

"But it's not my dream anymore. Enough about that. Let's go."

Nia's first adventure into scuba diving was as much fun for Roland as it was for her. As excited as she was about this new sporting venture, she wasn't too sure about the glass-windowed helmet. She kept wondering about the hose that ran from the helmet, wondering if the tenders above the water would supply her enough oxygen.

However, once in the water with Roland, exploring the mystical underwater world of the ocean, Nia felt like she was in another world. But it wasn't the only time she felt that way. She felt that way after the adventure, after Roland and she dined at a posh restaurant, scuba dived some more, and ate again. It was their communication that transported her to this other world. They talked about so many subjects, from comical events in their childhoods to politics, to just about anything that came up. Nia found Roland's thoughts and views, his humor, his experiences and his insights so intriguing, she was addicted to hearing more.

He felt the same. So the next day their adventure was water skiing. And by the end of the day, a day which he wished would have never ended, he felt like he'd been in another world too. Never had he found a woman so interesting, so warm and thoughtful, yet with so many intelligent views about things. They disagreed about as much as they agreed. And regarding those things they disagreed on, he found her arguments very compelling. She absolutely mesmerized him the entire day. He couldn't remember the last time he'd had so much fun with someone. And through it all, he'd fought his impulses to kiss her, even if he could not thwart the desire that surged within him.

It was there. In every laugh they shared. In every amusing disagreement. In every lingering look they exchanged across the table. He had enjoyed this woman so much, he would have wanted to kiss her even if he was blind and couldn't see how physically beautiful she was.

"Goodnight, Nia," he said, as they ended their two days together at her bedroom door. "It's been a lot of fun."

"It has, hasn't it?" Nervously, she looked down, then back up at him. "Sort of really like the brother and sister thing."

"Exactly." He glanced at her lips. They were so tempting, he forced his attention down the hall toward his room. "Better go to bed. I want to get an early start. Wade and his cousin will be in St. Croix soon and I have to get things ready at the office for them. I would also like to have a little dinner party here at the house for them."

CHAPTER NINE

Hearing the socializing of Roland and some guests out on the veranda, Nia stood in the dining room inspecting the table she'd just set. A silver centerpiece cast like a swan held more than a dozen roses. The ornament was beset by a steaming tray of lamb roast, mashed potatoes, creamed corn, a spinach casserole and buckets of Monet. A platter of Cajun shrimp and Buffalo wing appetizers had already been taken out to the guests by Roland. When they arrived, she was still getting things ready in the kitchen. She hadn't met them yet.

Nervousness churned in her stomach as she pondered whether these people would like the dinner she'd chosen and cooked. Her mother had been from the south, North Carolina, and Nia's tastes with spices and selections of meals reflected as much. Although, Nia enjoyed eating and experimenting with meals from other cultures. Overall though, the food looked delicious, but not as delicious as *him* when he walked in the dining room.

Admiring the spread, Roland shook his head. "The food looks great, Nia."

"Thanks. I try."

"You did more than try." He eased around the table toward

her. "You did a fantastic job. Those greedy people out there
are going to love it. And those Cajun shrimps and Buffalo
wings . . ." Closing his eyes, he smacked his tongue. "They
tasted like they were making love to my tongue. Making my
toes wiggle." He opened his eyes, deepening his gaze in hers.

Trying not to stare at him like she always wanted to, Nia
laughed. "You are so funny sometimes."

"And you're wonderful. Thank you for going to all this
trouble." He noticed her playing with her fingers. "And don't
be so nervous. They're going to love it." He came closer to
her, planning to simply grab her hand to ease her obvious
tension. An unseen force drew his arms around her instead.
Gently, Roland hugged her, and unable to resist doing the same
to him, Nia's arms went around him too.

A hug had never felt so good, he thought, and he was unable
to let go. "Don't be afraid. My friends don't bite. They're
going to love your food."

Feeling the mutual appreciation of him, Nia reveled in the
feel of him and closed her eyes. "I'm not afraid." *At least
now I'm not. I'm happier than I've been in a long time.*

When the dining room door swung open, her eyes opened.
The two jumped apart and their gazes leaped toward the door.
Nia saw a thirty-something man with a rumpled suit ap-
proaching them.

"This is Wade," Roland introduced his best friend. "Wade,
this is my exceptionally talented home management assistant,
Nia."

Nia found the job description funny. "How are you, Wade?"

"Much better, meeting you." Wade kissed her hand.

Moments later, Nia couldn't help being a sneak. She stood
on the other side of the dining room door, listening to the guests
commenting on how scrumptious her dinner was. She was
thrilled. Roland was her biggest fan. Even when the others
finished their meals and returned to the veranda, Wade and
Roland were having seconds and thirds alone at the table.

"Nia sure can burn," she heard Roland remark.

"And she sure is fine," Wade pointed out. "Super fine!"

Nia heard him smacking.

"Yes, Nia is a very beautiful woman," Roland agreed.

Nia was ecstatic to hear that he thought so.

"And I saw you two locked together in there." Wade snickered.

Nia listened closer.

Clearing his throat, Roland knew he had gotten carried away in that moment. "I was just comforting her. This is her first big dinner and she was thinking that the guests might not like it."

"Aw Roll, this is me you're talking to. You and that gorgeous creature have been alone for some days now, and you're either starting to fall, or you're just hot."

Nia listened even closer.

Roland acted like he didn't hear him. "So earlier you said your cousin had a situation at work, and that was why she couldn't make the trip with you. I hope she'll be coming soon."

"It was some obligation at the consulting firm where she works. She fired somebody and there was some investigation."

Roland didn't take firing people lightly. His dad was unjustly fired when he was a kid and it was one of the most depressing times of his life. "I hope she had a good reason for doing that. Jobs are hard to get. I don't fire anyone unless I really, really have to."

"I'm sure she had a good reason. But back to that fine lady you're keeping house with."

"We're not keeping house."

"Whatever you want to call it, I can understand why you hired her. She is *bad!* Beautiful eyes, beautiful body. I haven't seen legs and a butt that sweet in years."

Roland took a deep breath to contain his temper. He really didn't want to argue with Wade. "So is your cousin coming soon, this week, next week?"

"She'll call me and let me know. And I'll let you know as soon as I find out."

"Good. I look forward to seeing her again."

"So tell me the truth," Wade pressed. "Have you had any? Is she as good as she looks?"

Sourly, Roland wrinkled his mouth. "You know I would never tell you something like that. It seems the older you get, the cheaper and crazier you get."

Wade laughed at himself. "You want some, don't you? I can tell. It's written all over you."

"And like I was telling you outside, you should hear Nia sing. Oh, man can she blow."

"I bet she can," Wade laughed out.

But Nia had had enough. Armed with a huge leftover chicken leg from last night's dinner, she charged into the dining room, stood over Wade, and whacked him over the head with the meat and bone.

"Oh!" he screeched, grabbing his head. "Did a brick fall from the ceiling?"

Roland fought desperately not to laugh, but as he watched Nia marching out the door, he became furious. She had no right to attack his guest.

She was entering the bedroom when he caught her by the arm, whirling her around to meet his anger. "What is wrong with you attacking my guest, my best friend at that?"

"He deserved it." She jerked him off her arm.

"Why would Wade deserve being whacked over the head with a big chicken leg?" He almost laughed just saying it.

"Because he was insulting me and you let him."

"What are you talking about?" *I hope she didn't hear.*

"I was standing at the door and I heard him talking about me. Talking nasty."

He disliked her eavesdropping. Far worse, he disliked what Wade had said. "Look, Nia, I apologize for my friend. Sometimes he gets foul. But when you really get to know him, you'll like him."

"I doubt that."

"He was wrong. And I was wrong, too."

"You?"

"Yes, when I hugged you downstairs. I had no right."

"I hugged you back."

"Well, I just thought I might have overstepped my bounds. If I did, I'm sorry. Sometimes I'm very touchy."

"No harm done."

"Good."

He left the room and Nia relaxed across her bed. Footsteps approaching her room made her sit up. Thinking it was Roland again, she said, "Come in," in answering the knock at the door.

Seeing Wade, the disappointment was vivid on her face. "What do you want?"

"I just wanted to tell you I'm sorry." He tugged his glasses up by the middle. "Please accept my apology."

"Do you always talk about women like that?"

"Guys just have fun when they're alone, as long as it doesn't go too far."

"You went pretty far."

"I'm sorry. I was wrong. If I could take it back I would. I guess I learn something every day."

"I hope you learned not to talk about me or any other woman like that."

"I hear you. But you can't tell me that when women are alone, they don't talk about men—I mean talk about their bodies?" His two tiny dimples pinched his cheeks.

Nia speculated. Of course, she had been around women who discussed men's body parts and even shared some comical sexual performances. Though she wasn't about to admit this to Wade. "You're forgiven. So is that all you want?"

"No," he said, stepping closer to her, his expression becoming intense. "Be easy on my boy."

"What?" She was baffled by what he meant.

"Be easy on, Roland. I think he's starting to like you."

"I like him too."

"No, I don't mean that. I mean *like* you. He couldn't stop talking about you out on the veranda, telling everybody how nice you are, telling them how much fun you had together scuba diving and water skiing, and how good you sing. I've known him a long time and I can tell when *it's* starting. Love hasn't been too kind to him lately. And with you two living in the house together, it wouldn't be so hard to become very close. So be easy.''

Wade walked off, leaving Nia wondering. What made him think that Roland really liked her? Was he exuding that energy, which she felt so strongly herself? That energy that made her very aware that he was a man and she a woman, each time they were around each other. And why did he say love had been unkind? What happened to Roland? That night when they danced, he had revealed that someone betrayed him, but he didn't get into details. She guessed he'd been so involved with her pain, he didn't share his own.

But who could possibly have broken his heart? And how? But even if she discovered the answers it wouldn't make a difference. She hadn't changed her mind about what she was seeking in a mate.

Hours later, the guests had left. Wade and Roland were in the billiard room playing pool. Several times, they asked Nia to join them. Declining so they could male bond, she chose to relax across her bed with her latest romance novel.

The phone ringing made her put a floral-patterned bookmark on the page she was reading. Expecting a call from her friend, Alma, Nia put the book aside, and raised the receiver to her ear.

''Hello?''

''Nia?''

The voice was familiar. But it couldn't be ... ''This isn't—''

''It's Kal. Kal Hunter from New York. How you doing, baby?''

''I'm fine,'' she answered bewilderedly.

''I know that.''

"How did you get my number? How did you know where I was?"

"Did some checking."

"I don't like people checking on me. I like my privacy."

"How would you like to be rich and famous?"

"I'm happy with my life the way it is."

"What are you doing in St. Croix? Did you hook up with a fellow or was it a career move?"

"Career."

"What are you doing?"

She knew he would make a nasty comment about her way of earning a living. He was the type. She didn't care. She was proud of what she did. "I'm a maid."

"That's nice."

She was stunned. "Huh?"

"I said that's nice. My mom took care of me and my sisters off of a maid's salary. But I bet your employer can't offer you the kind of money I can."

"Are you still into that record stuff?"

"Baby, my business is starting to take off big time!" He could hardly contain his bliss. "My artists are getting airplay and the publicity is starting to kick in. And I still want you to be part of my label."

She still didn't want to deal with Kal, and she still wasn't about to abandon something solid for something so uncertain. "I'm not interested."

"Baby, you must be kidding. I know your mama didn't raise no fool."

"You're right she didn't. That's why I'm staying right where I am."

"I wrote some songs specifically with your voice in mind. I'll never forget how you sang. I can never forget that voice of yours."

"I'm not interested, Kal. Goodbye."

The phone clicked. Their connection was gone. Kal took a deep, irritated breath. "It's her loss."

* * *

The EEOC officers filed out of the Brayward & Boyce conference room, shaking hands with Suzanne and unsuccessfully attempting to do so with Bianca Coswell. Suzanne attempted to follow the committee members who had made a decision in her favor. Except Bianca blocked her exit out of the door.

"Excuse me?" Suzanne remarked with a smirk. "I have things to do and people to see."

"Not until I let you know something." Her large, hazel eyes were red from crying. She wiped both of them as she leered at Suzanne. "This is not over. I didn't have enough proof to show that you fired me unjustly. But the debt will be paid."

"Help yourself."

"I don't have to. Like I said, the debt will be paid. I don't know why you fired me, but it has nothing to do with my lateness, or even my performance. But I am one hundred percent of one thing and you should learn this in your life too . . ." A tear strode down her cheek. Not wiping it, she looked firmly at Suzanne.

"What should I know, deary?"

"You should know that my grandmother was a voodoo priestess."

Suzanne sniggered. "And you're going to put a hex on me?"

"No hexes here. I don't have to do that. My grandmother always shared her wisdom with me and one thing sticks out in my mind: evil is punished with a thousand times more evil. Meaning for you Suzanne, every dog shall have its day. You shall most definitely have yours."

"Wow, I'm soooooo scared," Suzanne teased.

"You should be." Rolling her eyes, Bianca flounced out of the room.

CHAPTER TEN

On the forty-third floor of the World Trade Center, among a paneled conference room embellished with plush, olive green carpet, Kal reclined in a homey chair around an oblong, oak table. Seated with his sixteen member staff of diverse ages, listening to their individual reports about their departments within his record label, he was extremely pleased with what he was hearing. His baby, Ecstasy Records was progressing faster and better than he projected it would.

Of most interest to him was the point in the meeting when his Promotions Manager, Dana, pored over her notes, preparing to share the breakthroughs of her projects. A divorcee and single mother raising three boys alone, she was a no-nonsense sister, who Kal admired personally as well as professionally. Always showing him he hadn't wasted a penny in hiring her, her brilliant efforts were a major impetus propelling his company forth.

Propping her palm against her satiny cheeks while placing her elbow on the table, she was reading her notebook when she realized everyone was silent, waiting to hear what she had to say.

Stark-faced, she looked up. "I would like to report that things are really looking good for Ecstasy. First of all, our male solo artist, Elan will be a guest actor on the soap opera 'All My Children.' "

"Freakin' A!" Kal exclaimed with a pound of his fist on the table. The others echoed his enthusiasm. "Tell us more, girl."

"Elan will be playing himself on the soap, and singing his song, 'Betcha Didn't Know I Love You', which is fast rising on Billboard's 100."

"Hot damn!" Kal shouted, making the others laugh.

"He'll also be performing on the Lady Of Soul Awards."

Everyone again expressed their approval.

"And there's more for Elan, more for him along with our male group, Torch, and female group, Flame, along with our esteemed CEO . . ." She glanced at Kal. "Well, we all have seen our label featured in this month's Emerge Magazine, and last month's Black Enterprise, but now we're going to be featured in several major newspapers across the country."

There was a thunder of cheers. Beaming, Kal couldn't stop shaking his head. "You go girl!"

Dana's countenance remained austere. "Torch will also appear on 'Planet Groove.' And Flame will be appearing on 'Soul Train'.

The room was in an uproar of uncontainable excitement.

Kal would have kissed Dana if she hadn't looked so forbidding. "You're bad, girl! You're too bad! A raise is on the way. A big one."

A pinch of a simper cracked Dana's bare lips. "And I have a couple of more things to report."

"Lay it on me," Kal beckoned.

"All the radio stations have received their copies of our promotion CDs for Torch's new single." She flicked a wayward dredlock off her eye. "And so far, I've heard from the program directors from our New York stations. "Both are going to play Torch's, 'Love Of A Lifetime' in the next two weeks. They'll be contacting us as to the specific day and time of the first air date. And BET will put the video for Love Of A Lifetime in rotation at the beginning of the month.''

Everyone went into hysterics with the last news, except Kal.

Weighing how this tremendous publicity would change his life, he was silent a moment. Mega success was imminent. Was he ready for it?

"So how's your search been going for the label's female solo artist?" the youngest member of the team, Brendell, asked Kal. With his youthful appearance—and hip hop style of dress, Brendell seemed much younger than his twenty-eight years.

Kal sighed his frustration. "I've been checking out the clubs and other sources, and I haven't discovered that voice I'm seeking yet. Whoever the sister is that sings the songs I wrote for our label's female vocalist, has to really, *really* blow. There's no half-stepping with those songs.''

Brendell nodded. "I hear that.''

"I'll find her," Kal assured him. "Somewhere out there is the first lady of Ecstasy Records." *Too bad it can't be Nia Lashon.*

Seven hours later, with dusk setting outside his recording studio's floor-to-ceiling windows, and with the candle-like atmosphere shading within it, Kal believed he had the perfect ambience for laying down one of the most impassioned tracks he'd written for a female vocalist. It was just too bad that he had to subject himself to preparing to hear Felicia sing the sensuous ballad. Watching her adjusting her headphones as he sat in the engineer's booth, Kal hoped these latest voice lessons she claimed helped her so much, truly had.

"Let me get a level on your voice," he spoke through a microphone, turning knobs and gazing through the glass at her.

"All right." Glowing with her eagerness, she belted out several notes and stopped. "Got it?''

Unimpressed, he nodded. "Yes, I have it. You're ready for the real thing?''

Her ear to ear grin showed how ready she was. "Un hunh."

Kal pressed the button for the prerecorded music to play. "Hit it."

The introduction began. Felicia came in on her cue. Barely a verse was sung when Kal stopped the music.

Her bottom lip dropped. Her arms outstretched. "What's up?"

"Come inside here, Felicia."

She didn't move. "But I thought you wanted to hear the new way I sound?"

"Baby, get your pretty tail in here."

She liked the way he said that. She came quickly, easing onto his lap and slipping her arms around his neck. "You want me to do it in a higher or lower octave?"

"I don't want you to do it at all."

Incensed, she sprang up from his lap. "You don't like the new way I'm singing?"

"Sit back down here." He tried to pull her back on his lap. It felt real good.

Jerking him off, she stepped back from him. "What you trying to say, Kal?"

"Felicia, why do you want to be a singer?"

Breathing hard, she folded her arms. "You didn't answer my question."

"Answer mine first."

She rolled her eyes at him. "I want to be a singer because I want to be a star."

"That's the wrong answer."

"What?"

"That's the wrong answer. That's not the reason you should want to be a singer. A real singer, a singer like Gladys Knight, Patti Labelle, Aretha Franklin, Whitney Houston, Mariah Carey, Nancy Wilson, and Ella Fitzgerald and Mahalia Jackson, all have one thing that is essential to good singing."

She unfolded her arms. "What's that?"

"They feel it. They sing from the heart."

Frowning, she folded her arms again. "I'm feeling it."

"No, I mean they *feel* what they're singing because it's

coming straight from their heart. Straight from it! Even super-
star recording artists who aren't considered great singers make
hit after hit song, because they feel what they're singing. Something from their heart touches the listener. They feel and they
want to make the listener feel it. They care about the listener.
They're not just trying to be a quote un quote, *star*. The most
important thing to them is entertaining their audience.

"They want them to feel in love, rid them of pain, give them
hope, make them see a situation for what it is, or tell a story
they can relate to. In short, they're singing because it's all
about their audience."

He didn't enjoy hurting her feelings, but that singing of hers
was getting on his nerves and wasted his time.

"It's like this, Felicia. You know I like you a lot. We have
a good time and we can still have it. But I can't sign you with
my label. No, your voice isn't great, but—"

"You have some nerve!" Angrily, she knotted her mouth
and swung her braids off her face.

"But even if wasn't great, I could work with it if I was
feeling something. All I feel is that you want to be a star, like
you said. But it has to be about your audience. They have to
enjoy you, and you should care that they do."

She sucked her tooth, shuffling toward the door. "Later for
you!"

The door slammed so deafeningly, Kal had to tap one of his
ears to see if he could hear. Relieved that he could, he wished
for one more thing: that Nia Lashon would come to her senses
and call him.

Smells so good, just like him. This was Nia's thought as she
stood before the washing machine, clutching one of Roland's
undershirts, inhaling its piquant scent. Most of his laundry was
swirling inside the machine, enveloped in white foam. Yet this
one piece compelled her to cling to it because the scent was
so highly concentrated on it. Holding it against the delicate

skin on her cheeks, Nia shut her eyes, remembering all the heartwarming things about him as a man and as a person.

In the short time she'd known Roland, he'd made some impression on her, making her feel more attached and interested in him every day. It wasn't supposed to be that way. How could she make herself stop all the wondering, feeling, wanting?

The phone's ring pierced the haze of her thoughts, making her hurry to the wall shelf where it sat. "Hello?"

"Hello, Nia?"

Roland's voice made a flutter in her stomach.

"How was your day, Roland?"

"Great. But it hasn't ended yet. I'm going to be a while longer, and I need you to do me a favor."

"Anything." *If only I could do anything to you.*

"There's a blue folder in my study. Has about twelve pages in it."

"Okay."

"Could you bring it over to my office?"

"At the resort?"

"Yes. I thought it would be a chance for you to see the place too."

She was excited not only about visiting the resort, but his thoughtfulness. "I'd love to see the resort."

"Great. And do me another favor?"

"Anything."

"Wear something formal, a gown or something. A guest is having a party in the ballroom area. And you're going to have to pass through there to get to my office. If you're not dressed in formal attire, security probably won't let you up."

Nia questioned why Roland wouldn't tell security to let her up regardless of what she was wearing. On the other hand, she liked the idea of getting dressed up for a change.

"I have a gown I wore to a wedding."

"Great. So how fast can you get here? I'm sending a driver to pick you up."

"Oh, boy." Calculating how long it would take her to get

ready and find the folder, she estimated, "About a hour and a half."

"Fine. I can't wait to see you in that gown. Can't wait!"

And I can't wait to see you, period.

Raspberry fragrance bubble bath was still invigorating Nia's senses when she stepped out of the tub onto the lush, pink carpet. Patting the towel on the pellets of water speckled over her warm skin, her mind replayed the way Roland said he couldn't wait to see her in the gown. Whatever his expectations were, she didn't want to dash his hopes.

Inside the bedroom, she opened the cherrywood Victorian dresser and took out a pair of turquoise satin panties. There was a matching bra, but the dress she was wearing required a strapless one, or none at all. Since she didn't have one, she was opting for the latter.

Once her panties were on, along with some French coffee-colored hosiery, Nia opened the wall length closet and ferreted out a silver lamè evening gown with a V-neck and spaghetti straps. Slipping it on over her head, shoulders and down her curvy figure, she began to feel pretty even before she looked in the mirror.

Turning from side to side, she liked the way the gown fit, not too tight, not too loose—just right. She also liked how the fabric felt so soft and feminine against her skin. The way the silver color accentuated the rich, brown tone of her complexion made her even happier.

She disliked foundation on her face, particularly in a tropical climate, so she chose to simply apply a small amount of blush, lipstick and eye shadow, all in shades of Raspberry Ice. Complimenting the look, she sprayed her hair with a dash of oil sheen and brushed it back in one neat bun. Tiny silver ball earrings, and the same color bag and shoes completed the look. When Nia took one final look in the mirror, she was pleased with the woman reflecting back at her.

* * *

Exotic flowers, statue-waterfalls and ponds with real live swans were some of the lovely attractions that captured Nia's attention upon the driver parking the limousine in front of one of Destiny Resorts International's many buildings. Being escorted along a white, pebbled walkway to the entrance, Nia felt a tinge of nervousness and didn't know why. Yet the feeling vanished, conquered by bewilderment when they ventured a few steps inside the building. Guided by the hand of the driver, there was total darkness. Neither was there anyone in sight or any sound of anyone.

"SURPRISE!"

Unexpectedly, the lights came on in a luxurious ballroom, complete with a band and at least a hundred elegantly dressed people, all beaming at Nia. Roland and Wade were among the crowd. Above them all was a huge banner bearing the bright red inscription WELCOME TO ST. CROIX, NIA.

In shock that Roland had gone to such lengths for her, Nia was momentarily speechless, her hand clutching her wildly beating heart.

Roland walked toward her. "I just wanted to welcome you. You didn't have to leave your life in New York and come here to help me. And believe me, folks. I needed help. I'm a lousy housekeeper."

Everyone chuckled, including Roland.

"I appreciate you, Nia. I hope you'll be very happy on this island and working with me, and I just wanted everyone to know how special you are and to meet you."

Glowing, Nia had to fight the temptation to cry. "I know I haven't been working with you long, but in the short time I have worked with you, it hasn't seemed like work at all. It feels like I'm on vacation. And if I seem special, it's because you're making me feel that way. Thank you, Roland."

Her arms went around him. It felt so good, she had to force herself to let go.

Starting at the front of the ballroom, working their way to

the back, Roland introduced Nia to every guest, making sure each was informed that not only was she a great home management assistant, but an awesome singer. The only disappointment of the evening was her not getting an opportunity to dance with Roland. The reason being that many were pulling him in their direction, engaging him in lengthy discussions. Others were interested in Nia, in sharing information about the island, and about themselves.

Wade did manage to steal her from a conversation, escorting her to the middle of the dance floor. The band was performing Stevie Wonder's, 'You and I'.

Laxly, Wade placed his willowy arms around her waist. "So, were you surprised?"

"Nope," she teased him. "I pretended."

"You weren't pretending." His dimples appeared for her. "You were about to cry you were so surprised."

Nia had hoped her sentimentality hadn't showed. She was hoping it didn't show even then. It felt like she was dreaming all this, dreaming since she first stepped on the island, dreaming that she even knew Roland.

"These are good people," Wade stressed. "I've met some of them on my trips to see Roland in the past, but most of them I don't know."

Nia scanned her eyes around at all the guests. "I noticed that some of the people Roland introduced me to were the head of charitable organizations. Do these organizations book the resorts often? How does he know them? So many."

Wade glanced over at Roland. "No, he doesn't know them from booking the resorts. Roland donates money to these organizations. Lots of it. That's one of the reasons why he wants to get the business on track. He wants to do a lot of good things for people."

Another attractive characteristic, Nia thought.

All the guests were gone except for Wade when Nia and Roland finally had a chance to spend some time together. Roland wanted to show Nia around the building before leaving.

He turned to Wade. "We'll be right back. Nia hasn't seen the place."

"You haven't?" Wade asked.

"No, but this kind gentleman is going to give me a tour." Nia stared up at Roland. Roland stared back down at her. Wade stared at them both. He could see it. The *look* they were giving each other. The *look* that promised that something was going to happen between these two before the night was over.

Roland had showed Nia nearly every public suite in Destiny's corporate headquarters when they found themselves strolling in the hallway near his office.

Still feeling like she was dreaming, Nia leaned against the wall. "I can't get over you doing this for me."

"Doing what?" With his hand propped against the wall and over her shoulder, he knew he could never get enough of looking at her. "You mean this little party?"

"Little party?" She was tickled. "That was a big affair. And I want to say thank you again. It really was one of the nicest things anyone ever did for me." She felt like crying, but she refused to make herself look silly.

"You look so . . . so beautiful." Emotion lowering his voice, his gaze ran down the length of her gown, returning hungrily to Nia's eyes.

The look made her so warm and uneasy, she knew she needed an escape, or she may have found herself in a situation she had wanted to avoid.

She peeked around him toward his office door. "Aren't you going to let me see what your office looks like?"

"Sure." Reluctant in turning away from her, he unlocked the door, outstretching his arms for her to enter.

"Nice," she complimented him, once standing in the center of the cozy but very traditional room. The window view was the best thing about it. Drawn to it, Nia beheld a dark, sparkling sea, brandishing a yacht that sailed in the distance. "This is a nice view."

"I like it too," he said, strolling up behind her, stopping close enough to smell her hair. Raspberries, he thought. Gazing down at the back of her body, loving the way the clinging dress draped over her tiny waist and round hips, he wondered if all of her smelled like raspberries. With it, he wondered how close he could get to her without being too close.

Her eyes now shifting from side to side, Nia sensed his longing to be nearer. She could almost feel his hands raising from his sides to touch her. It all prompted her to seek a diversion, the huge closet across the room.

After opening it, she peeped inside. "Big and roomy." Nia closed it. As she did, her arm collided with the light switch. Stark darkness pervaded the room. Not even the window shed them light. "I'm so clumsy," she scolded herself, fumbling for the switch. She couldn't find it.

Neither could Roland in reaching for it too. "It's all right. I'll get it."

But in his attempt to locate it, his hand hit something that made him motionless, that made him swallow the excitement in his throat.

"Sorry," he said, attempting to move his hand from the soft roundness of Nia's breast. However, it was her own hand that didn't allow him to move it.

With her palm laying against his hand, she held it there. More than that, the pleasing, sensitive feeling of him touching her that way, made Nia guide his hand to an even more dauntless place—inside the top of her dress, where she wore no bra.

Gently squeezing her nipples, Roland was soon fed off her sharp intakes of breath. Becoming addicted to the provocative sound, feeling it stimulating the untamed tempo of his heart, he offered her what he couldn't restrain any longer: the sweltering lusciousness of his lips touching hers, caressing hers, tasting hers.

For Nia, merely the touching of his lips alone was enough for her to feel a sultry surge of awakening below her belly. But combined with his deft fingertips tantalizing her nipples and soon fondling her entire breasts, she was overcome by his lips merely touching hers, and beyond overcome when he offered the honeyed tip of his tongue.

Accepting this gift into her mouth, she soon felt his full tongue thrusting beyond her lips, swirling erotically inside her nectar. Never had she tasted anything this good. Never had she felt hands that touched her so sensually, making her feel so incredible he was almost stealing her breath away. If she could have bottled his kisses and his touch, she would have labeled it: *this is the sweetest gift Nia ever had in her life.*

Throwing her head back as his searing kisses began to divide between her lips and neck, she felt her arousal reaching its peak as his head bent toward her breasts. Carefully, Roland slid off the straps of her dress, making the slinky lamè fabric fall and bundle around her feet, leaving her only in panties and hosiery. Afterward, she eased him out of his jacket and far more quickly assisted him out of his shirt. Before long, their bare, damp chests were touching in the dark.

Her insides wet and throbbing for him to do more, Nia was just about to unbuckle his pants when the light flipped on. Yet neither Roland or Nia had found the switch. Their eyes shot to the door. Standing by another switch, Wade stood looking as stunned as they were.

Straightaway, Nia raised her dress to cover herself.

"I—I didn't mean to interrupt you guys," Wade apologized. He forced himself to look only at Roland. "The security guy was looking for you. The guy that is supposed to relieve him called in sick and he can't stay. He—"

Just then, the phone rang, cutting Wade off. Thinking someone calling his office past midnight might be an emergency, he answered it, "Roland Davenport."

Embarrassed and feeling foolish, Nia wanted to get away as soon as possible. Fully dressed now, she fled out the door.

Wade trailed her out to a cab. She had just rode away by the time Roland reached Wade. They could see the taxi's taillights moving farther and farther away.

"She said she would see us at home," Wade told him.

"Why couldn't she just wait to go home with me?" Roland asked, scratching his temple.

"She was embarrassed, Roll. Couldn't you see that? And who was that on the phone at this hour?"

Frustrated, Roland bit down on his bottom lip. "Could you believe of all the times to call me, my mom picked tonight and at that moment? She tried me at home first."

"Is everything all right with the family?"

"The family is fine. She just wanted to talk. But who I'm worried about is Nia. She and I definitely have to talk."

CHAPTER ELEVEN

Suzanne strode out of the Capelle Beauty Salon, one of her favorite retreats, feeling like a new woman. Her skin had been deep cleansed with a facial peel. Her body was massaged with the magic fingers of their finest masseuse. Her feet were attended to by an actual podiatrist, and her short healthy tresses treated with rare, conditioning herbs, discovered by a world-renowned hair expert.

Striding down Madison Avenue, browsing in the boutique windows, it was essential that she find the ideal wardrobe to harmonize with her fabulous appearance. After all, she was about to head to the beautiful, tropical island, St. Croix, and face its most beautiful resident, Roland Davenport, once again. It had been a long time since Suzanne had been this excited about a man. Not even Kal had raised her temperature the way Roland did when they first met. Visualizing Roland's sexy face and body, her lips curled with images of mischief she could make with him.

Strolling by one dress shop's window, Suzanne wasn't captured by anything striking, and was about to walk away. That's when, abruptly, a sight did arrest her attention. Closer she stepped toward the glass window, gawking at a thirty-something man who sat on a sofa inside the boutique. Soon she was walking inside.

"Mikel?" Suzanne said, forbiddingly confronting a face she wished she'd never seen before.

Mikel Hardaway wasn't pleased to see Suzanne either, even if it was interesting that she hadn't changed much since high school. "How have you been, Suzanne?"

"Much better than you." She'd read about him losing his high profile investment banking position due to layoffs in a business trade publication. That was the main reason she wanted to see him anyway. To let him know she knew he was down and out. "Must make you feel bad to lose such a high paying job like that."

Mikel's fleshy eyes rolled slowly over the face he'd woke up to for nearly six months of his life. Mean by nature, Suzanne hadn't changed. More than that, she wanted him to pay—pay for not loving her.

"I've made a lot of good contacts," he told her, "and I've had some promising interviews and one offer."

"Good for you," she said with a giggle.

Mikel glimpsed up at a woman and two small girls shopping in the sportswear section of the store. "And I hope all is going well for you, Suzanne."

"Couldn't be better. I'm about to fly down to St. Croix to work with a resort chain for a while."

"Sounds interesting."

"It is. In fact, love is waiting for me there, too."

"Your husband?"

"No, but *real love* just the same." She narrowed her eyes in his.

Mikel hung his head, recalling the mistakes he'd made. The biggest one of his life was marrying a woman he didn't love—Suzanne. Why had he let her get him drunk that night so long ago, weakening him into sleeping with her when he had a wonderful girl that he loved deeply? The indiscretion resulted in an unwanted pregnancy, and a marriage that both their parents forced Mikel into. After Suzanne miscarried the baby during the second month of her pregnancy, Mikel took that as a sign that their relationship was not meant to be. Unfortunately, by then it was too late to mend the precious heart he'd broken.

"You ever see Nia?" Mikel asked. Again, he glimpsed over at a woman and two girls. They had moved to the accessory section.

"I saw her several times. The last time she was working right where you expect trash to work—at that club Big Boys."

He shook his head. It was amazing that the jealousy was still there—jealousy that had nothing to do with Suzanne knowing how much he had loved Nia. "Did you ever tell her?"

"Tell her what?" But Suzanne knew what he was talking about. She regretted sharing anything with him.

"You know what I'm talking about, Suzanne."

"I don't care what you're talking about. You're a nobody anyway. You weren't nothing when I married you and you're nothing now."

"I'm happy. Are you?"

One of the little girls who he'd been observing ran over, all smiles. "Daddy, Mama is ready to pay for the stuff. She needs your credit card."

"Be right there, sweetheart." The girl ran off, standing by her mother, who now stood in the line for the cashier. Worry lines set across the woman's face as she looked from her husband to the stranger that he didn't seem pleased to talk to.

"So you're married," Suzanne remarked.

"Eight years." He stood, looking in the direction of his wife. "Good luck in St. Croix."

Mikel strode off. Suzanne walked out the boutique door. When he reached his wife, he explained who Suzanne was. Afterward, he stood by his wife, holding his credit card as the cashier rang up an abundance of extravagant items. Contrary to what Suzanne insinuated, money wasn't his problem. Matter of fact, he had few problems.

Mikel considered himself lucky to have a lovely wife, a nurse, who had given birth to his two beautiful girls. There was only that certain something that crept up into his mind from time to time, nagging him whenever he examined his past. It was the age-old question: what if? What if Nia and he had never broke up?

The door to Nia's bedroom was locked when Roland arrived home from the surprise party. Assuming she was sleeping, he preferred not wake her. So the next morning he was looking forward to seeing her at breakfast. Not that he cared about eating. Not that he cared about anything more than seeing her. What happened between them was all he could think about. *She* was all he could think about.

By the time he left for work, Nia hadn't come down for breakfast. At work, the day was long because there were too many thoughts about her. There were even calls home. His answering machine message was all he heard. Deciding he had to see her immediately, he shortened his work day, telling Wade he was leaving early.

Entering the house and the living room, he called out, "Nia? Nia?" There was no answer. He headed to her room. She wasn't there. He searched throughout the other rooms. When he reached his own bedroom door, an explosion of coconut lured him in. Standing by his dresser, Nia stood pouring incense leaves in his burner.

"I—I saw that you had run out of incense," she said, not looking at him. "So I wanted to fill it back up for you."

"Why did you leave like that last night?" He moved close to her, hoping she would meet his eyes. "And why didn't you have breakfast with me this morning? Are you avoiding me?"

Nia continued shaking the leaves into the burner, peering down into it. "Roland, I don't want to get into it."

"Nia, we have to talk about what happened."

"Nothing happened. We just got carried away. Happens sometimes. We'll forget it ... eventually." Finishing, she wiped her hands on a handkerchief and made a step toward the doorway.

Roland blocked her. "We can't deny what we felt last night. We can't deny what we're feeling right now."

Being so near him again, Nia hung her head. She was ashamed of how weak she was last night. She was weakened by a man who would wind up treating Nia as appallingly as her mother's rich lovers treated her. Hadn't Roland admitted that he wanted nothing more than flings? Hadn't he stated that his commitment at this point in his life was with rebuilding his company? Yes, he had. Even so, as he touched Nia's chin, lifting it, forcing her to finally meet his eyes, the rumblings of desire that began their ascent, removed all reasoning for her not to push him away.

"I want you, Nia," Roland confessed with a husky breath. "And I can see that you want me, too."

"No, I can't." Aroused already to an aching point, Nia knew she had to resist this time, and tried to go around him.

He caught her by the mouth, pressing his firmly against hers. In the same moment, he wrapped his arms around her back, pressing his body inflexibly against her, too. Unable to fight the titillating rush stirred by his succulent mouth against hers, Nia surrendered inside the warmth of his arms, carrying hers around him, too. Instantly, she was aware of the muscles on his chest and arms, but more aware of the concrete-hardness that rocked torpidly against her, making her throb below her hips, craving to feel him in the flesh.

Heightening her desire with teasing grazes of his tongue across her lips, he soon thrust it beyond her trembling lips and within the sweetness that was their first step into heaven. Grasping him tighter with every taste, feeling her tongue thrashing erotically across his, Nia knew there could be no greater pleasure in life than being seduced by this man. Her ears, her heart, her stomach, her legs all pulsated with arousal, but nowhere was her desire for him more intense than the moist place between her legs.

"Have to have you," he whispered breathlessly between kisses. "So bad."

Gazing down at her body, he separated from Nia with just

enough room between them to raise her arms and pull her tank top above her head. He tossed it across the room. Looking back at her, his eyes never leaving hers, he then fingered around to the back of her black lacy bra. Nia felt her breasts being freed and quickly he slid the straps off her shoulders. Neither saw the fabric tumble to the floor. Roland was too busy staring at her round softness. She was too busy being turned on by the desire in his eyes.

"They're so pretty," he said, his voice buried low in his throat with breathless excitement. He couldn't stop looking at her.

"I love looking at you, too," she said, her voice also stifled with her uncontainable hunger for him. With his love-drugged eyes looking down, studying her face, he enjoyed her easing off his jacket and helping herself to unbuttoning his shirt. When he was finally as bare-cheated as she was, Nia felt her breath catch in her throat, and her hands glide along the many mountains that formed his upper body.

She couldn't utter a word. Mesmerized by his sexiness, she simply examined, stroked and soon glided the tip of her tongue in spirals along every deliciously bare inch of him.

"Umm," she heard him groan. "Umm."

Nia was so delirious she didn't know if she could handle it when Roland unexpectedly kneeled down as they stood. Her legs tremored in anticipation and because of the unknown of what he was about to do to her next. Swallowing the excitement rising in his throat, and looking up at her hazel eyes, his hands reached up for her belt buckle. Undoing it, Nia felt his fingertips accidentally brushing below the pants line, and the hairs on her lower body seemed oversensitized. When the buckle was finally undone, Roland indulged himself in unzipping her jeans. Soon she watched his turned-on expression as he slid the dungarees and panties down past her hips and off her legs.

Her thighs captured his fascination immediately. Staring at them, Roland began rubbing his face against them. Trembling from the sweet feeling of his skin against hers and the tickle of his facial hair, she was far more thrilled when his lips began kissing her thighs. Not only there, but kissing her entire leg, her ankles, calves, then working his way back to the top. Nia couldn't help closing her eyes, savoring the sweet feeling, hoping that he would never stop.

He did stop abruptly. Praying he would soon continue, Nia didn't open her eyes, but merely waited. Before long, she felt his warm hands moving her legs farther apart. Unexpectedly, then she felt the warm, firm, wet tip of his tongue entering her. Tickling at first, it made her scream out. But soon the tickling sensation subsided as his tongue began to disappear inside her. Intolerable pleasure gushed through her as he moved his mouth back and forth methodically, occasionally deepening or softening his force.

Screaming, Nia knew she couldn't withstand any more when her body shook repeatedly with orgasmic sensations. Her legs were so weak, her overall body was so weak, Nia knew she would have collapsed if he hadn't picked her up, laying her gently on the bed.

Staring at her naked, sweat-oiled body trembling against his blue satin sheets, Roland couldn't remove his pants and shorts fast enough. Nia's lust-drugged eyes were unspokenly pleading with him, "Please love me. Please love me." Climbing up toward her on the bed, Roland was more than ready to fulfill the request.

Nia's eyes couldn't help but widen, seeing him fully naked for the second time. He had to be the most beautiful masculine creature that ever walked the earth, and as her eyes remained stuck in the area below his hips, she was certain no other man could have been more physically blessed.

Reaching Nia, Roland laid on top of her carefully, making sure he didn't smother her with all his weight. His tongue entered her mouth just as he reached down lifting himself so that his steel-like erection entered her, too. Ever so slowly he pushed, making her aware that he was thick and reaching so deep into her, making her aware that he was also extraordinarily long.

"Oh," he groaned as he began to move. "Oh, yes."

Swaying his hips slowly, Nia's smoldering movements matched his. But speeding up his rhythm, his dance of love became more erotic, rendering Nia with ecstasy beyond anything she'd experience thus far with him, beyond anything she could even describe. She could only hold tight, feeling him, loving him, giving him all in her power to give. And then with one final thrust of himself, Roland's limbs shuddered uncontrollably, while Nia's body tensed with such excruciating pleasure she couldn't scream or utter a syllable. She could only feel the tears of joy strolling from the corners of her eyes.

Waking up hours later with her head laying against Roland's chest, Nia asked herself if she was dreaming. Yet as she awakened more, she felt compelled to sit up. Peering down at Roland sleeping beside her, she felt the awareness below her belly that indicated she'd been with a man—the awareness that guaranteed her she was not dreaming. She had made love with Roland and now she was lying in his bed.

Gazing up at the window, she was surprised to see the darkness outside. They had been sleeping too long, but she was grateful that he hadn't awakened. If she was ashamed to face him before, she was a thousand times more ashamed now. Because she couldn't suppress her attraction to him, she had allowed herself to be used.

Gathering her clothes, Nia quickly and quietly dressed. Noiselessly, she then closed Roland's bedroom door behind her. With her bare feet thumping lightly into the carpet, she couldn't wait to get inside her room, lock the door and lie in her own bed. There she could think. She could think about how to get rid of that tug in her heart. That tug that kept warning her that she was dangerously close to falling in love.

Dreaming about making love to Nia, Roland was more than happy when he awakened to realize he really had been intimate with her. Turning aside to feel her, see her, smell her, hear her voice and hopefully have a replay of the splendor they shared, he was disappointed that she wasn't in the bed with him any longer. After what happened between them, he hoped she felt as addicted to him as he did to her. With the aftershocks of her sweet love still rippling through him, he didn't ever want to leave her side. Never had a woman made him feel the sensations he felt with her.

Knowing that she'd probably gone to her room, he swung his legs over the side of the bed, stretched and stood. He noticed the darkness outside the window, then turned to the clock on his night table. It was well past midnight and he was hungry. Not for food.

Though putting sex aside, he was enjoying Nia even before they made such incredible love. He loved talking to her, seeing her, just being around her. Overnight, it seemed she had changed his view of the world, of his life. No longer did he wonder at what time in the future would he get seriously involved again with a woman. He was already involved. And if the maddening pounding in his heart was any indication, it was serious.

Thinking and thinking about her, he couldn't sleep. He longed to go to her room, but since she might have been sleeping another thought came to mind. He wanted to do something for her. Something to let her know how he felt. He thought of the twenty-four-hour flower shop nearby the hospital. He would go get some roses. They would be sitting right outside her bedroom door when she woke in the morning.

Purposefuly, Nia decided to leave her room when she knew Roland had left for work. After being such a fool with him, it was hard for her to face him. It was also hard to think about continuing to be his maid.

Opening the bedroom door, she was debating how she would survive if she resigned. That's when suddenly the sight of a big bunch of roses at her doorstep halted her tracks.

"Do you like red roses or the other colors?" Roland asked. From the hallway, he was approaching her with a huge smile.

"What are you doing home?" she asked, not touching the roses. "Aren't you supposed to be at work?"

Roland was expecting some warmth after what had happened, a smile or merely the sight of her picking up the flowers to enjoy their fragrance. Instead Nia looked angry. Was it his imagination?

"Nia, what happened between us was unforgettable. I have so much I want to tell you."

"I don't want to hear it."

It wasn't his imagination. "Why not?"

"You heard me. I don't want to hear it. And I don't want your roses." She picked them up and threw them at him. "I'm not for sale! Remember that!"

"I wasn't trying to say that you were." He didn't understand her behavior. This couldn't be the same woman who was so loving yesterday. "I—"

"No one buys me. Not you or anyone. And what happened last night will never happen again. So you better get your groove on somewhere else. Find yourself another sex partner."

"Sex partner?" He couldn't believe she thought that's all she was to him.

"Look, Roland, it meant nothing to me like it did to you. You're free to be with all the people you want to be with, and I'm free to look for a real relationship."

He still didn't understand her. Wasn't what they shared real enough? Wasn't the warmth, the friendship, the connection they shared outside of the bedroom real enough? Didn't he qualify for a candidate for a real relationship? Or did she still think he was so shallow, he was incapable of love? Why did she stereotype him so terribly because of his success? That way of thinking made no sense.

Getting angrier by the second, he decided he didn't have time to figure Nia out. There was important work to do at the office. Suzanne, Wade's cousin would arrive in Christiansted tomorrow. There were documents he needed to prepare for her. Without saying goodbye, he began walking down the hall.

"Are you going to work?" she asked.
There was no answer.

After an afternoon of grocery shopping the following day, Nia opened the front door and heard Roland and Wade's voice in the living room, accompanied by a disturbingly familiar female voice. Knowing Wade's cousin was expected today, Nia headed to the room to introduce herself.

The woman's back faced her, but even that made Nia feel strange. The short hair was cut too evenly. The linear suit was even in the style a certain person wore. There was also the upright posture. It couldn't be *her*, Nia thought, then suddenly the woman turned around.

CHAPTER TWELVE

With her astonishment enticing her further into the room, Nia questioned if life was playing a cruel joke on her. Suzanne couldn't have been standing in this living room in St. Croix, again making her heart race from merely her presence.

Equally stunned at encountering Nia, Suzanne stepped across the room toward the doorway, questioning why Nia was standing there. Wherever she came from, Suzanne was more than willing to assist in her return.

"What in the devil are you doing here?" Suzanne asked with a wry chuckle. "In St. Croix of all places? In Roland Davenport's house? How do you even know him?"

"Nia lives here," Roland answered, uncomfortable with the women's reaction to each other.

"You two know each other?" Wade asked.

"Very well," Suzanne responded.

Wade shoved his glasses up by the middle. "Where do you know each other from?"

"New York," Suzanne answered, her glare unmoving from Nia. "We go way back to junior high and high school days."

"You've known each other longer than Wade and I have," Roland commented.

Still in shock at seeing Nia, Suzanne nodded dazedly. "Why is she living here?"

Nia took a deep breath, hoping to tame her raging heartbeat. "I work here."

Suzanne frowned. "You work here? Doing what?" She glanced beyond Nia to the grocery bags in the hallway. "Are you the cook?"

"I'm the maid."

Roland stepped nearer to Nia. Standing by her side, he explained to Suzanne, "Nia is assisting me in managing my household."

"Call it what you will," Suzanne told him. "A maid is a maid."

Roland disliked the distaste in her tone. "I'm very glad that Nia is here. And you should be too since you'll be staying here a while. She's very good at everything she does."

Wondering to what depths he meant the last line, Nia glimpsed at him. He glanced at her, too.

Suzanne studied the two. "How long have you been the maid here, Nia?"

"Not long."

"I guess you enjoy providing service."

"I like it here." She exchanged a look with Roland.

Suzanne didn't miss it. "How did you get this job?"

"I met Nia at a hotel," Roland interjected. "She was working there, and I offered her the position."

Suzanne didn't like the way this sounded. Nia had probably used her feminine wiles on him and he hired her just like that. "Did you check her qualifications?"

Nia was insulted.

Roland was a bit angered. "Why are you asking me that?" He couldn't see how this was Suzanne's business.

Sensing his cousin was alluding to something that wouldn't be pretty, Wade cleared his throat. "Cuz, aren't you hungry? Let's go get something to eat. I'm in the mood for Italian."

Suzanne ogled Nia. ''Isn't the maid going to cook tonight?''

''Since I was shopping all day, I was going to warm up leftovers.''

''Leftovers?'' Suzanne spat.

''Don't knock it,'' Roland added. ''That roast beef was delicious. But Wade and I had decided to take you out, Suzanne.'' Softening his look, he gazed at Nia. ''Will you please come with us?''

More and more, Suzanne deplored what she was seeing and hearing. ''You want the help to come to dinner with you?''

Apologizing with his eyes, Wade looked at Nia. Trying not to lash back at Suzanne, he simply shook his head.

A vein was bulging in Roland's temple. ''I don't appreciate you referring to Nia like that.''

''But she is the help. And not even qualified help. Do you know where she used to work?''

Nia was shocked into silence at Suzanne's lingering hostility. For a moment, she could only look at her.

''At a hotel,'' he shot.

''No, I'm talking about before that.''

''I worked at Big Boys, a men's club,'' Nia defended herself.

''It was a sleaze club,'' Suzanne countered. ''One of the sleaziest in New York.''

''It was not!''

''It was. And do you know what she did there?'' With her nose squiggled up, she eyed Nia up and down. ''She was a stripper. A stripper. Probably a hooker too.''

''I WAS NOT!''

Promptly and tenderly, Roland brought his arm around Nia's heaving shoulders. If Wade's cousin wasn't a woman, Roland would have slapped her for attacking Nia the way she had. Since she was female, he gathered his emotions, baring them in his voice.

''Even if she was a stripper that would have been her business, and people earn their living however they see fit as long as they aren't hurting anyone. But I know firsthand that there was nothing dirty about Big Boys.''

Wade nodded his agreement. "It was a classy place. There was a fire there and it has been renovated. Our fraternity party was held there this year. But even before the renovations, it was classy. I used to like to go there because the waitresses wore sexy uniforms."

Suzanne's face lit up. "You see! They were half dressed."

Roland shook his head. "Suzanne, I don't care what Nia wore at her other job. She's doing a wonderful job here."

"But you can do better," Suzanne went on. "You can get a maid from an agency, one who has education and proper credentials."

Nia stepped directly in front of her nemesis. "Suzanne, if you don't want me to do anything for you in this house, I'll be glad to oblige you."

"Lazy too, hunh?"

"Lazy my foot! Goodnight."

Nia hurried out of the living room and up the stairs to her bedroom. By the time she placed her hand on the door knob, Roland was placing his hand atop hers. Slowly she curved around.

"I apologize for Suzanne speaking to you that way," he said. "I had no idea you two knew each other, and no idea she had something against you."

"She always had something against me."

"What? It's deep, whatever it is."

"You know, I've asked myself that question for years. I really don't know what she has against me. I should be the one who has something against her."

"Why do you say that?"

She didn't feel like conjuring up the old pain about Mikel. "I'll tell you another time."

He liked hearing that. "Does that mean you're still going to talk to me? Does it mean you forgive me for getting mad the way I did?"

"I like talking to you, Roland. And yes, I'll forgive you if you forgive me for getting mad too."

"Nia, I . . ." His gaze heated in hers. "I *loved* what happened. I can't stop thinking about it. I can't stop thinking about *you.*"

She couldn't stop thinking about him either. Nevertheless, she had to. She couldn't let him make love to her again. She couldn't be used again. She didn't solely want to be his sex partner.

"I better get some rest, Roland. I think I'm going to have a long day ahead of me tomorrow, with a new guest being here and all."

She turned her back to open the door. He ached to go inside with her, if only to be with her alone and nothing else. Respecting her wishes, he simply walked away.

"Goodnight, Nia."

"Goodnight."

After Roland, Wade and Suzanne left for the office the next morning, Nia spent her day fulfilling Suzanne's requests. As Nia served the three breakfast, Suzanne had specified her desire for satin sheets on her bed instead of cotton. She wanted peach potpourri poured in her incense burner instead of coconut. She wanted her bathtub sanitized again because she saw a bug in it. She also wanted her carpet not only vacuumed, but shampooed because dust must have been embedded in it. It made her sneeze.

By the time the three arrived home, relaxing around the dinner table, inhaling the aromas of the delicious meal displayed before them, Nia had satisfied Suzanne's every request. So when Roland asked Nia to join them, she truly believed Suzanne would be civilized toward her.

"The food looks tasty," Wade complimented Nia. He was digging his fork in a juicy portion of lobster. Chewing its succulence, he shook his head with tightly closed eyes. "Tastes just as good as it looks."

Swallowing a Cajun seasoned home fry, Roland's pleased expression showed that he was enjoying his food too. "You're really a great cook, Nia. You're really good." His eyes lingered in hers.

Fed off the ravenous look, Nia heard his unspoken whisper of wanting her again. As wrong as she knew it was to desire him back, Nia could feel the rising tide of her longing, prodding at the bottom of her stomach, letting her know all too well that she wanted him, too.

"The food is good," Suzanne complimented her. "Very well seasoned."

The compliment drew a look of surprise from all three, especially Nia. "Thank you, Suzanne."

"Now I can't cook worth a poot," Suzanne went on. "But I can make damn good reservations though."

Wade laughed, but seeing that no one else did, he stopped. He stuck his fork into his salad. "I love the dressing you put on your salad, Nia."

Swirling a chunk of lobster in butter sauce with her fork, Nia's lips couldn't help curling with pride. "That dressing recipe came from my mother."

"Your mother?" Suzanne questioned. She scratched at the mole by her mouth.

"Yes." Nia sipped some fruit punch, then set the glass back on the table. "My mother had a lot of different recipes."

"That's surprising," Suzanne remarked. She was chewing a crouton.

"Why is that surprising?" Nia asked.

"I just don't know when she had time for all this cooking, the Suzy Homemaker bit."

Listening intently, Roland had just finished his fries and was now working on his lobster. "You knew her mother?" he asked Suzanne. "You two must have been close."

"I didn't know her that well, but I knew *of* her."

Wade tensed. He could tell when his cousin was setting someone up for something.

Nia half frowned, half smiled. "I don't understand when you say that you knew of my mother."

"You know what I'm talking about, Nia." Suzanne stared at the colorful salad bowl near Wade. "Pass me that, cuz?"

Nia's hand blocked Wade from passing it, forcing it back

in the place where it sat. Nia leered at Suzanne. "What are you trying to say about my mother?"

With narrowed eyes, Roland looked at her too. More and more, he was regretting that he decided to do business with Wade's cousin. The woman had problems.

A mocking grin spread Suzanne's thin lips. "Come on, Nia. You know your mother had a reputation."

Nia leaned forward, holding her arms at her sides to keep her fists from leaping over at Suzanne. "How my mother lived her life is no concern of yours."

"Suzanne, I'm really not in the mood for a replay of last night," Roland warned.

"Neither am I," Suzanne insisted. "But Nia and I both know that Nia's mother slept around with rich, married men."

Nia shot up from the table, hurrying around to Suzanne's side. Wade and Roland reached her before she reached Suzanne.

"You have no right to talk about my mother!"

"Why are you so testy about it?" Suzanne asked. She was smirking.

"Wouldn't you be testy if someone had insulted your mother?" Roland asked. He escorted Nia back to her seat.

Nia sat, but her eyes burned into Suzanne. "Why do you hate me, Suzanne?"

"I don't hate you." Suzanne reached for the pitcher containing the punch. Pouring some into her glass, she looked thoroughly amused. "What makes you think I hate you?" She returned the bowl to its place on the table. "If anything, you hate me." Peering over her glass at Nia, she sipped.

"Now why would I hate you?" Nia asked.

"It looks like the other way around to me," Roland interjected.

Throwing his eyes heavenward, Wade shook his head. "I wish we could change the subject. This is getting ugly."

Ignoring her cousin, Suzanne grinned at Nia. "You can't get over it, can you?"

"Get over what?"

"What I did to you." Suzanne smiled.

"You mean by being mean and spiteful to me when we were younger? You mean by insulting me and even telling a gang of girls to beat me up so that they broke my ribs and put me in the hospital?"

"My God, Suzanne," Roland exclaimed. "You did that to Nia?"

"Hell no!" Suzanne protested, the amusement faded from her face. "I didn't tell anyone to touch her."

"You did," Nia argued. "One of the girls told me, but she didn't want me to tell the police. She thought the other girls would jump her."

Suzanne waved her hand at Nia. "You're lying. You just want it to look like I have something against you when you know it's the other way around, and you know why."

The conversation was so upsetting, Wade wasn't hungry anymore. Aggravated with his cousin, he gawked at her. "What are you rambling about, Suzanne?"

"I'm talking about what I took from Nia."

"What?" Wade asked.

"I took her man."

Nia rose from the table.

"She wasn't woman enough to keep him."

Trying to figure out why she was doing this, Nia could only look at her.

Roland stood also, leering down at his unwelcome guest. "Get out, Suzanne."

"Get out?" Suzanne knew he couldn't have been saying what it sounded like.

"You heard me. Get your gear and go to one of the suites at the resort. It's on the house. Just as long as you get your things and get out of my house!"

"I didn't mean to cause trouble, Roland."

He didn't want to hear it. He didn't even want to look at her. "You can't treat Nia like that and stay here. That's unacceptable. She's done everything she could to make you feel welcome."

Suzanne refused to apologize or even look at Nia now. She

knew her enemy was loving having this gorgeous man defending her. But the thing that bothered Suzanne the most was the reason why Roland was defending Nia. It was obvious to her that Nia wasn't merely his employee. She was much more to him than that.

"I'll go with her," Wade told Roland.

"You don't have to leave, Wade," Roland assured him.

"I know. But she's family. Where she goes, I go."

At the front door, Roland watched the taxi that drove Suzanne and Wade off the estate. Afterward, he went up to Nia's bedroom. She was standing, peering out the window.

"Nia?"

She turned around as he entered the room. "I saw them leave."

"Yes, it's too bad about Wade." Roland stepped near her, detecting a glaze of water covering her hazel eyes. "But Suzanne had to go. I'll still try working with her because I signed a contract with her and Wade, but she can't stay here, not treating you like she did."

"Thank you for standing up for me." Her deep gratitude to him, impulsively made her draw her arms around him in an embrace.

Loving the way it felt to be close to her again, he closed his eye relishing the moment. "She can't hurt you anymore. You don't even have to see her unless you want to."

"I tried not to let her get to me. I tried not to let her upset me, but I can't help it."

"May I ask you something, Nia?" He was still holding her, still closing his eyes because the warmth of her felt so good. "Is what she said true?"

He felt her nodding against his chest.

"Yes, my mother was a mistress. In addition to attending two of the same schools, Suzanne and I lived a few blocks from each other, and had two friends in common. We never hung out at my house, but several times they walked me to my door. On two occasions they saw two men leaving my house, kissing my mother on the cheek, and getting into their fancy cars. One of them Suzanne recognized. He was a doctor, who worked with her father. They were both cardiologists in the same practice. He had a wife and kids. Suzanne loved throwing that in my face.''

"She's rotten.''

"And yes, it's true that Suzanne did take a man from me.''

"Is he the one you were telling me about that night when we danced?''

"Yes," she said, feeling his hold on her becoming tighter. "He was the one.''

He listened as she shared more about her mother's lifestyle. It all made him understand her reaction to the roses. Then she talked more about losing the man she loved to Suzanne. Mikel made her keep her heart at a distance from anyone else.

"People will betray you, Nia. I know firsthand. You can't let it stop you.''

Wade had implied that someone had hurt Roland. Nia's curiosity was piqued. "Who betrayed you, Roland?''

At first he was reluctant to drudge up the pain, especially when he felt he needed to be strong for her at that moment. However, he was feeling closer to her with each second. If there was anyone he could unburden himself with about the pain of lost love, there was no one better than the woman who'd quickly made him forget that love.

When he finished telling her about Cameron, Nia looked up at him seeing even more attractiveness, even more to admire in his integrity. It all made her body heat with throbbing desire. "I would never betray a man who loved me that much.''

Staring down in her eyes, he raised his hand and softly strode his finger across her cheek. It was so soft, he was reminded of her body. Thinking of how good she felt always turned him on, regardless of where he was or what he was doing.

"What would you do if a man loved you more than that?'' he whispered from the arousal that began to choke him even in his throat.

"More than that?'' she asked, feeling his fingers gliding

along her cheek until it reached her mouth. Was he talking about his feelings for her?

"Yes, more than that." Roland was whispering and tracing her mouth with his fingertips. Teasing her so she was weakening for him to do more and more, he dipped his finger at the trembling crack between her lips. Her lips parted. He removed his finger and replaced it with his tongue.

Nia felt her body come alive with a heat that ricocheted all over her body, but blazed most intensely between her legs. Feeling his tongue tasting the honeyed walls of her mouth, Nia felt herself climbing higher and higher to the brink of ecstasy. Before she knew anything, his hand was reaching to the back of her sundress, unzipping it. As it sailed to the floor, he wasted no time in freeing her of her purple silk bra and its matching panties.

Bare before him, Nia was so turned on by the look in his eyes, she was nearly dazed when he guided her toward the bed. He sat at the edge guiding her hips in front of him, grazing his fingertips along their sides.

For a long time, Roland stared into her hazel eyes, then lowered his gaze until it reached her silky belly. Kissing it, while he reached up to caress her full breasts, Nia felt her body aching for that most sacred part of him. He wasn't going to indulge her just yet, not with that. Rubbing her thighs, he eventually rubbed between them, stroking her fluffy hair and her secret place. Tantalizing her with tender touching on the sensitive outer skin, he maneuvered his finger inside, igniting her arousal so she couldn't help writhing her hips.

Slipping his finger out of her, he gripped her round buttocks. Pulling her forward by them, his face kneaded into her downy hair, working its way down until he reached the sweet opening he hungered for. Nia cried out at the first stab of his warm tongue within her.

Thrilling her with his insatiable taste for her, Nia felt her insides overflowing with wetness. The pleasure he was giving her was beyond what she felt before with him, beyond anything she had known. She didn't want him to stop. Addicted to the intense sweetness, she held his head hoping that his miraculous powers could make it last forever. But it was she who ended it all when the rapture became so intolerable that her body went into near convulsions. On her stomach, Roland laid her on the bed.

Hearing his heavy breathing, she also heard him removing his clothing as he stood at the foot of the bed. Not soon enough, she then felt him sucking her toes, kissing her ankles and the backs of her calves.

She was on fire when his lips reached her buttocks. Kissing each one ever so slowly, Nia couldn't help moaning, "Oh, don't stop."

"I won't baby," was his husky whisper.

Continuing his love crusade, he kissed her back, along with her shoulders and the back of her neck. His tongue darted inside her ear, driving her wild. At the same time, he reached underneath her, lightly squeezing her nipples before thrilling her entire breasts with his hands.

"I want to feel you," she heard him murmur, then abruptly felt his hardness gliding along her inner thigh. Turned on by everything he was doing to her, a thrust of himself inside her as he laid against her back had to be his greatest gift of the night.

As he moved inside her moist walls, Nia felt coils of heat racing from the bottom of her feet to the top of her head. Rocking her hips with the same lustful hunger that possessed his, she knew that heaven was no farther than this seductive creature loving her. Sweet sensation after sweet sensation erupted with that passionate opening that was the gateway to her heart.

"Oh, that's so good," he cried. "Please don't stop. Don't stop, baby. Keep giving it to me. Just like that . . . like . . . Oh, my God . . . Oh . . ."

Loving his pleasured moans, Nia yearned to give him even more rapture. Exciting him with deep-throated kisses, she maneuvered her body so that she was on top. Immediately his hands reached for her breasts, teasing them, stroking them, taking them into his mouth, and she quivered with desire just from that.

Kissing him still, she reached down and brought her hands around his masterpiece. Gripping her hands around its thickness, soon she felt it melt inside her, filling her completely with its extreme length and hardness.

For a moment, each was motionless, simply savoring the luscious feel of the other. But as the fire in her loins exploded from being so connected with him, Nia began to move so erotically the joy was almost unbearable for both of them. Frowning as if she was hurting him, Roland raised up and grabbed her, pressing her into him. He couldn't get enough of her.

Burying his face into her breasts, he kissed them before an agonized expression suddenly masked his handsome features. Through half closed eyes, Nia watched, knowing her own expression probably reflected his. She was feeling *it* too—joy so extreme her body shook uncontrollably with his.

"I love you, Nia," she heard, mixed with his heavy breaths. "I love you so much."

"I love you, too."

CHAPTER THIRTEEN

With her head laying against Roland's chest, Nia had never felt more loved, more womanly, more safe in her life. The magic between them was almost too good to be true. Every moment or so, Nia even pondered if she was dreaming.

The kiss Roland planted on her forehead assured her she was not.

"I can't believe this is happening," she thought aloud.

Roland was gazing dazedly at the ceiling. "I can't either. I never felt like this before. I loved, but it was never, ever like this."

No words could have made her feel more special than those. He was touching her heart with his body and his mind.

"Sometimes I feel like I'm dreaming," she heard herself say. "It's like, can something this good happen to me? Can a man like you really come into my life and love me?" And she did feel loved. The right kind of loved. It felt *so* right.

Touching her chin, Roland gently curved her face upward to meet his eyes. "Believe me, this is no dream. I love you.

And I know it's just going to get deeper and deeper. Yes, I'm going to do everything in my power to make my business a major success again, but my first priority is going to be loving you.'' He pressed his lips lightly against hers.

She gazed in his eyes, touched by the sincerity in them. ''I've always felt alone, even though I had family. But now I don't feel alone anymore. I feel like I've found the person God sent here for me.''

''You have. I'll be here for you. In good times, in bad times, in sickness and in good health. I'll do anything to make you happy. Give you anything you want, and if I don't have it I'll find a way to give it to you. And your dreams . . . Nia, I'll help you reach those too.''

''I have my dreams. I'm happy working here.''

''And I'm glad you're happy to work here. But baby, God gave you something. I truly don't believe he would have given it to you *so good* if he didn't intend for you to use it. What about singing at the resort? One song would even do. Just to get your feet wet.''

She shrugged her shoulders. ''I don't know, Roland. Every time I've tried to do something big in the past, it just never worked out. It just breaks you down so bad, sometimes you just don't want to even try things any more. It's like God is telling me it's just not for me.''

''You're wrong, baby.'' He leaned over, gazing at her. She was so beautiful, he couldn't imagine life without seeing her eyes, her lips, her smooth, dewy skin. ''Sometimes we fail. Even winners, those success stories have failed lots of times before they reached their goals, but the people who win are the ones who keep trying no matter what. They try because their dream is in their heart and no matter what they do it stays there. So they have to follow their heart. You have to follow your heart, Nia. I see that look in your eyes whenever we talk about your singing. You want to do it so bad you can taste it.''

Looking at his lips, there was something else she wanted to taste. ''I'll give some thought to singing at the club.''

"Good." He relaxed back on his pillow, putting his arm around her shoulders, and easing his finger toward her mouth.

Feeling it gliding along her lips, Nia suckled it in her mouth. "You know everything, don't you, Roland?"

He liked the way she tasted his finger. It reminded him of what she tasted on him during their numerous passionate encounters during the night. "I know what you like, that's one thing I know."

She laughed. "You think so?" She felt his finger pulling back. He took hers and placed it in his mouth. "Umm," she purred.

"You like that?"

"Love it." He was winding his tongue around her pinky.

"I can do a lot more." He reached down, rubbing her silken belly and raising his hands to stroke her breasts.

Her eyes fluttered closed. "You're driving me out of my mind, you know that?"

He rolled on top of her. "You haven't seen nothing yet."

When Roland hummed into his office the next morning, he found Wade sitting on the opposite side of the desk, already busy at work.

Watching Roland place his jacket over the back of his chair, Wade could tell that something significant had happened between Nia and his best friend during the night. Not only was Roland humming when he never hummed, but he looked plain silly to Wade.

Sitting with his legs crossed in a swivel-back chair, Wade had studied his friend enough. "What happened to you?"

Roland bit his bottom lip, then grinned. "Nothing. Just happy about everything. You and . . . and your cousin are going to help me get on track with the company. Everything is just going well." He opened his briefcase.

Wade uncrossed his legs. "Now you know good and well you're not just happy about that. This is Wade you're talking to. Wade from the frat party days. You're not looking like that just because of this company. A woman has got to you.''

Roland's grin spread. ''You think you know so much about me.''

''I know what I see, and a woman has got to you.''

He tried to stop smiling, but he couldn't. ''It's Nia. We came to an understanding.''

Wade leaned forward, resting his hand on the front of the desk. ''An understanding?''

''Yes, we know how we feel about each other.''

''And how is that?''

''Good. We feel real good.'' Roland started laughing, drawing a laugh from Wade too.

''Congratulations, man.''

''Congratulations about what?''

Suzanne didn't bother to knock as she entered Roland's office.

''Morning, Suzanne.'' Roland was so happy, he didn't want to get off to a bad start with anyone today. He wanted to start fresh with Suzanne.

''Morning, Cuz,'' Wade added.

Roland smiled up at her. ''I hope you like your office.''

''I sure do.'' She helped herself to a seat in front of his desk.

''And I hope you find your suite comfortable too.''

''It's very comfortable.''

''Great.'' Roland nodded, and wondered what Nia was doing. He couldn't wait to get home. ''So I guess we all should get to work.''

By the end of the day, Roland had developed an admiration of Suzanne. No, he couldn't forget how she mistreated Nia. What's more, a part of him had hoped she wouldn't be an asset to the company. That way he could have some contractual leeway to get rid of her. Suzanne's skills were not allowing that.

She had such brilliant strategies for moving the company

forth when they had a conference call meeting with his investors that all of them were in awe of her genius. At day's end, as the three of them packed up their briefcases, Roland couldn't help complimenting Suzanne.

"I'm really glad we decided to bring you in."

"I'm glad too," she said, snapping her briefcase shut. After locking it, she observed the two men.

Wade nudged Roland on the arm. "Didn't I tell you she was a genius?"

"And you were right."

Suzanne observed them continuing to pile papers in their attaches. "So what are you two doing this evening?"

Wade looked at Roland. "I don't have plans."

"So why don't you celebrate with me?" she asked.

Wade thought a minute. "Sounds good. Where are you going?"

"I want to go on this glass-bottom catamaran one of the managers was telling me about." She was talking to Wade, but looking at Roland. Looking downward, he concentrated on packing his attache.

"*The Renegade* is a really nice one," Roland informed her.

"That's the one I want to go on. Would you like to come along?" Suzanne was freely ogling his body since he wasn't watching her. All day she had sneaked looks at him. "It should be fun."

Fun for him would be the red teddy Nia promised to model for him when he came home from work. "I'll pass this time," he said.

Suzanne was so desperate for him to come, she contemplated a different approach to get what she yearned for. "You don't want to be around me, Roland." Pitifully, she gazed down at the floor, then raised her gaze. He was looking at her. "And I can understand why. I was rotten to Nia. I'm sorry."

He was surprised that she was apologizing. He wished she would have made amends with Nia instead of him. All in all though, he was grateful she realized her mistake. He smiled at her. "Everything is cool."

"It is?" She brightened. "Can we be friends?"

"We are friends."

"No, we're not. I thought our working *so well* together today meant something."

"It did. I'm glad to have you working at my company."

"If you were really glad, you would celebrate our working together and you would join me and Wade on an innocent little boat ride. It wouldn't even take long."

The Renegade sailed across the ocean, destined for Buck Island. Listening to a guitarist playing an enchanting Caribbean rhythm, Roland, Wade and Suzanne swayed their heads. When the guitarist switched gears and the splendor of George Benson's classic Masquerade flowed through the air, Suzanne slowly rocked her body in front of Roland.

"Want to dance?" she asked him.

"I'll sit this one out."

"Go on and dance," Wade urged. He had been looking out over the water, thinking that it appeared as blue as the Caribbean oceans depicted in postcards. "Loosen up some, Roll. You only live once."

"That's right," Suzanne agreed, tugging him toward her.

Reluctantly, he permitted her to guide him to the middle of the floor. There, her arms locked behind his neck. He slackly held her around the waist.

"Ooh, this song makes me think of things," she told him.

He was noticing how adroitly the guitarist's fingers were strumming his strings. The music was bewitching him. He regretted not asking Nia to come along. "So what does the music make you think of?"

"This music makes me think of lovemaking." She nestled her head in the crook of his shoulder.

Roland was still fascinated by the musician. "This guy is good."

Suzanne glanced at the guitarist. "I'm good too."

Now she had Roland's attention. "You're very good at business. I have to give you your props."

"Thank you." She smiled. "But I'm very good at more personal matters too."

"They're lots of nice guys on the island who'll find that information quite pleasing."

He switched his attention back to the musician.

"Are you afraid of what I just said?" Suzanne asked.

The question drew him back to her.

"Why would I be afraid of a statement you're making about yourself?"

She locked her hands tighter around his neck and brought her body nearer to his. "Because I'm telling *you* that I'm good. I don't care about these other guys on this island."

Taking a deep breath, Roland told himself that she was not coming on to him. It had to be his imagination.

"I think you look so good," Suzanne raved on, "and I admire you so much as a man."

"I appreciate that."

"And I want to go to bed with you."

Roland was tickled at her boldness. In fact, ever since Cameron shattered his confidence by cheating on him, he'd really enjoyed when women let him know they found him attractive. In any case, he was so in love with Nia he couldn't imagine being with another woman.

"I'm in a serious relationship. But I'm very flattered, Suzanne."

She half smiled. "Who is the lucky lady?" But she already knew.

"Nia."

Suzanne snickered. "That's really funny."

His dancing steps slowed. "What's funny about it?"

"Because she can't make you happy. She's boring. That's why I took her man."

Roland ripped Suzanne's hands off his neck. "Don't start up again."

"But it's true. She is boring. Look at what she's doing with her life. Isn't that proof?"

"She's doing very fine, thank you."

"But look at you, Roland. You're the owner of the premiere resort chain in the world and look who is by your side—a loser."

She tried to put her arms around his neck again to resume dancing. Like her touch burned, Roland sprang back. "Nia is no loser. Not only does she have a good heart—something you wouldn't know about—but she has a talent that she's going to share with the whole world one day."

Suzanne had heard Nia sing before, and she was certain he was referring to that. As much as she didn't want to admit it, she did recognize Nia's talent. Despite it, Suzanne knew Nia didn't have the spunk to use it. "It'll never happen. Nia doesn't have what it takes."

"That's what you think," Roland argued. "She's going to be performing at my resort one of these days real soon, and when she does, you can have a front row seat."

Nia paced back and forth along the plush azure carpet inside the dressing room of the Paradise Cove Lounge. One of Destiny Resorts most elegant entertainment lounges, some of the top singing acts in the country had graced its stage. Now that was what worried Nia. Would she measure up?

"Stop walking, baby," Roland urged her. He relaxed his bottom on the edge of the vanity. "You're getting me nervous."

"I can't help it." Nia threw her hands up in the air. "I haven't sung before a crowd since high school. What if I just don't have it anymore?"

"It's there, big time." He strolled over to her, welcoming her in his arms.

She nestled her cheek against his chest. "Oh, Roland, what did I get myself into?"

"Into something good. I've heard you rehearsing. You sound fantastic." He pulled back from her so he could look in her face. Gently gripping her shoulders, he gazed deep in her eyes. "You can do anything, Nia. Anything you put your mind to. Always remember that. And always know that I'm here for you. Because we're going to be together forever. *Forever.*"

He bent his head toward hers, preparing to taste the succulence he had desired all night. But just when the door swang open, the host of the evening flashed his mile-wide smile at Nia. "Showtime!"

Accompanied by Wade, Suzanne sat at an alcove table in the Paradise Cove Lounge. She didn't want to come to see Nia shine in the spotlight. However, knowing how long it had been since Nia had sung, she guessed that she wouldn't shine. Suzanne believed that Nia would make an idiot of herself. Wanting to see that happen was the sole reason she attended the performance that Roland had invited everyone in the company to.

Though when Nia began to sing, her voice filling the air like a flute from heaven, Suzanne gazed over at Roland's face. He was standing on the side of the stage. The look in his eyes for Suzanne was all it took for her to excuse herself from Wade, and walk quietly away.

Moments after, when Nia returned to her dressing room, the thunderous applause could still be heard. She was ecstatic. When Roland joined her backstage, hugging her, raving about the people giving her a standing ovation, Nia was far more thrilled. Entering her dressing room, Wade was also clearly moved by the performance he'd just heard.

"Nia, I never would have known you could sing like that."

"Thank you, Wade. I can't believe I did it."

Roland planted a kiss on her lips. "You did it and you're going to do more. As talented as you are, you need to get a record contract. I'm going to hire a lawyer, get you a demo tape done and we're going to get a deal."

Nia thought for a moment. She'd recently read some impressive articles about Kal Hunter and his label, Ecstasy Records, in some newspapers. She'd even heard of a group called Torch, who she'd read were on Kal's label, being played on the radio. Perhaps it was time to give Kal a call. "I know someone who has a successful record label. He'll sign me. His name is Kal Hunter."

CHAPTER FOURTEEN

Standing before the closet mirror in his office, Kal tugged at the emerald green tie an old girlfriend had given him. With the tie straightened, he didn't move away from the honey-colored man staring back at him. Kal inspected other things about himself. His graceful African nose, his dusky, see-through-you eyes, his dazzling mustache. By anyone's standards, he considered himself a good-looking guy. Women loved to mingle their fingers through his black, curly hair, and often complimented him on the way his lips were shaped. He'd been told more than once that he had "kissing lips."

Turning away from the mirror, heading to his desk, he wondered if Nia Lashon would be one of those women. He still couldn't believe she had called him, requesting a meeting about signing with his label. His mother had always told him if you ask God long enough, he would have no choice in answering your prayers.

There was a knock at the door, and Kal felt himself feeling what he'd rarely felt before: nervous.

"Come in."

When the door was opened, he saw that Nia looked as beautiful as he remembered her. He pecked her on the cheek. "How you doing, girl? Looking good."

It was the guy who sauntered in behind her who didn't look so good to Kal.

"Hello," Nia greeted Kal. "Kal Hunter, this is Roland Davenport."

"How you doing?" Roland asked, extending his hand.

Lightly, Kal shook it. "Is he your lawyer?"

"No," Roland answered, not appreciating this guy acting like he wasn't there.

"Who are you, then?"

"I'm her man."

Roland and Nia soon faced Kal across his desk.

"So Nia," Kal began, "my offer still stands. I want to sign you on my label."

"Do I have to audition for anyone?"

"I make the decisions on who gets signed and I've already heard you. You sold me, baby." His gaze searched her face, falling down her neck and lower to the hint of cleavage revealed from her blouse. Swallowing the lust in his throat, he wished this guy hadn't come with her.

Roland didn't miss Kal mentally undressing Nia. Yet he knew the man could look all he wanted. She was in love with him. Every second they were together, he felt it and she showed it.

"So what are you offering Nia, financially?" he asked Kal.

Kal half smiled. "She's going to get a nice package." He then reached in his drawer, pulling out a folder containing some papers. Handing them to Nia, he explained, "This is some information about the company, and a contract I had drawn up for you."

"A contract?" Nia browsed through the documents.

Roland frowned as he looked across at them. "Let me see those, baby."

She handed them to him. "Everything okay?" She watched him examining the papers.

Roland looked up at Kal. "No, everything is not okay. First of all, Nia is not signing anything without her attorney."

Kal smiled, disguising how much he couldn't stand this guy. "I didn't say she had to sign right now."

"But you didn't say that she didn't either." Roland glanced down at the papers, then looked back up at Kal. "And I really don't like these figures. Where did you get them from anyway? There were no negotiations on her advance or royalties."

Kal nodded. "True."

"So new papers need to be drawn up," Roland stated. "Ones with better figures than those."

"What if I can't do any better? What if that is my only offer?"

Roland chuckled. "I'm a businessman too, Mr. Hunter. If there is a product that is essential to my company moving forward, I will sacrifice to attain that product. My girlfriend's voice, as we both agree, is an outstanding product that you find essential to move your company forward, is it not?"

"True."

"Then if you want her voice featured on your label, and not on any of your competitor's labels, then you have to do better with the advance and royalties."

Kal looked from Roland to Nia. To him, Nia was looking at her man like he was the stars and the moon. Perhaps if he gave her a large advance and royalty percentage, she wouldn't look so hard at Mr. Know-It-All.

Kal scribbled some figures on a paper. He slid it across the table in front of Nia. Her eyes widened, seeing the enormous amount of money he was offering her. It felt like she was dreaming again. She slid the paper in front of Roland.

"That's better," he thought aloud. "Much better."

"Cool," Kal said, staring at Nia. With her shining, dark hair besetting her doll-like face, she looked so good, he was wishing more and more for a chance to be alone with her. "So are those numbers nice enough for you, Nia?"

Dazedly, she nodded. If someone would have told her she would one day be offered such a huge amount of money, she wouldn't have believed them. With that kind of advance, not to mention the royalties, she and her siblings would be very comfortable. Unimaginably comfortable.

"Kal, this is very generous of you," she told him.

"You're worth every penny."

She smiled. "I'm sorry I doubted you in the past. Sitting here, seeing how far you've come, I can only admire you."

Kal was loving this. "That makes me feel good. Touches me right up here." He placed his hand near his heart.

"So how many songs will I be recording?"

"Thirteen. For a CD. Do you read music?"

"No." She looked alarmed.

"Ah, don't worry about it. Reading music is not essential to singing professionally. It helps to know all you can, but it's not necessary. As long as you feel it, it'll be all right. And I must warn you, recording songs professionally is not as easy as it seems. First, we're going to do a scratch vocal, which is your voice with the basic keyboard and maybe drums or a drum machine. After that, we're going to arrange other complimentary instruments around your voice and key. Then you'll have to sing it again with the new, more elaborate musical arrangement."

"That's no problem."

"But there can be problems. Sometimes you have to do a song over and over until you practically can't stand the thing. But in the end, when you hear the finished mixed product, you'll be proud that you worked so hard."

"I can imagine."

"But how long will all this take?" Roland asked.

Tired of sitting, Kal shifted his weight in his seat. "It could take anywhere from three months to a year and sometimes even longer than that. It all depends." He looked at Nia. "On you, young lady. Things can get done a lot quicker, depending on how long you're willing to work."

"A year?" Nia thought aloud. That sounded too long to her.

"Could be a year," Kal added.

Nia looked worried. "That wouldn't be good. Roland wants

to stay in New York with me while I record, but he also needs to be with his business in St. Croix.''

Kal liked what he was hearing. A separation is just what they needed. ''What type of business are you in?'' he addressed Roland.

''I own a chain of Caribbean resorts. Destiny Resorts International.''

''I see.'' Having heard of the resorts, Kal was impressed, but wouldn't show it.

''I tell you what, Kal,'' Nia said.

''What's that?''

''If you want to sign me, you'll have to do something special for me.''

''And what's that?''

''I want to record the songs in St. Croix.''

Kal was glowering. ''What?''

''You heard me. If you want me, you'll have to set it up so that I record there. I have to be with Roland.''

Touched by her gesture of love, Roland stared at her speechless.

Kal really couldn't stand this guy now. He could cost him money. ''Do you know the expense I'd have to incur and the inconvenience to set that up?''

''I can imagine. But if you want me, those are my terms.''

Once Kal and Nia began their recording sessions on the island of St. Croix, he didn't mind the expense and energy she'd cost him. He'd flown in musicians, paying for their flights and living arrangements. What's more, there was the expense of the house he was renting, along with the studio costs. If he were in New York, he could have used his label's studio. Nonetheless, he was a firm believer in getting what you paid for.

This was never more apparent than when Nia touched his songs with her golden voice. Every day he looked forward to their sessions, not merely because she would knock him and

everyone else out with the prowess of her voice, but equally
because he genuinely enjoyed being around her. She was easy
to talk to. Moreover, he was pleasantly surprised at the range
of things she would talk about. From books, to sports, to politics,
to spirituality, to religion, she was so well-versed, she intrigued
him even more.

Every day when Roland came to pick her up, all Kal could
do was think what a lucky man he was to have her in his life.
And more than once, he was tempted to flirt with her like he
had in the old days. However, as he came to know her, he
realized he wanted more than that. He wanted more than some
hot sex with Nia. What he wanted was for her to look at him
the way she always looked at Roland. He also wanted all the
good stuff that went along with that look.

On a sun-blinding Saturday afternoon, Kal was jogging along
the shore to avoid kicking sand on the myriad beach goers
when he spotted a sight that was so nightmarish it had to be a
mirage. To get a better view, he left the shore side, persisting
to tell himself that the nightmarish image had to be a hallucina-
tion. Yet the closer he came, the more obvious it was he was
actually seeing *her*. Clad in a bronze-colored bikini, Suzanne
Greer lounged in a folding chair with her eyes closed.

"Are you on vacation?"

The nagging sound of Kal Hunter's voice opened Suzanne's
eyes. "What are you doing here?" she asked, wishing the sight
of him standing before her was a bad dream.

"I'm enjoying the island. What about you?"

Suzanne scanned the area, before leveling her eyes at him.
"Are you following me? Do you have police watching me?"

Kal frowned. What kind of funny grass had she been smok-
ing? "Why would I be following you?"

"You accused me of burning down that club." Suspiciously,
she looked around again.

His brow raised. "And you think I'm down here to get you
arrested for it?"

"I wouldn't put it past you." She looked behind her.

"Well, I'm not here for that. I'm down here working."

"Working?"

"Business is booming, baby, and I'm recording Nia Lashon's first CD."

"Nia's recording an album?"

Suzanne didn't know that. Surely, Roland wouldn't have told her. Ever since she propositioned him on the boat and berated Nia, he didn't speak to her about anything other than business. Wade would never talk to her about Nia either.

"That CD is going to leave you bankrupt," Suzanne predicted.

"Now why do you say that?" He sat on the sand in front of her.

"Because she has no talent."

Kal was intrigued by this jealousy Suzanne harbored for Nia. "You didn't come down here to do it, did you?"

Suzanne was baffled. "To do what?"

"To do what you started at Big Boys."

"Pardon me."

"To kill her."

Suzanne looked tickled. "Now why would I want to kill that slut? Because of you? I can't stand you anymore."

Kal scratched his head at that one. She did have a point. She couldn't stand him. "So what are you doing here?" The sun rays made him squint up at her.

"I'm working too."

"Doing what?" A woman passing by, who wore a snakeskin thong, lured his attention. When she was out of his line of vision, he returned his interest to Suzanne. "Tell me what you're doing? I'm curious."

"If I tell you, will you promise to go away?"

"I promise."

"If you must know, I'm doing some work at Destiny Resorts International."

Kal blinked. He thought that was interesting. "Did you know that Nia's boyfriend is the owner of that resort chain?"

"It's just a coincidence that we're in the same circle. My cousin and Roland are best friends and frat brothers. And Roland *is not* her boyfriend."

"According to him he is."

"He won't be for long."

Kal observed Suzanne's squared jaw line become more pronounced. *Don't tell me she likes him too.* "Don't tell me you have an eye for Nia's man?"

"He isn't Nia's man! He's just marking time with her."

"And waiting for the real thing, you?"

Suzanne just looked at Kal. Shaking his head, he returned the stare until two more women passed wearing thongs. His scrutiny trailing their bodies, he realized he was enjoying this island more and more. Perhaps he would never leave.

Watching Kal behave like a pervert, Suzanne began to realize something. The something she realized excited her. She had almost missed it. Kal being in St. Croix could have been the best thing to happen to her.

"How are things going with you and Nia, Kal?"

The question drew him back to her. "What do you mean?"

"I mean, I know you had a thing for her. And since you're working together you probably spend time together. Is she responding to you, or does she only have eyes for Roland Davenport?"

"Why do you ask?"

"Because maybe I can help you get her."

"Now why would you do that for me?"

"Because you can do something for me."

"And what's that?"

"You can help me get Roland. I have a plan."

Kal leaned back, looking at her, weighing what she offered. A while back, he might have been interested in a scheme to get Nia in his bed. Yet solely being intimate with her wasn't his objective anymore. Not only did he want her to look at him like she looked at Roland, but he wanted her to say his name the way she did his, and feel proud of him the way she was proud of Roland. Furthermore, he didn't want any schemes to make this happen. The turn-on for him was for her to be turned on by him naturally.

Kal stood, dusting the sand off his sweat suit.

Looking desperate, Suzanne gazed up at him. "So what do you say?"

"I say good luck."

He was walking away when she called to him, "Kal?"

Stopping, he looked over his shoulder. "What?"

"If you change your mind I'm staying at the resort, suite 1409. The desk clerk will page me."

The work week went by with a whirlwind of excitement at Destiny Resorts. The corporate star who was responsible was none other than Suzanne. Everything she touched had turned to gold, from her successful advertising campaigns to her revised budget plans. Most spectacular, the corporation's profit and loss statements were showing a significant growth in revenues in the short amount of time that Wade and Suzanne had come aboard. The investors were elated about her performance. Roland had expressed his gratitude, too.

Now it was 5:00 on Friday afternoon. As much as Suzanne enjoyed the weekend, she didn't look forward to this one. She was lonesome. She had had plenty of men asking her on dates. If only the one she wanted to go out with would have asked her. Outside of work issues, he wouldn't speak to her.

Suzanne could have reasoned that she wanted Roland because it would have been fun to steal him from Nia. And his being involved with Nia did make him more tempting. However, she was attracted to him long before she knew Nia was in the picture. More and more, as she watched him every day in action, she admired how he ran his multi-million dollar corporation. She admired his intelligence, his wit, his charm, his talk, his sexiness, and just about everything about him. How was she going to make him feel the same way about her?

Her secretary's intercom intruded on her musings.

"Yes, Libby? What is it?"

"Mr. Davenport called. He said that if you hadn't left for the day already, he wanted to see you."

"Does he want me to come to his office?" Suzanne asked, excitedly.

"No. He'll be by yours in about ten minutes."

"Wonderful," she said under her breath. "Wonderful." A scheme laid vividly across her mind.

"Ms. Greer, is there anything else you need me to do for you?"

"Nothing, Libby. Go on home and have a good weekend."

"You too, Ms. Greer."

The door was ajar when Roland approached Suzanne's office. Thinking nothing was inappropriate about going in, he pushed it open and proceeded inside.

Shocked by Suzanne wearing only a pair of pink panties and a bra, he made an about-face. It didn't matter that she was holding her dress in her hands. He hurried back toward the door.

"Don't leave!" she ordered, halting his tracks. He didn't turn the slightest bit around. She was pretending to wipe a stain off her dress. "I spilled something on myself and I was trying to get it off my dress."

With his back to her, he said, "The door was open. So I thought it was okay to come in."

"I forgot to close it. Everyone is gone anyway."

"Didn't your secretary tell you I was coming by?"

"No," she lied.

"I told her to tell you that."

"It must have slipped her mind."

He took a deep breath. "Anyway, I came by to tell you that I really appreciate what you've done for the company. This week seemed like a big turning point."

"Thanks, Roland. It means a lot coming from you."

"You're wel—"

"Ouch!" she cut him off.

"What's wrong?" He felt so ridiculous talking with his back facing her.

"Something bit me. It bit me in the middle of my back. I can't reach the spot. Could you?"

Roland would have laughed if the game she was playing hadn't been so outrageously obvious. "No, I can't check your back. But the nurse is still here. She's here until 7:30. Stop by her office when you get dressed and she'll check you out. Have a nice weekend."

The candle-like ambience of the studio surrounded Nia and Kal as they finished their session for the night. The musicians were gone. The engineer had left too. Yet Kal didn't want to leave Nia alone as she waited for Roland to pick her up.

"I can give you a ride home," he offered, plopping down next to her on the sofa.

"That's okay. Roland will be here any minute now. I called him at his office and his machine picked up. I'm sure he's on the way. Probably stopped to get a drink with Wade or something."

Having the first chance to really look at her during the day, he thought to himself again how damn lucky Roland was. If he could have just tasted those plump lips once, that might have been enough sweetness to last him for a lifetime.

"I really like that last song," she told him. She was trying to ease the discomfort of how hard Kal was staring at her. "People are really going to relate to those words."

Thinking about the ballad while gazing at her, Kal agreed. "Lots of people out there are fighting the feeling. They feel such a powerful attraction to a person, but they deny it. They fight for all types of reasons. Sometimes they're just scared of getting hurt, of getting rejected. There are all kinds of reasons why people fight the feeling."

"Where did that song come from, Kal?"

His lips tipping up at the corners, he laid back into the beige leather cushions of the couch. "It came from a personal experience." He looked down, dabbing at a crinkle in his pants. "I was denying how I felt about this beautiful lady. But the more I spent time with her, the more I realized it wouldn't go away. What I was feeling just became stronger."

"It's a passionate song. You must have really cared about her."

"I still do care." He looked over at Nia.

The opening of the door brought Roland's excited energy into the room, piercing the mellow atmosphere they had shared.

Kal wished Roland would have stayed away just a little while longer. "How you doing, Roland?"

"Great. And you?" Roland never felt easy when in conversation with him. There was always something strained in the air between them. He turned to Nia. "Had a good session?"

"A fantastic one. You should hear this song that Kal wrote."

"Sing it to me later." He moved toward the door, opening it for her. "Sing it to me at the beach."

"Ooh, is that where we're headed?"

"For a night of passion," Roland teased.

Within minutes, Kal listened to Roland's Jeep driving off down the highway. He wondered if that "night of passion" bit was spoken for his benefit. If it had been, it surely reached its target. All he could imagine was Nia in Roland's arms, laying by the silken waters. The image was so disheartening, he felt like writing a song about it.

Unexpectedly slowing the Jeep before they reached their destination and parking it along the highway, Roland reached inside his briefcase, removing a squared, sandwich-sized black velvet box. With an intense expression, he extended it to her. "I was going to wait until we reached the beach to give it to you, but I just can't wait. I really get turned on making you happy, seeing those eyes just light up."

Half shocked, half delighted, Nia's lips parted, but no sound came out. She was looking from Roland to the box. "You didn't have to buy me anything, Roland."

"I wanted to, Nia. And I want you to know it's not because I'm trying to buy you, like those men did to your mother."

She lowered her head.

With caressing fingertips, Roland lifted her chin. Her exotic, hazel eyes sparkled like a vision in a man's most amorous fantasy. They were so exquisite, Roland looked forward to gazing into them all night.

"I wanted to give you something for one reason," he said, "and one reason alone. I just wanted to make you happy, Nia. And making you happy is one way I express my love."

With his words touching her heart as deeply as the passionate look in his eyes, Nia moved her face across toward his. Ever so lightly she pressed her lips on his and simply held them there. "I love you so much, Roland." Her emotions had choked her voice into a whisper. "You just don't know how much."

When her french manicured nails ultimately wrestled the box open, a three tiered-diamond bracelet glittered in front of her. Without delay her arms came around him, swallowing his broad chest in a spirited embrace. "Thank you," her whisper stroked his ear. "It's so beautiful."

"Like you," he said, his eyes closed, his arms holding her just as fervently. God knew, he loved this woman. "And Nia, there's so much where that came from. I want to take you shopping tomorrow. We'll go to all the clothing boutiques, the jewelry stores, the art galleries, the book stores, even to the car dealer. I saw you checking out a red sports car the other day. I want to give that to you."

"Roland, you don't have to do that."

"I know I don't have to." He drew back from her to look in her eyes. "Please let me spoil you. I'm not buying you, Nia. I'm just expressing my love. Please let me. If I can give you something that will make you happy, what's wrong with doing it?"

Nia gazed down at the beautiful bracelet he'd given her. She loved it. She looked over at him. But there was nothing more that she loved than him. There was nothing she wouldn't do to make him happy.

"Nothing is wrong with it, Roland. We can do whatever you want. If giving me beautiful things makes you happy, then I'm happy to receive them."

Lacing his fingers with hers, he raised her hand to his mouth and kissed it. Afterward, he started up the Jeep's engine. "Now let's get to the beach. I've been thinking about you all day. I can't wait to make love to you."

The tranquil waters of Cramer Beach made soft lapping sounds with every stir of Nia and Roland's bodies. Standing in the warm water face to face, feeling it undulating across their shoulders, they were grateful they'd discovered a deserted section of the beach. Free to express their love in whatever way they wished, Nia reached under the water toward his swim trunks.

"Did you miss me today?" she asked him, fingering the elastic of his shorts.

Feeling her fumbling near his erotic zone, his eyes drifted closed. "I always miss you, Nia."

"How much did you miss me?" She placed her mouth against his, teasing him with the tip of her tongue. She raised her hands to probe the muscles of his chest and arms. He was the sexiest man she'd ever known.

Roland accepted the succulent gift of her tongue, fully opening his mouth, then thrashing his own sweet weapon across hers until he became extremely aroused. Kissing her, with the warm water splashing against their skin, he soon reached her bikini bottom. Tugging the middle of the skimpy brown fabric aside, his fingers easily discovered her sweltering garden. After a caress, he was stimulated to become one with her. With one light push forward of his hips, he found himself in the glorious moistness of her love.

Savoring him motionlessly at first, Nia abruptly began to dance to the provocative cadence Roland led with. The billowing of the water further guided their movements. But all too swiftly the fire of desire blazed from their feet to their middles. The tremors of pleasure that shook their bodies with their maddening joy caused what seemed like a hundred ripples throughout the water.

Some time later, with dusk painting the sky a stunning shade of orange, Nia flattened her back on the beach blanket, entranced with its resplendence.

Laying down also, mostly on his side, Roland leaned over her, his elbow making a dent in the sand. "Why do you drive me so crazy?"

She giggled, feeling as silly as she sounded. "You're the one that drives me crazy. Why do you make me feel so good?"

"Because you make me feel good back." He laughed. "I can't wait for my parents to meet you. They're going to be here next week, you know."

"What!" Nia sprang up into a sitting position. "You're joking, right?"

"Not at all." Grabbing her hand, he sat up too. "Their forty-fifth wedding anniversary was coming up so I offered to fly them in from Atlanta. We're going to have a party for them in the ballroom where I had your party."

Worry lines marred Nia's forehead.

Roland had never seen her like this. "What's wrong, baby?"

"I'm just scared, that's all."

"Scared of what? My parents? They are the most harmless, sweetest, easiest people to get along with on the earth."

"What if they don't like me? What if they want me to be more like your old girlfriend, Cameron?" *What if they treat me like Mikel's parents did?*

Roland put his arms around her, swallowing her in a hug. "They're going to like you, Nia. But even if they didn't, someone else loves you to pieces. And that's me. I love you more than you'll ever know."

CHAPTER FIFTEEN

Donning a salmon-colored crepe de chine evening gown, Nia circulated around the crowded ballroom, nervously awaiting the guests of honor's arrival. Across the room, she observed Roland greeting guests who entered the door. Every so often, he would wink at her. It was his signal that everything would be fine. It made her feel better.

There were plenty of people for Nia to converse with. They ranged from all the employees whom Roland had invited, to those who had attended her party to his relatives flown in from various parts of the States. When she saw Kal striding in, sporting a black suit with a matching fedora, his was one of the most welcome faces of all. Nia had invited him because she planned a special treat for Roland's parents.

She wanted to sing one of the songs from the upcoming CD, but since Kal was cautious about exposing his music to the public before it was officially released, he proposed an alternative. He would play the piano while she sang. The song she selected to perform was one of her favorites, "For You" by Kenny Latimore. It was ideally suited for the occasion.

When Roland's parents finally arrived, they were as sweet,

wonderful and harmless as Roland had described them. They talked with Nia about their fun and hard years together, and loved talking about their youngest son, Roland. It was easy to see that they adored him. Nia could understand why.

When it was time for her to present her gift, Nia positioned herself at the center of the stage. All the lights were lowered except the spotlight on Kal and her. Roland's parents sat at the front of the ballroom. Nia smiled down at them before raising her hand, signaling to Kal. The introduction of "For You" began to play. Nia's voice came in masterfully on cue. In a matter of moments, Roland's parents were slow dancing. Others in the audience joined them.

In a red charmuese gown with a daring side split, Suzanne made an appearance into the ballroom at the point when Nia finished her song. She was glad she had missed it.

"What are you doing here?" Kal asked her, after maneuvering through the crowd toward her.

Suzanne barely heard him, distracted by a small crowd gathering around Nia. "Who are those people?" she inquired, tossing her head in that direction. Roland and Wade were among the crowd.

Kal glimpsed the pack of well-dressed folks. "The older couple are Roland's parents. Some are his brothers and there's a sister. And I think there are some other relatives over there too."

"Is that so?" Suzanne turned away, giving her full attention to Kal. "So you're Nia's piano man tonight?"

"I'm my own man all the time," Kal corrected.

Suzanne paused at that one. "Did Roland invite you?"

"Nia invited me. Did Roland invite you?"

"Yes," she said, even though she was surprised by the invitation. Other than work issues, he rarely made any contact with her.

"Did you ever get what you wanted?" Kal shot her a knowing look.

"Did you?"

Kal smiled, peering over at Nia and Roland. They were

laughing and talking with his parents. He shifted his concern back to Suzanne. "I guess if we're both asking, neither of us got what we wanted."

"Are we going to do something about that?"

Staring over at Nia, Kal still didn't feel right about conspiring with Suzanne against her. Added to it all, he was still debating whether Suzanne had set that fire in New York, nearly killing Nia. "Count me out."

Suzanne rolled her eyes. "Where's that spunk that's driving you to the top of the record business?"

"It's there in full force. But I don't need a plan to get me a woman."

Suzanne was amused. "You still don't have her."

"Everything takes time." He glanced at a glass full of wine someone was holding and had a taste for some. "I'm going to get a drink from the bar. Would you like one?"

"I'm not in the mood for a drink. I want to know if you'll be in on my plan. I know it will work."

"As I said before, count me out."

Frustrated with Kal, Suzanne turned her head toward the direction where Roland and his family were. Laughing and talking, Nia seemed to be a big hit with the folks. Suzanne wondered what Roland's parents would think if they knew how Nia grew up, and what type of woman she was raised by. Moreover, what if they turned on her like Mikel's parents did long ago? Eavesdropping on that scene as she stood by an open porch window, Suzanne had found the moment so enjoyable. Peering across this room, she began to wonder if history could repeat itself.

But witnessing how effortlessly Nia was bonding with Roland's parents, Suzanne knew she would need some ammunition to impair Nia's life this time. Thinking of her position in the company, Suzanne smiled as a possible plot formed in her mind. It wasn't guaranteed to work like the one she wanted to execute with Kal's assistance. Regardless, it was something that could possibly damage the connection Nia was forming with Roland's family. The unpredictable scheme had to take place under the ideal conditions.

Observing Roland's parents' table much of the evening, it took a while before nearly everyone had dispersed from it. Many of those who swarmed around the couple began socializing with other guests. Aside from Wade being one of those who was left at the table, much to Suzanne's regret, Roland and Nia walked off arm in arm to another suite, disappearing from sight. Forcing herself to ignore their seemingly growing attachment to each other, Suzanne chose to direct her energies more usefully. Specifically, on a certain popular table. Roland's parents were now sitting alone. It was the moment Suzanne was waiting for.

"Good evening, folks," Suzanne said, easing into a chair opposite Roland's parents. "I hope you're having a happy anniversary." Straightaway, she could see that Roland was the male version of his mother. The gray-haired beauty bore the same bewitching features. "I'm Suzanne Greer, one of Roland's business associates." She extended her hand.

A tall, strapping man, Roland's father bared a set of unnaturally white teeth. He offered Suzanne his hand also. "Nice to meet you, dear. I'm Langston. This is my wife, Kate."

Kate's red-glossed lips curled up beguilingly, her smile reminding Suzanne so much of Roland's. "So you and my son work together?"

"Yes, we do. Very closely. I'm also Wade's cousin."

Langston smiled. "Now that's a fine young man. I've known him a long time. Since Roland and he were in college together at NYU. It makes me feel good that they've both done so well. Now they're working together. Isn't that nice?"

Suzanne suddenly looked saddened. "It could be nice if the company was doing well. Things have been rough lately."

Kate's lineless forehead suddenly formed a furrow. "What do you mean things, have been rough?"

"Yes, what do you mean?" Langston looked as concerned as his wife.

Suzanne scratched the corner of her mouth. "I really

shouldn't be talking about it. But I truly care about Roland. And I know how hard he worked to accomplish what he did."

"Please, dear," Langston implored. "If it concerns my son, we want to know about it."

Suzanne stared at the concerned faces of the two. After a moment of pretending to reflect, she said, "You promise me that you won't say anything to Roland or anyone about what I'm about to tell you and show you."

Kate nodded. "We promise." She was looking more worried.

Suzanne's eyes scanned around the room, then returned to their distressed faces. "It's that woman Roland is seeing. She's the problem."

"Nia?" Langston said with surprise.

"What about Nia?" Kate asked. "She seems like such a lovely girl."

"And so talented too," Langston added.

Suzanne shook her head wildly. "She fools people."

Langston frowned. "You're losing me, dear."

Suzanne moved inward, causing their faces to lean toward hers. "She's not what she appears to be. She grew up hard and it's still in her."

"What do you mean by hard?" Langston asked.

"Sir, I mean that her mother wasn't a nice lady and she passed her ways down to her daughter." She peered around the room, searching for Nia and Roland. Fearing that they might return to the ballroom to interrupt and ruin her, and knowing that taking the couple to her office was necessary for her plan to work, she asked, "Will you join me upstairs in my office? We can talk more freely and I can show you something very important."

Once in Suzanne's office with the door locked, the three circled an oak table that she used for conferences.

"So you were telling us about Nia and her mother?" Langston pressed. He hoped his son hadn't become involved with a woman who was no good for him.

"Yes, I was." Suzanne folded her hands in front of her. "There is no other way to say it but to come straight out."

Pausing, she took a deep breath. "I've known Nia since we were children. I've tried to be nice to her, but I think she had problems because of how she lived . . ."

"Problems?" Kate repeated.

"Yes," Suzanne went on. "Problems because her mother was a prostitute."

"A prostitute!" Langston gasped.

"A prostitute!" Kate was gasping too. Pressing her fingers to her cheek, she looked as though she were about to faint.

"Are you sure, dear?" Langston asked.

Suzanne nodded. "Absolutely. Like I said, I've known her since childhood. We lived a few blocks from each other. We also attended the same junior high and high school. Private schools, at that. Her mother didn't work. Not a regular job, at least. So her *occupation* is how she could afford to send Nia to the finer schools."

"My Lord." Kate was shaking her head as if it were the worst thing in the world. "That poor child. Poor Nia."

Suzanne blinked. She couldn't believe this woman was sympathizing with Nia.

"I pity the child," Langston echoed his wife's sentiments. "Children have no say in what their parents do to raise them."

This was not going the way Suzanne had hoped. Desperation called for other tactics. "I wouldn't pity Nia if I were you. She used to do the same thing as her mother."

"What!" Langton gasped again.

Kate nearly fell out of her chair. "Please, don't tell me that."

Suzanne held in her laugh. "It's true, Mrs. Davenport. Nia was a hooker. She worked out of a club called Big Boys in New York."

Langston was scowling. "So when did she stop that and start singing?"

Suzanne looked off in silence.

Langston didn't like what the quiet was telling him. "Don't tell me she's still doing it?"

Suzanne shook her head. "I don't know, Mr. Davenport. Sometimes I wonder. She treats Roland so bad, disappearing for days sometimes. Who knows. And she also embarrasses him in front of me and Wade, disrespecting him and doing all kinds of terrible things to the man. She's the reason the company is going down.''

Kate was angry. ''What does she have to do with the company's decline?''

''A lot,'' Suzanne answered. ''You see, she gets Roland so upset with all the stuff she does to him, he can't concentrate. He can't really operate this company. What's more, she's draining him financially. She's always asking for things—expensive things. And Roland is just so in love with her, he gives it to her.'' Suzanne thought about the rumors she'd heard in the company. Everyone was talking about a red sports car Roland had bought Nia. It was a Lambergini, one of the most expensive cars around. ''Just recently I heard that she asked him for a $100,000 car and she knows his finances are in trouble.''

Kate was rubbing her temples. ''But she seems like such a nice girl.''

''But she isn't.'' Suzanne stood. ''Let me show you something.'' Knowing she had one final part of the plan to execute, she went to her computer and turned it on. While the couple spoke in low tones behind her, Suzanne located a file containing some of the company's financial reports. After doctoring a statement that demonstrated a great profit so that it showed a great loss, she carried the printout over to the table.

Sitting down again, she slid the report in front of Roland's parents. ''You see.'' A pink nail pointed to some discouraging numbers. ''This is all the money that Destiny Resorts is losing. It's a result of Roland not functioning properly as a CEO, and it's also a result of him withdrawing huge sums of cash every time Nia requests it.''

When Nia returned to the ballroom without Roland, it was because an aunt had dragged him off, demanding a tour of the building. Having enjoyed Roland's parents so much Nia felt like she knew them longer than she did. She anxiously made her way to their table again.

"Have you two done anymore dancing?" she asked, making herself comfortable in the chair opposite them.

Kate forced herself to smile. "No, we didn't dance."

Nia gazed at Langston. "Don't tell me you're tired, Mr. Davenport? The night is young. You better get your wife and get on up there and dance."

Nia laughed, but when she noticed no one was laughing with her, she stopped.

In fact, Langston appeared very austere. "Do you go dancing often?"

"Not much," Nia answered. The way he was looking was making her feel funny. Something was different.

Rearing back, taking a good look at her, Langston folded his arms. "What did you do before you became a singer?"

Nia's lips curled with the sweet memories of how she'd become Roland's maid. She had really enjoyed her work. "I used to work as a maid. That's how I met Roland. I was his maid."

"He told us about how you met," Kate said.

"But what did you do before becoming a maid?" Langston pressed.

Recalling the skimpy uniforms she'd worn at Big Boys, Nia looked uncomfortable. The uneasiness and reluctance made Langston and Kate look at each other.

"I was a waitress," she eventually responded, drawing their attention to her.

"Where?" Langston asked.

"In New York." *What did I do?*

Langston unfolded his arms and folded them again. "Where did you work as a waitress in New York? What kind of place was it?"

Nia felt more and more like she was being interrogated. "It was a club."

"What kind of club?" he queried further.

Nia hesitated. Why was he asking her these questions? Why

were they acting so strange period? "It was a men's club. A—
a classy one."

Kate and Langston traded looks again.

Langston leaned toward Nia. "Look, young lady, let me tell
you something. I think the sun rises and falls on all my children.
In my eyes they are the cream of the crop. And when they are
choosing partners to share their lives with, I want them paired
with the cream of the crop. Now if you're *not right*—and you
know if you're not—then you need to be with your own kind."

Having finished giving his aunt a brief tour of the building,
Roland strode back in the ballroom, searching for Nia.

Kal came up behind him. "Looking for Nia?"

Roland turned toward him. "Yes. Have you seen her?"

"She left."

"Left?" Roland asked, with all the shock bared on his face.

"She just left, man. Said she wasn't feeling well and was
going home in a cab. I offered to take her home, but she
preferred taking the cab."

Roland couldn't imagine why Nia would have left so unexpectedly. For that matter, she wouldn't even let Kal drive her
home. Roland hadn't missed the way he had looked at her all
night. He saw the way he looked at her all the time. It never
made him comfortable to think about them working together,
either. At the same time, he understood that it was important
to trust in order for a relationship to be successful. He trusted
Nia. It was a struggle to trust Kal.

"I'm sure she'll be all right," Kal interrupted his thoughts.

"I don't know," Roland responded, his features distorted
with concern. "It's strange that she just left like that. I think
I'll go home and see what's the matter and tuck her in bed."

Watching Roland walk off, Kal wanted to snatch him back
and let him know what a street fighter from the hood could do.
From Kal's perspective, he was always showing off that Nia
was his lady. It started back in his office in New York, when
Roland told Kal he was Nia's man. It progressed to that remark

about passion at the beach, and now it had ended with that comment about tucking her in bed. Kal was tired of it! So tired, he was going to have a talk with Suzanne. Perhaps there was something they could work on together.

Déjà vu. That's what the episode with Roland's parents was like, Nia thought. Believing this, she tossed and turned in bed that night with Roland sleeping by her side. She hadn't told him how cruel his parents had been to her. She didn't want to be the cause of a rift in the relationship he cherished with them. Neither did she want to bring any ugliness into their own involvement. It was a nightmare she yearned to forget. But his parents' words kept replaying in her head. It reminded her so much of the past.

Mikel's family were the first to detest her being with their son. Now another upstanding set of parents didn't want her anywhere near their child. They didn't think she was good enough for him. It was one of the most horrible feelings she had ever felt in her life.

Nia was glad the Davenports were gone, and in spite of how they treated her, she hoped they arrived safely in Atlanta. Far from her, she wouldn't be exposed to their emotional abuse again. She could concentrate on the most important thing to her: loving Roland.

Wanting to spend time with Nia kept Roland away from the office during the next couple of weeks. Something was bothering her. Roland sensed it, despite her claims that nothing was wrong. Lovemaking was always unbelievably magical between them, so Roland attempted to cure the mysterious malady by granting her overdoses of it. To further boost her spirits, he treated her to breakfast in bed, read her romantic poetry, pampered her with unending bubble baths, bestowed on her toe-curling massages, and took her to dinners, plays, movies and nightclubs. That was all during the first week. The second week consisted of a trip to Paris. When they returned home, Nia was the happiest woman alive.

As soon as Roland set foot in his office the following Monday, he was harshly and shockingly awakened from his vacation. Suzanne and Wade were in his office. With what seemed like tons of papers surrounding them.

"What the hell is going on in here?"

Sighing, Suzanne rolled her fingers back through her hair. "Roland, Wade didn't want to bother you on your days off."

Frowning, Roland stepped further into the mess. "Bother me about what?" Turning and turning, he couldn't stop looking at all the papers.

Looking exhausted, Wade patted Roland on the shoulder. "Roll, we have a little bit of trouble."

"What?" Roland was still turning, astonished by the chaotic state of the room.

Suzanne stifled her laughter. She had caused Roland's trouble as soon as Kal agreed to a partnership in her scheme. It began with an anonymous call to the IRS. According to Suzanne, there was something askew taking place with the books at Destiny Resorts International.

"We're being audited," Wade answered, attempting to assuage Roland's bewilderment.

"It's tough," Suzanne remarked with a shake of her head. "But we have to deal with it."

"No, we don't," Roland disagreed. He was still gaping at all the papers. "That's what we have accountants for."

"Not for this job," Suzanne stressed. "Roland, we're just getting on our feet and we can't leave anything for chance. We shouldn't let anyone else take this on. We have to get in there and make sure things are one hundred percent fine ourselves."

"She's right," Wade agreed. "You need to go through everything yourself. Piece by piece. You're the one with the most at stake. And we're here to help you along the way, not merely because of our reputations and association with Destiny now, but I refuse to let all I've worked for be lost by some trivial tax matter. I have to make sure everything about your books is exactly the way it should be. Now you can hand it over to the accountants if you want, but Suzanne and I both agree that that would be the wrong move right now. You're the CEO. It's up to you, Roll.''

Digging his hands in his pockets, confusion spun inside Roland's head. Undeniably, he was tempted to hand the responsibility over to the accountants. Nevertheless, Wade and Suzanne did have a point. Something this important and detailed was better handled by those in charge, particularly in light of a corporation trying to regain its losses.

What was most daunting about this situation wasn't so much the work involved as it was the potential strain on his personal life. Examining the company's books would mean long days at the office. It would mean cold, lonesome nights for Nia.

Nia was determined to be understanding of Roland's situation. It was only temporary anyway. So she occupied herself with maintaining the house and with the recording sessions at the studio. During the evening hours that she once spent with Roland, she played music, read books, watched videos and spoke to friends and family on the phone. By the time Roland would arrive home, often after midnight, Nia would be showered, perfumed, wearing a negligee and ready for love.

Much the opposite, Roland would feel tired and not like talking. Worse, their lovemaking became different. With every fiber of his being, Roland burned to make love to Nia, and he would. But he was so exhausted for indulging in all the foreplay and variety of positions that always ensured their sexual encounters to be unforgettable. Roland possessed the energy solely for the most basic lovemaking. After they were satisfied, he would roll off of Nia and promptly go to sleep. There wasn't any more after-play caressing or playful, tantalizing conversation.

From her perspective, this crisis at work was changing him. She strived to pretend that it wasn't really bothering her. Unfortunately, it did. Especially when she would call at night while he was working late, just to hear his voice. However, he would have his voice mail turned on because he was too busy to merely say that he loved her.

One day at breakfast, Nia had to get it off her chest. "Why do you turn on your machine at night in the office? Sometimes at night I just need to hear your voice."

Chewing a muffin, Roland frowned. He hated putting the machine on so that she was unable to get through, for he craved her voice every night in that stuffy office. On the other hand, Suzanne thought that the fewer interruptions they had, the sooner they could have their books prepared for the auditors. Wade agreed.

"I don't want to turn on the voice mail, but we're running against a deadline."

"Would one little call make such a big difference? I wouldn't keep you on long."

"Bear with me, baby. This grueling schedule I'm keeping will be over soon. In fact, I'll take you out Saturday night. We'll have dinner and see a good movie. I hear that one with Oprah Winfrey starring in it is in the theaters now. The one called 'Beloved.' "

Nia was excited. She wanted to see that movie because she loved Oprah. Plus, she'd read the fabulous reviews.

On Saturday, Roland had to work. Regardless, he promised he would end his work day early and arrive home by 7:30 in the evening to take Nia to dinner and a movie. All day, Nia looked forward to it. When 7:30 arrived, she was comfortably dressed in a plain white top, beige khaki pants, and some brown flat sandals. And when he wasn't there on time, she called him. The voice mail was triggered. So she sat around and waited for him to walk through the door or call. Neither happened. When 9:15 came around, she phoned him again. Again, there was voice mail. Striving to be more patient, once again she hoped he'd walk through the door or call.

By the time 12:45 AM rolled around, Nia was still dressed and sitting on the couch. When Roland strode in the door and flipped on the light switch, he was stunned to see her sitting in the dark. She was livid.

"I'm sorry, baby. Can you believe I fell asleep?"

"No, I don't believe it!" she snapped.

He approached her. "I really did. Fell right asleep in my office. I've been so tired lately. I really wanted to see that movie too. And overall, I just wanted to spend some time with you. Can you forgive me?" He sat on the couch and grabbed her hand.

She snatched it back from him. "No! I'm not going to forgive you. You are taking me for granted lately!"

"I'm sorry. But I did fall asleep. I can't wait 'til all this stuff is over. I'm so tired."

"So am I. Of being treated bad." She stomped off, walking up the steps. "I'm sleeping in my old room tonight."

At the recording studio, Kal could see that the time had come to execute his role in Suzanne's scheme. Kal knew that Nia was more than ready for it. She didn't have that love-glow when she came into the studio anymore. She didn't talk about Roland endlessly like she once had. She didn't wait for him to pick her up anymore. Kal knew all too well why.

"Something wrong?" he asked her.

All the musicians and the engineer had left.

"Why do you say that?" She was packing her lyric sheets and tapes in a portfolio.

"You just don't seem happy today. And not just today either. Lately, you just don't seem like yourself."

"I'm happy." Tears tried to creep in her eyes. She blinked them away. "Doesn't my voice sound the same to you?"

"Your voice gets better every day. You have some golden pipes, girl."

"Thanks." He made her laugh.

"If you want to talk about anything," he went on. "I'm here."

Nia looked up at him and smiled. Kal had been so kind to her. He'd made her dream come true and believed in her. Other than staring at her a little too long sometimes, he didn't even flirt like he used to. She was grateful for his friendship. Even so, she felt like being private.

"There's nothing to talk about." She resumed placing the papers and tapes in the portfolio. "Everything is fine."

"Good." Standing beside her, he began gathering his sheet music that was scattered in front of them. "So tell me, why don't you go with Roland to those business meetings?"

Puzzled, she looked up at him. "What meetings? You mean at his office?"

"No. I mean those meetings at the restaurants at night. I would want to take my lady along."

She knew he had to be mistaken. "Roland hasn't had any meetings at restaurants at night. He's at the office working on the books with Wade and Suzanne."

"Maybe he's taking a break when I see him. But I've seen him when I'm heading to the studio for one of those night sessions with the musicians. I've seen him a lot over the past month."

Nia mused on that. For the last month, Roland had been working on the tax predicament.

"Was he with Suzanne and Wade?"

"No, he was with some lady. They must have some big deal going on, huh?"

Nia's heart began racing with her crazy thoughts.

"When do you see him?"

"When I've seen him it has been as early as seven o'clock and as late as midnight."

Roland didn't know why Nia was acting mad all night after he arrived home. Yet he was too bushed to have a confrontation. He peeled back the covers and nestled underneath them. Except when she slipped beneath the covers from her side of the bed, he didn't feel *that* tired. He inched close to her and began rubbing her through the red chiffon fabric of her teddy.

"Get off of me!" she ordered suddenly. Too angry to look

at him, Nia stared straight ahead. "Just get off." She sat up, flattening her back against the headboard.

At once, Roland moved his hands back. "All right. You had a bad day or something or you're just mad at me again for working late?"

Her hazel eyes lunged at him. "*Who* have you been taking to a restaurant?"

He didn't like this question. "I take myself at lunch time."

"I'm talking about at night time. And I'm talking about in the last month, since you've been working *so late.*"

His head tilted with uncertainty. She couldn't have been implying what it sounded like. "You want to ask me something?"

She studied him as he sat up. "Are you seeing someone?"

Was *Nia* really asking him this? "Someone like who?"

"You tell me."

"Nia, I barely have enough energy for one woman these days. How could I have enough for two?" He chuckled, but stopped, realizing how serious she was. She was actually accusing him of cheating. It hurt. "I'm in the office busting my butt, and you're accusing me of having another lady."

"You sure have taken me for granted."

"I apologize if I have."

"That's all you do lately. Apologize. I'm sick of your apologies."

"And I'm sick of your whining," he let slip out.

The words stunned her so, Nia went silent, silent and staring at him, and staring and wondering. Where was the man she fell in love with? She didn't recognize him anymore. As swiftly as he'd entered her life, he had left it.

"I'm sick too, Roland," she said, getting out of bed. She hurried to the dresser and began removing items. "You don't make love to me the way you used to. If I call you at night at the office, I can't reach you. You don't even seem excited or interested in taking me any place. And now I learn you've been seeing another woman."

"I haven't been seeing anyone! Who told you that lie?" He

still couldn't believe she was accusing him of something he didn't do. *Nia* was accusing him of cheating on her. Who was this woman standing in this room? Certainly not the one he'd fell madly in love with.

Watching her gather some items and place them in a small suitcase, Roland was too angry with her to stop her from leaving. He couldn't even recognize her as the woman he'd held so many times in his arms. Where had she gone? Where was all that warmth, that tenderness, that affection?

When Nia was finished packing and getting dressed, she headed toward the door, only stopping when she thought of something his parents had said. It made her look over her shoulder at him. "Goodbye. Maybe you've found *your kind.*"

Roland stood by the window, watching the taxi drive off of the estate. When it was no longer in his line of vision, he lumbered across the floor, eventually plopping on his bed. Thoughts, so many thoughts crammed his head. One stood above all the rest. What did she mean by that remark *your kind?*

CHAPTER SIXTEEN

Nia's music became her lover. Day by day as she recorded the CD in the studio, she thrust her heart deeper into every song. It was all she could do to keep her spirit from dying. The absence of Roland's love in her life was felt all the time.

When she woke in the morning, she thought of him. And when she looked outside the window and saw the sun, she wondered why it looked so differently than it did when he was in her life. Somehow the sun didn't have the same magnificence, without him to share it with. Going about her day, Nia was obsessed with more thoughts of him. She wondered what he was doing. Where was he? How was his life progressing? Did he ever think of her?

The evenings were probably the worst to brave without Roland in her life. There had been so much laughter, warmth, closeness, communication and so much passion in their nights. He was her soul mate, her best friend, the one who knew her like no one else, and she knew him like no other. So in love they were once, they could make love by just looking at each other.

In the cozy townhouse Nia rented, she sprawled on her couch.

Listening to Mary J. Blige's ballad "Missing You Like Crazy", she could definitely relate to the song. The talented songstress could sure sing that song with some heart-tugging feeling, Nia thought as the tears began gathering behind her eyes.

She was blotting the last moist spot on her cheek when the doorbell rang. Confident that her face was now dry, she looked through the peep hole, and upon seeing Kal, she opened the door. Weeks ago, she had sent for the rest of her things at Roland's house so she could move them in her new home. Kal had helped her move in, and often dropped by in the evenings. Usually they would talk about the album. Sometimes Nia would cook for him.

"What are you doing tonight?" he asked. Another track on Mary J. Blige's CD was playing. "Ah, this album is one of the best I've heard this year." He started rocking his head to the uptempo rhythm.

"I like it a lot too," Nia agreed, resuming her spot on the couch.

Kal relaxed on the plush, magenta carpet near the CD rack like he usually did. He loved to read the backs of the covers to see the songwriter's and producer's names. "So do you think your album is comparable to this one?" He picked up Mary J. Blige's CD cover, reading the names of each cut.

"I think when we finish we'll have a lot of hot tracks. Thanks to my super-talented songwriter and producer."

Kal's penetrating eyes shot up. Itching to get up and hug her, he smiled instead.

"The songs can't come to life without the right singer to do them justice."

Just then, Nia felt tense around her shoulders. It probably had to do with the way she was laying on the sofa. Throwing her head back, she began to roll it around to assuage the tautness.

When Kal saw her doing this, he waved her down toward him. "Come here. I can do something for that."

"I'm okay. Just tight around my neck. Think I need to exercise more."

"Come here," Kal insisted. "You need a massage around that area and I'm the best."

That was funny to her. "Why does every man think he's a massage expert?"

"I don't know about everybody else, but *I am* an expert."

"Sure, sure, sure," she joked with him.

"Come on over here if you don't believe me."

Nia came down from the sofa and eased over to where he sat by the CD rack. Turning her back to him, she was immediately soothed by dexterous fingers magically slackening the tenseness around her shoulders.

The massage was so relaxing she couldn't resist when his hands traveled lower on her back, massaging all the strained areas on it too. So wonderful it felt, her eyes drifted closed.

Kal's fingertips gliding up her neck, tracing beneath her jaw line and lightly tugging her face so that she felt his warm breath nearing her lips, was all that opened Nia's eyes.

"I can't, Kal."

"Nia, you have to forget him and move on."

"I haven't forgotten, and I don't want to use you that way."

"Use me up."

She would have laughed if she hadn't realized he wasn't joking. His gaze burned into hers with his seriousness. "I won't pressure you. But when you're ready I'm here. And I'll never hurt you like he did."

With his hands buried in his pockets, Roland gazed out of his office window at the sun splashing down on Chenay Bay Beach. Slivers of crystal looked like they were chopped up and dusted over the vibrant blue ocean. Yet somehow the water didn't look as breathtaking as it did when Nia was in his life. Having someone that wonderful who loved him made watching a sight like this a sacred gift to behold.

But not only the water was treasured then. Everything was. Sunsets were like watching magic. The moon was an aphrodisiac. A cool breeze on a summer day was paradise. The flowers looked prettier. The air smelled fresher. People seemed nicer. Life was suddenly alive. Roland was alive.

Now the world was something he merely existed in. He worked, he talked, he laughed, he did everything that seemed as if he were functioning, but all the while he felt as though he was immersed in a fog. Forever hovering dismally around him, it was always moaning: *your life will never be the same without her.*

Wade excitedly entering the office lured Roland's attention away from the window.

"What's going on?" Roland asked. "You look happy about something."

Wade was ecstatic. "We passed the auditor's inspection."

"Great," Roland said, wishing that he really cared. Whether they passed it or not, he knew the outcome wouldn't have affected how he was feeling.

Wade didn't care for the way his friend was looking and sounding. "Why aren't you thrilled about this, Roll?"

"I'm glad."

"You don't sound glad." Wade never thought he'd ever see Roland so down. "You don't sound like you care one way or the other."

"Of course I care. I wanted to pass the audit."

"Everything is like it should be now." He removed his glasses to rub his eyes. "Everything except you and Nia. Why don't you call her, Roll?"

"I'm not calling her. I don't even have her number. I don't even know where she lives. And I'm not about to try to find out her address and number. She should call me. She left me because of some foolishness."

"It wasn't foolishness." Wade put his glasses back on. "She thought you were cheating because you neglected her."

"She thought I was cheating because someone lied to her."

"Forget all this thought stuff. Go find that woman and convince her of the truth."

"She doesn't want me. If she did, she never would have left. Let her go. I'll be all right."

"You're missing her, Roll."

"I'm not missing her. I'm not even thinking about her."

"If you say so. Anyway, some of the employees, including Suzanne and I are going on this yacht tonight. Would you like to come?"

"No. Think I'll get some sleep tonight."

"You always say that lately. You just want to go home and mope about Nia."

"I do not."

"You do too. If you weren't so hung up on her, you could go out and really enjoy yourself. But since you can't do that, what does that say about you?"

"What time does that boat leave?"

"Seven PM sharp."

"I'll be there. I'll show you something."

The Sun Princess sailed out from the shore with more than five hundred partygoers enjoying food, drink, games and a spectacular jazz band. Once tasting the scrumptious West Indian dishes, socializing and relishing the mellifluous music of the band, Roland was glad he came. He knew it wasn't good for him to spend another evening at home alone.

Suzanne popped alongside him as he made his second trip to the buffet table.

"Bet you're glad that tax business is over." she said.

"Oh, yes," he answered, helping himself to a shrimp cocktail.

"Now we can focus on other things, like making you a billionaire."

Roland liked the way she thought. "You think big, don't you?"

"I think about a lot of things," she said, sincerity lowering her voice.

Her emotionalism made him look over at her. Something about her face was vulnerable. He had never seen her look like that before. It was almost like a little girl's face.

"Roland, I heard through the grapevine that you and Nia broke up. And although I still feel the same way, I'm not going to put any moves on you. I just want you to know that I'm here. Whenever you want me, whenever you need me, I'm yours."

Looking in his eyes, she held his hand.

Kal and Nia had been enjoying the limbo rock game on the lower deck of the Sun Princess when they were lured up to the next level by the sound of the sensational band. What Nia didn't expect to see however, was a discouraging sight over near the buffet table. Her heart did a jolt, seeing Roland on the yacht. Far more unnerving, he was holding a woman's hand. Suzanne's hand.

Kal saw the two right after Nia did. It couldn't have been a better scene or had more perfect timing even if Suzanne and he had planned it.

"You want to go over there and talk to him?" Kal asked.

Wildly, Nia shook her head. "No, I just want to get off this boat. But for now let's go back downstairs."

"But I thought you wanted to hear the band."

"Not anymore."

Kal trailed her steps down the winding metal staircase.

CHAPTER SEVENTEEN

Cheers, howls, barking and all sorts of roars bellowed from the recording team throughout the studio as Nia sang the last entrancing note on the CD, entitled *Nia Lashon*. Side by side with the engineer in the booth, Kal wasn't boisterous, like the musicians who hugged and picked up his star. Instead, he opted for celebrating with the bottle of champagne he'd been carrying in the bag with his sheet music.

Entering the area where the rowdiness was taking place, Kal opened the bottle and began pouring Monet everywhere and on everybody. Nia was screaming when the bubbling liquid cascaded down her skin.

In a secluded corner of the room, she caught up to Kal, punching him in the arm for acting so crazy and drenching her.

"What did you wet me up like this for?" Laughing, she was picking up parts of her blouse and pants, shaking them.

"Because I felt like it," he kidded her. "Right now, I'm so happy and pleased with what we just finished here, I feel like doing any damn thing I want, including wetting your butt up with champagne."

"I didn't know you were this crazy, Kal."

"There's a lot you don't know about me. Now let me take you home so you can get some dry clothes on."

Prattling about the CD all during the drive to her house, Nia and Kal couldn't even quell their exhilaration about it inside the house. Kal had hundreds of ideas about promotion and was eager to speak to his promotions manager, Dana, in the morning. Nia was sharing ideas about the video concepts. Kal promised to promptly contact a talented teenaged film director he knew. He was positive the young talent could cinematically interpret Nia's vision for several of the songs.

After Kal became cozy near the CD rack like he normally did, Nia decided to go upstairs, shower and change into some dry, spiffier clothes. Kal had suggested they go out for a night on the town to celebrate. Nia was so high from her victory, she didn't think that was a bad idea at all.

Inside her bedroom, she took some undergarments out of her drawers and headed to the bathroom. After turning on the shower knob, the ballooning water below assured her, the drain was clogged. She'd call a plumber in the morning. For now she could use the hallway shower. Simply closing the door would have to do too, since the door had no lock.

The warm stream cascading down over her bare flesh was so soothing. Her thoughts were not. She had been laughing and talking and busying herself all day. And although her success made her high, behind it all, in that innermost place in her heart, only God knew how much she ached. A day like this, a day this victorious, she should be spending with Roland. After all, if it weren't for him, there might not have been a Nia Lashon CD.

He was the one who loved her and encouraged her so much, Nia truly believed there was nothing she couldn't attain in life if she wanted it bad enough.

But Roland wasn't part of her life anymore. He never would be again. Obviously, he had moved on. Possibly even with Suzanne. Roland didn't love her anymore. If he did, he would have come by the studio sometimes. He knew she would be there. With his resources, he could even have discovered where she lived, or found out her phone number. But he hadn't. He hadn't because he didn't desire her anymore. Perhaps he'd done what his parents clearly wanted him to do: be with his *own kind*.

If only him not loving her could have made Nia stop loving him. Unfortunately, that seemed impossible. The ache in her heart that spilled her pain from her eyes soon told her that.

"Why does it hurt so much, God?" she cried. "Why do I love him so much? Please make it stop. Show me a way to make it stop."

Beyond the shower curtain, above her faint sobs, Nia heard the bathroom door opening. She could have stopped the curtain from being pulled back and exposing her. She didn't. Through teary eyes, she plainly watched as Kal's hungry stare roved over her naked, drenched flesh.

Neither spoke a word. She even helped him out of his shirt, pants and briefs. Stepping in the shower with her, it was obvious that he was a beautiful man—a beautiful man who was extremely excited by her.

He came behind her, placing his middle against her back. He groaned as his hands reached around to the front of her breasts, stroking them ravenously. Lifting her head as he moved his face around to kiss her neck, all Nia could think about was how much she wished Roland was doing this to her.

"I can't," she said, as his hand roamed lower in the front of her. "I can't do this, Kal."

"Yes, you can," he whispered, twisting her around so that he met her lips. "You can do this, baby. I want you. You want me. It's been a long time coming."

"No," she protested, trying to pull out of his embrace. He was holding her tighter and his breaths were erratic.

"Please, Nia."

"No, no." Harshly, she pushed him back, grabbed a large towel and wrapped it around herself. "I'm sorry."

Avoiding looking at him, Nia quickly stepped out of the

shower, leaving a heavy breathing Kal inside. She was halfway to her bedroom when his fingers dug deep in her wrist, spinning her around.

Rage exploded in his face. "Why did you do that to me?"

"Kal, I'm so sorry. I just can't make love to you. I can't be with any man right now. I'm a one-man woman."

"And that man doesn't want you anymore! Can't you get that in your head? Didn't you see him with Suzanne? Weren't you listening when I told you about the other woman I saw him with?"

"What he may or may not have done doesn't matter. No, I'm not with him. But I can't stop feeling what I'm feeling for him. Maybe in time it'll go away."

His nostrils flared. "And what's supposed to happen to us in the meantime?"

"We can be friends like always, and business partners."

"Friends! Friends! I can get a freakin' friend anywhere!"

He stormed off down the hall.

She called to him, "Kal? Kal?"

Unresponsive, he continued walking.

Nia went inside her bedroom and then winced from the violent slam of her front door.

Hours later, Nia lay awake in the darkness of her bedroom. Everything was keeping her from sleeping. There were thoughts of Kal, of the CD, and mostly of Roland. The restlessness soon had her sitting up. After reaching for and turning on the Tiffany style lamps, she glimpsed the unopened mail she'd carried up to her room earlier in the day. Things had become so hectic she'd forgotten to open the numerous letters.

Now giving them her attention, there were a few bills, some junk mail, a fashion catalog, and surprisingly, a letter with no return address. On first sight she hoped it was from Roland. Nonetheless, the style of the handwritten address indicated it wasn't from him. Even so, the writing was familiar. Curious, Nia opened the envelope easily with a long, fuschia-colored nail. Unfolding it, she noticed it was misted with a familiar cologne: *Pierre Cardin*. There was only one man she knew who wore that brand. A strange sensation blew over her. She began to read.

Dear Nia:

I know it's been a long time since we've talked, seen each other or have even been friends, but lately I have thought of you so much, I had to write. With all the computer technology at our fingertips these days, it wasn't hard for me to find a service on the internet that located lost loved ones and friends. Hence, that's how I found out your address. But that wasn't how I found out you were living in St. Croix. That I learned from an article in a newspaper. There was an article about the record producer, Kal Hunter, and the recording artists on his flourishing label, Ecstasy Records. The article did a fine piece featuring the newest powerhouse addition to his label—you. They stated you were in the studio recording your debut album. I was so proud of you.

I'm glad your life is going well. I'm glad you didn't waste your singing talent. I always told you that God's gifts to us, we should never waste them, but use them to bring joy to yourself and to others. It's so wonderful that you are doing that.

As for myself, I'm doing well. I was an investment banker, but was laid off. I'm seeking another position, but sometimes I feel like I want to start my own business. Maybe the layoff was God's sign to me to start my own business. Despite being unemployed though, my life has turned out pretty well. I'm married to a lovely young lady, who is a nurse, and I have two beautiful girls.

After what happened between us, after I hurt you so deeply, I know you're probably thinking that I have nerve writing you. And I do. However, as I said, I've been thinking about you a lot lately. And I wanted to let you know what truly happened to change the course of our lives.

I loved you, Nia. Deep in my heart I always will. You were the stars, the moon and the earth from where I stood. But I was immature and didn't know myself nearly as well as I do now.

After running into Suzanne one night in a bar, foolishly I began drinking with her. It lead to the greatest mistake of my life: sleeping with her. That resulted in an unwanted pregnancy.

When our parents found out, the fact that you and I were about to be married didn't matter. My parents knew hers, and prudes that they were, they dismissed my upcoming marriage to you, and urged me to marry Suzanne. I did it for the sake of my child. But Suzanne lost the baby a few months after our wedding. With that, she lost me. But I was lost to her already. I was in love with another woman. Day and night I thought about her, missed her, ached for her, body and soul. That woman was you, Nia. One night I told Suzanne that. Because she loved me, she was devastated. We divorced shortly after.

So you know now what really happened with our lives. I know this letter won't make you forget what I did to us. But I do hope it will help you forgive. Also I must mention that I ran into Suzanne one day. She mentioned heading to St. Croix. If you happen to see her, beware of her. She's always hated you, and my ego would have loved to believe that it is because I loved you. But I know better. I know the real reason Suzanne harbors bitterness toward you. It has nothing to do with me. Though it is not my place to tell you the reason. I can only pray that her heart will soften and she can tell you about it with love, and not bitterness.

For now, know that I wish you all the best in life. You gave me wonderful memories that I will cherish for a lifetime. Also know that regardless of how my parents

treated you, you are no pebble to be swept aside. You're
a precious diamond to be treasured and loved.

                                        All my love,
                                        Mikel

As soon as Nia finished the letter, she held it near her heart. Now she understood what happened so long ago. Now she knew that Mikel didn't just steal her heart and throw her away. He called her a precious diamond to be treasured and loved. But she didn't need him to tell her that to know that she was. He also expressed how much he once loved her.

Now she was certain she wouldn't be able to sleep tonight. On top of the thoughts that had kept her awake before, she would be thinking about the letter, about her life, about Suzanne. What was Suzanne keeping from her?

To laud another significant increase in Destiny Resort's profits, Roland decided to share an afternoon of horseback riding with Wade and Suzanne. It was Suzanne's idea to spend some time with his Palomino and Appaloosa horses. On that first day she arrived in St. Croix and visited Roland's mansion, Suzanne had seen the horses and drooled over them.

Now sweeping her right leg over the Palomino as she dismounted it, she was still drooling.

"This is a beauty," Suzanne said. She rubbed its golden coat, imagining that it was Roland's chest. She always wondered what his muscular chest would feel like against her hands. "Riding a horse is so much fun."

"I always loved riding," Roland admitted. He was tying his horse to a palm tree's trunk. It was also a Palomino.

They spotted Wade galloping on the Appaloosa near the small domed bridge that adorned Roland's land. He waved to the two. Shortly after, he vanished in the distance.

Roland sat beneath the tree opposite the one the horse was tied to. Tipping his head back against the trunk, he felt tired. Lately, he was always tired. He'd visited the doctor to see if anything was medically wrong with him. It turned out that he was in excellent health. When he was with Nia, he had had plenty of energy.

"You're a good rider," Suzanne remarked. She relaxed on the ground next to him.

"You're not bad yourself," he complimented her.

Abruptly, she laughed.

"What's funny?" he asked her.

"Us."

"What about us?" Her smile was making him smile.

"Not long ago you couldn't stand my guts. Now look at us. We're actually friends."

Musing about that, Roland nodded slowly. "Yes, we did get off to a bad start. But I like how things are now."

"You do?"

"Yes, I do."

She looked off, hearing Wade's horse, but not seeing it. "But don't you want more?" She looked over at him. "I sure do."

Roland stared at her. With her angular face, model-like features, and short, silky hair, Suzanne was a pretty woman. She had a pretty body too. She was also highly intelligent and fun to be around, when she wasn't being manipulative and cunning. That being as it may, Roland knew she wasn't the woman to make him forget Nia. Getting involved with Nia's foe was as sleazy to him as getting in bed with her sister. Bad as Nia had treated him, and as abandoned as he felt by her, it didn't justify any type of intimacy with Suzanne.

Wade galloping by on the Appaloosa lured Roland's gaze to his direction. Showing off, Wade swung his legs to each side, and even rode backwards. All this he did before weaving throughout close-set trees, soon disappearing again.

"He's crazy!"

Shaking his head in conviction of his words, Roland moved to his side to get Suzanne's reaction to her cousin's antics, and he nearly bumped into her face. In the time that he watched Wade, she'd come so close to him he could feel her breath on his cheeks.

Staring at him, Suzanne's eyes spoke so clearly of what she wanted. Within that second, her lips sought it. He was so beautiful to her, inside and out, and if she could just claim his heart this time, all her efforts wouldn't have been in vain. Most of all, she would know that the powerful emotions she felt for him were reciprocated. The tremor in her legs every time she saw Roland, and the raging in her heart whenever he was near assured Suzanne that this wasn't about Nia. Her affection for Roland was about feeling something she'd never felt before, not with Mikel, not with Kal, not with any other man. If she were blessed with him feeling for her what she felt for him, it would somehow make up for every wrong she'd ever experienced in life. Even the wrong she tried every day of her life to forget.

With Suzanne's first feather-brush of her lips against Roland's, he leaned back from her. Instead of receiving his message, it seemed to Suzanne as if he had invited her to indulge in much more. Again, she proceeded forth, her lips trembling in their quest for his.

"No, Suzanne," he fought her mouth forcefully pressing against to his.

"Why?" she questioned, her breath catching in her throat. "I know you want me."

"No." He pulled back more.

Yet she came at him harder, her lips soon crushing his, her hands soon roaming. As her mouth fought to possess him, she grasped his fingers, lifting them to the warm mounds cupped in silk beneath her blouse.

She had just begun to moan when Roland took his hands and lips away.

Suzanne was stunned. "What is wrong? I know you want me. I've seen how you look at me. I know you think I'm attractive."

"Yes, Suzanne, I do think you're attractive," he acknowledged.

Pleased to hear that, she reached up to caress his face. All the riding and the sunshine made it dewy. It beckoned her touch.

Grabbing her hand, Roland carefully guided it back down at her side.

Suzanne looked like she was about to cry. "Roland, why are you doing this? You're sending mixed messages. You just told me I was attractive."

"But that doesn't mean you and I should be together."

"It means something."

"Suzanne, let's forget this."

"I don't want to forget it! I want you and I know you want me too. It's been building up between us, and now it's time to give in to it. It'll be so good, Roland. So good. I promise."

"It won't work."

Suddenly realizing why he was so reluctant, she chuckled wryly. "It's because of her, isn't it? She's the reason you're fighting me. What in God's name do you men always see in her?"

"Don't start, Suzanne."

"No! I want to know. She's pathetic and she's a nobody. She was born from a nobody! She's trash just like her mother!"

"I've had enough of this." He started walking off toward the house.

Suzanne caught up to him. "I'm sorry. I didn't mean to go there. I just want you to think about you and me."

Halting his steps, he faced her with empathy. "Look, I really don't want to hurt you, but there is no you and me. And there isn't going to be."

"But Nia doesn't love you."

"Leave Nia out of this."

"If she did, she would be here now."

"Stop it!"

"She doesn't! You know she doesn't. And I do!"

The confession shocked them both into silence. Suzanne had shocked herself. But now that her heart had spoken, she hoped his would speak the same.

"What do you feel for me?" She interrupted the quiet.

"Friendship," he answered. "Just friendship."

Suzanne laughed. That way the truth wouldn't hurt so bad. "Friendship, and that's all? That's all?"

Roland peered down, then looked back up at her. "You know where my heart is, Suzanne. Deep down, you know."

Suzanne wasn't going to let him see her cry. She wasn't going into hysterics. She wasn't going to do anything that would expose the ache ripping inside.

"Fine! Forget you then!"

She flounced around and stomped off toward the woods.

In the forest behind Roland's house, Suzanne found refuge. Collapsing on the dirt, she didn't care if her clothes became soiled, or if bugs crawled on her, or even if a snake slithered nearby. Getting rid of the pain was all she cared about—the pain of unrequited love.

Sure, people had loved her in her life. Wade loved her. There were men who had loved her. Her parents loved her. They loved her so much they adopted her. All in all though, the people she had loved most never loved her back.

Mikel's love was never hers. Neither was Kal's. And now, horribly, Roland had rejected her too. Then there was that other love she craved. Nia had stolen all of them from her.

Wade had dismounted the horse and was harnessing it to a tree trunk when he heard odd, muted sounds. Cocking his ear toward the direction where it came from, he trampled toward it. A woman was crying. Soon he saw Suzanne.

"What happened?" He rushed to her, cradling her tightly in his arms. An astonishing sight to him, he realized he had never seen Suzanne cry. Even at family funerals when everyone was in hysterics expressing their grief, including him, Suzanne's eyes remained dry and clear.

"Did you get hurt on the horse?"

Unable to look anywhere but down, she attempted to say

something. Except all the wailing drowned her voice, hurling her words back in her throat and back down inside her heart, where there was such an ache her sobs could only grow louder.

"My God, cuz, what's wrong? I've never seen you like this. Where's Roland?"

Finally, she looked at him. "I want you to get him," she managed in a whisper.

Wade's bottom lip dropped. "What happened with you two?"

"He led me on, that's what!"

Wade took a deep breath. "Suzanne, you didn't try to seduce him, did you?"

"You sound like that's so horrible."

"Cuz, you know he's still in love with Nia."

The sobs returned, mingled with her voice. "What's wrong with me, Wade?"

His own eyes getting teary, he nuzzled her head against his chest. "Sweetie, nothing is wrong with you. You're beautiful. You're smart. He just isn't the man for you. So many other great men are out there. Give one of them a chance."

"What's wrong with me, Wade?" she questioned again. She began rocking. "Why is it that the ones I love never love me back?"

"Don't talk like this, girl." He wiped the line of water that rolled down his own cheek.

"After all I did to get him too." Her cries grew louder.

Wade looked puzzled. "What did you do?"

"Everything and he still didn't love me."

"Everything like what?"

She was crying louder, rocking harder. "I—I lied to his parents about her. And I . . ." There were louder cries. "And I asked Kal to help me."

Wade did not like the way this was sounding. "How did he help you?"

The sobs were louder, louder, louder. "I . . . I called the tax people and lied about the books. I didn't want him to spend any time with her."

Still holding her, Wade was shocked into speechlessness.

"And . . . and when we worked late trying to fix everything, I didn't want her to talk to him. I wanted her to think he lied about where he was."

He was still holding her. She was still rocking. "So that's why you suggested that we leave all the machines on when we were working at night?"

"Yes." Her cries weaved louder through her words. "And then Kal . . ." Her shoulders shook as she became more emotional. Wade's shirt was soaked.

"What about Kal?" He held her tighter.

"Kal told her that he saw Roland with a woman. That fool believed him. I wouldn't have believed him, because I love Roland. I love him, Wade." She grabbed his shirt tightly between her fingers. "Would I have done all this if I didn't love him?" She stopped rocking.

Slowly Wade raised Suzanne up from his chest. Searching her damp, reddened face, he felt a mixture of disgust and pity. "You have to tell Roland what you did, Suzanne."

"Tell him?" Feeling as if she was awakening from a fog, she moved back, frowning at him. "I can't tell him this. It was for your ears only. I just couldn't keep it inside." She began drying her eyes with her fingers. "Let's go. I want to get as far away from this house as possible. Who needs him?"

"You obviously did, to go to such lengths."

Wade was suddenly looking at her so angrily, she felt betrayed. "You should be on my side. I'm your cousin."

"And he's my friend. And you ruined his relationship. How could you do such a thing, Suzanne? All my life I've seen the rotten things you did. And most of the time, I overlooked them. You know I did. But this was so calculated and cruel I can't just stand by and do nothing. I can't see my friends hurt because of your wickedness." He stood, extending his hand down to her. "Come, let's tell him."

Suzanne stood, but didn't accept his hand. "You must be out of your mind if you think I'm going to subject myself to that. I told you, Wade! I told you only! It's between you and me.''

"Not anymore." Wade walked over to his horse and began untying it from the tree.

In disbelief that he was about to betray her, Suzanne gawked at him. "You're not going to do that to me are you? We're cousins, for heaven sake."

Wade mounted the Appaloosa. "Yes, I'm your cousin, but what you did was wrong."

The horse galloped off.

After Wade shared the story of Suzanne and Kal's treachery with Roland, Wade saw the outrage on his friend's face and feared for his cousin Suzanne.

"I have to find her," Roland said.

"Wait until you cool off a bit," Wade urged. "Suzanne is pretty upset about you rejecting her that way."

"I wasn't talking about Suzanne."

CHAPTER EIGHTEEN

Nia hadn't been able to reach Kal for four days. She had gone by the studio, his home, and had left several messages all of which went unanswered. It all was in hopes that they could straighten out their friendship. What occurred to her in her shower had definitely put a cloud over their relationship, possibly changing it forever.

So when the doorbell rang shortly after the eleven o'clock news went off on Thursday night, Nia was sure it was him. No one else would have come to her house at such a late hour. Elated that they could now talk, she didn't bother to look through the peephole. She eagerly opened the door. Shock colored her face.

"Hello, Nia."

His voice vibrated through the silence, triggering bells that went off in her ears. She felt her head pulsing, even if visually it sat motionless on her shoulders. Tremors on the insides of her legs hid her extreme shock. The dramatic rise and fall of her chest didn't even reveal that this person standing before her was no ordinary presence in her life. But it was her eyes that unspokenly conveyed that this man had meant something to her—meant so much that he had been with her every second of every day even though he was nowhere around.

"So you found out where I lived?" she managed above the shock.

Roland couldn't answer immediately. He didn't process the question right away. The sight of Nia had somehow drawn him into another world.

So many days and nights, he had imagined seeing her again, being face to face—now that he was before her, he needed simply to savor the moment. The ache that she'd left in his heart, the one that didn't stop him from thinking about her day and night, the one that made his heart now nearly stop, had given her an almost mystical quality in his mind. There were times when he even questioned whether had he once loved a woman as passionately as he loved her. Now seeing her in the flesh, her hazel eyes sparkling at him, her lips so full and moist, her sultry body reminding him of passionate nights they shared, he was certain he had loved that deeply. For that emotion was never felt greater than at this moment.

"I did investigating and found you," he said.

"Why were you looking for me?"

"May I come in? There is something you have to know."

Uncomfortably, Roland stepped inside, looking around as he did, seeing mostly gold and black furnishings.

"Nice place. The color scheme is real cozy."

"Thanks. Have a seat." She gestured to the couch behind him.

With her leg folded beneath her, she sat on the loveseat.

There was a strained silence as they stared at each other.

"You look great," he told her. "Really great."

"So do you." She scratched her ear. "But what is it that I have to know?" Was he going to tell her he still loved her?

Roland then recounted the story Wade had told him. When he finished telling Nia how they were manipulated and betrayed by Suzanne and Kal, Nia couldn't sit.

"How could Kal do such a thing?" Holding her arms, she

wandered aimlessly. "I can see Suzanne doing something like this, but Kal . . ."

Roland eased up behind her. "Nia, I—"

"He was such a good friend to me. He—"

"Nia!"

Summoned by the urgency in his voice, she turned around. Roland was so close to her, Nia saw her reflection in his eyes.

"I missed you," he confessed. Fascinated by the smoothness of her cheek, he began stroking it.

The delicate teasing closed her eyes. "Oh, I missed you, too." She could feel her breath escaping her.

"I thought about you every day." He traced his finger across her lips and down her neck. "In the morning when I woke."

She reared her head back. "I thought about you all during the day."

His mouth brushed her neck. "I thought about you as I worked, as I walked down the street, as I drove home. And at night . . ." He carried his lips up along her neck, soon reaching the quivering line separating her lips. "At night I thought about this."

With the tip of his tongue, he painstakingly sought the sweetness beyond her lips. Closing his own eyes because it felt so good, he couldn't help seeking more and more. Forcefully putting his arms around her so that her head rested in the bow of his muscular arms, his head glided from side to side as he tasted her ravenously to fulfill his rapidly increasing desire. Her luscious nectar turned him on even more than it had before.

Laying back into what felt like heaven, Nia knew nothing recently that had felt this good. Not singing. Not laughing. Not fantasizing about the passion that they used to share. Thrash after thrash of his tongue across hers startlingly informed her that she was feeling more desire for him than she ever had before. A sweltering sea stirred tempestuously at the base of her stomach, and she knew he was the only captain to tame the storm.

Reaching underneath her blouse, he was delirious about her

wearing no bra. Caress after caress of her softness, and he was aching for her touch.

"Feel me, Nia. Touch me," he groaned.

Stroking his chest and arms, she soon freed them of clothing. Her heart raced, seeing and touching the bare flesh that she hungered to feel for so long. Crushing herself against him, she heard him moan out the joy that she felt, too. Moving her backward, he took a head to toe look at her body. Then without saying a word, he began unzipping her skirt.

Clad only in her panties, she kissed him deeply and felt his hands pulling her panties off. Aching to do more to him, she helped him shed his pants also, and afterward she eagerly reached into his briefs and felt the luscious splendor that was so ready for her.

"Oh, that feels so good," he cried out with a husky breath.

His shorts were now off and Nia kneeled before him. Her kisses and caresses of his love were making him delirious. Knowing it felt so unbearably good that he couldn't possibly end their pleasure too soon, he kneeled down with her, steadying his eyes on her beautiful face.

He kissed it, kissed every ravishing feature, kissing even below, down her neck, down her belly, kissing and kissing, gently laying her back with his lips. Leaning over her, he eventually reached the sweetness between her legs. As she held the back of his head, his sword-like tongue entered her secret place.

She couldn't stop herself from writhing with excitement as he thrilled her, tasted her, slowly and tenderly, then ever so lustfully. She wanted him to do this forever. But her body had a will of its own, soon shuddering so uncontrollably, Roland could only stroke her, soothe her and prepare her for what was coming next.

He raised himself, then grabbed her arms, raising them above her head. Holding her by her two wrists, he kissed her deeply, before opening her legs with his thighs. One light push into her honeyed walls and he let out a sigh of pleasure.

"I love you," he moaned, moving slowly. "Oh, baby, I love you so much."

"I . . . I love you too," she whispered, feeling the intense pleasure pounding between her legs.

Harder and faster she felt it. Sweeter and deeper. Her body flooded with ecstasy, and with one final forceful penetration of his love, Nia felt her being floated to a place that had to be heaven.

Suzanne sat in the diner chairs of Brady's Bar and Grill, anxiously looking around for the vagrant she had met on the beach during a midnight stroll the previous night. A stocky man of about forty, he was dirty, hungry, and penniless she learned, when he begged her for money for a sandwich.

She had dismissed him with a scornful expression and a wave of her hand. She wasn't even worried about him attacking her with the huge knife glittering from his pocket. Yet when he was about a yard away from him, Suzanne realized something. That knife could be very useful. Backtracking to him, she offered him a smile and a proposition that would reward him $5,000.

The man found the reward exceptionally seductive. Regardless, he was abhorred by what she wanted him to do for it. Suzanne increased the payment to $10,000. His eyes grew bigger. Nevertheless, he still abhorred the task. Before they parted, she scribbled the phone number to the new townhouse she was living in. This morning the vagrant called her, informing her where to meet him.

Now spotting him lumbering into the pub far filthier than he was last night, Suzanne gestured for him to come to her table.

Sitting down, his red-rimmed eyes steadied in hers. "I want to see the money."

"It's right here," Suzanne said and peered around. Finding that no one was paying them any attention, she raised a stack of money, which displayed a hundred dollar bill on top.

The vagrant swallowed and reached for it.

Suzanne snatched the money back, lowering it to her lap. "You do it first. Then get the money."

He leaned forward. "How do I know if I can trust you?"

Her nose squiggled up from his horridly acrid breath. "I could say the same for you if I gave you the money."

"This don't seem fair."

"Are you going to do it or not?"

Suzanne was mysteriously missing after Roland learned what she had done. Because she was missing from work, missing from her hotel and unreachable by her beeper or cell phone, Kal was the first to confront for the betrayal. Roland and Nia finally caught up to him one day at the recording studio. Pecking on a piano key, he was alone.

"Kal?"

Kal swerved around to the sound of Roland's unwelcome voice, and saw his enraged face beside Nia. Looking from face to face, he smirked. "So you have your girlfriend back, Mr. Davenport."

"No thanks to you."

"I had nothing to do with your breakup."

"Liar!" Nia shouted. "You broke us up. You and Suzanne. We know about it. Suzanne told Wade everything."

Kal appeared unbothered by their knowing the truth. "So what; I lied. Big freakin' deal. If you two were all that tight in the first place, no one could separate you." Pausing, his stare burned into Roland. "And if you were so much of a man, no other man could take what's yours."

Roland's eyes narrowed. "I've lost nothing but time. As you see, my beautiful woman is with me."

"She was with me too." Kal glanced at Nia. "And I don't mean she was holding my hand."

Nia couldn't believe this was the same Kal whose friendship she had grown to cherish.

"It's not like he's trying to make it out to be, Roland," she defended. "That's why he's angry with me. We didn't—"

"I don't care what it is, baby," Roland cut her off. "Whatever happened, happened when we weren't together. I don't need to hear about it."

"And I don't need to hear any more from either of you." Kal moved toward the door and opened it. "I have work to do, so if you will excuse me?"

Nia stepped toward him. "Speaking of work, when is the album going to be released?"

"It's not."

"What?"

"It's not going to be released."

Roland stepped so close to Kal, their noses were nearly rubbing. "You have a contract with her. She worked hard on that CD and you're going to release it."

Amused, Kal eyed him up and down. "You may be king over there at the resort, but I'm king of Ecstasy Records and if you happen to read her contract I have the say-so when and if the CD will be released."

Roland was amused by Kal too. "You mean to tell me you're going to base a business decision on some rejection, some ego bruising. Nia's CD could net you millions and you're going to let it go—let it go because you're thinking with your head, and I don't mean the one on top." Looking at Nia, he grasped her hand. "Let's get out of here, baby. We hang around here too long, we might get stupid too."

Kal sat on the bar stool at Brady's Bar and Grill, sorely regretting how he had handled Roland earlier. What he should have done was lie and tell him how he turned his woman out in graphic detail. That would have knocked him off his high horse. Better than that, he should have punched Roland out.

After ordering a Heineken, he nearly drank it all in a second. He was trying to drown out the image of those two together again. He couldn't get over the way she looked at Roland's

side. She was so devoted to him, so into him. It all made Kal
wonder what Roland had that he didn't. He was rich like Roland.
He was just as handsome. He had the equipment to satisfy her
sexually; Kal made her aware of that in the shower. So what
was it? What was it that Roland did to her to claim her heart
like he did? What were the ingredients to the spell he cast?
What did he say and do to mesmerize her so?

Rubbing his forehead as his questions grew, Kal found himself with company. One of his musicians, Curtis, was sliding
on the bar stool next to him. Kal had spotted Curtis' bald
head earlier as he sat around at a table with some women.
Nonetheless, Kal wasn't in the mood for socializing. So he
decided to sit at the bar.

"Man, you won't believe what I just heard," Curtis said
eagerly.

Kal glanced over his shoulder at the women Curtis had been
sitting with. All looked like they were disgusted by a drunk
sitting at an opposite table.

"What won't I believe?" Kal asked. Curtis was bursting to
tell him.

"You see that bum over there? The one drooling at my
friends."

Kal looked back over his shoulder again. All four women
were rolling their eyes at the bum. Wretchedly, there were no
other tables available to distance themselves from him.

Kal turned aside to Curtis. "What about him?"

"He told one of my friends over there that he's getting ten
grand and he wants to spend it on her."

"Good for him." Kal motioned to the bartender for another
beer. "Another one here, man." He pointed in front of him.

The bartender nodded.

Looking back at the vagrant, Curtis shifted his weight on
the bar stool. "You wouldn't be saying good for him if you
heard what the bum was saying." He looked over at Kal.

"What did he say?"

The bartender set the drink in front of Kal. He started sipping.

"Said some chick is paying him to kill this woman. Guess what her name is, the one who is going to get killed?"

"I have no idea."

"Nia Lashon."

Kal nearly choked.

CHAPTER NINETEEN

"Who is going to pay you to kill Nia Lashon?"

Kal sat opposite the outspoken vagrant, resting his knuckles on his chin and his elbow on his thigh.

Samuel Caldwell's red and pink lips curled, making his leathery face look younger. "I'm not really going to kill her. I just told that rich woman that to get the money. I'm going to pretend. And when I get the cash . . ." He looked over to the table with Curtis and his lady friends. "I'm going to get me one of those honeys over there. I haven't had a woman in ages."

Kal could see why. "Was her name Suzanne Greer? The woman who propositioned you?"

"Her name is Suzanne. Fine thing too. Tall, nice body."

"How are you supposed to pull this off? This pretend murder?"

Samuel smiled again. "Well, that's the tricky part. You see, this Suzanne has given me a picture of the girl. Now she's a looker too. Whooh."

"Yeah, yeah and what else?"

"Well this Suzanne found out that this Nia lives in a townhouse. I'm supposed to watch the house and wait until the time is right and then strike.''

"Strike how?" Kal leaned forward. Though as soon as he did, the odor from Samuel's mouth made him rear back. "What are you supposed to kill her with?"

"With my knife. Here it is." Samuel reached inside his tattered jacket pocket. A twelve-inch blade was pulled out.

"Put that away," Kal urged, looking around.

Samuel complied. "But I can't do that. I can't cut up no lady."

"So how are you going to pull it off? You still haven't told me."

Samuel scratched his bulbous nose. "Well this Suzanne wants me to show her a body in order to collect the money."

"Damn her!" Kal cursed.

"But the thing is, I have this friend, Abby. She's about the size of the girl in the picture. She don't have no place to stay like me. And Abby said she'll pretend to be this Nia lady. I'll thin some ketchup with water, then smear it on her face so Suzanne won't see her features, and their hair already looks about the same length and color. Then Abby will lay down on the beach and pretend to be dead. And I'll collect."

Kal had stopped listening to Samuel well before he stopped talking. The part about Suzanne wanting to see a body had seized him. If she was this desperate to hurt Nia, then she was this desperate back in New York. Now he was certain that she had set that fire. But why? Was this all about jealousy over men? It had to be, he answered himself. For what else could it be?

As furious as Kal was at Nia, the last thing he wanted was to see her die. Fortunately, this guy was harmless. But what about the next person Suzanne hired to end Nia's life? What if it was a professional hit man? Suzanne had to be stopped.

Kal pulled out his cell phone and dialed Nia's number. The phone rang several times before the answering machine triggered. He hung up and dialed Destiny Resorts. Two rings and he had the switchboard operator.

"Where can I find Roland Davenport, the CEO?" Wherever he was, Kal was sure Nia was with him.

"Would you like to leave a message, sir?" the pleasant female voice on the other end asked.

"Hell no. I don't want to leave a message. I want you to find out where Roland Davenport is because I have to see him. Now! It's a matter of life and death."

Accompanied by Samuel, Kal tracked down Nia and Roland at Roland's mansion. Not at all happy to see Kal and this slovenly stranger, Roland didn't ask either to sit on his study's sofa.

"What do you want, Kal?"

Kal reached to his side, clutching Samuel's shoulder. "My friend here has something to tell you." He looked over at Nia. "It's about you. Your life is in danger."

After Samuel Caldwell shared the details of what Suzanne was hiring him to do, Roland quickly notified the authorities. When they arrived, Samuel shared his story again. This time however, his story was recorded as an official police statement. Suzanne had committed a crime. Now they had to trap her to be punished.

A sting operation was set up. Samuel would call Suzanne and tell her he had just fulfilled her request—that he killed Nia. At that point, he would invite her to see the body at midnight. It would be laying in a secluded section of Highland Bay Beach. Samuel would give her directions on how to reach the isolated area.

However, when Suzanne arrived there, the police didn't feel that Samuel's friend Abby would do, posing as Nia. They wanted Nia herself to pretend she was dead. And all the while, Samuel would be wired, and asking questions that would make Suzanne answer accordingly, verifying her guilt. Videotaping would aid in the sting. Then last but not least, the money would exchange hands. Once that was done, Suzanne would be arrested.

* * *

"Are you sure you want to do this?" Roland asked Nia in bed that night.

Tomorrow night was the night. "I'm sure." She was staring at the ceiling, looking like a frightened little girl to him.

"Because we can use Samuel's friend Abby or some other person that resembles you."

"No, I want to do it, Roland. I want to see Suzanne's face when I get up. I also want to know why she hates me. I can feel that the reason is more than meets the eye."

Uninvited, Kal sat in the van with the authorities and Roland as they waited on the transmitter to hear Suzanne's meeting with Samuel. She was expected at any moment. While the authorities checked their audio and video equipment, Roland couldn't help wondering aloud about Kal.

"Now you know you have no business here," Roland said. He was sitting on the floor of the van opposite Kal. Kal was also on the floor.

"I want to make sure everything turns out all right. After all, if I hadn't came across Samuel, none of this would be happening."

"Does that mean you're willing to get over this *thing* you have and release Nia's CD?"

Kal smiled with his lips, but not his eyes. "I'm not releasing anything. I just came here to see that Suzanne gets what she is due."

"So you're saying that you're not here because you care about Nia?"

Kal gazed over at the men handling the equipment because he didn't feel comfortable anymore with Roland looking in his eyes. "I care about lots of people. But as far as Nia's career goes, she could do what the hell she wants with her life! *I'm not* releasing that CD."

Just then, they began to receive something on the transmitter.

Roland and Kal hurried over to it, joining the officers as they listened. The video monitor began to show a picture also. Suzanne had arrived.

Looking around to see if anyone was watching, Suzanne followed Samuel as he led her to the body.

Finally standing above the bloody form, Suzanne momentarily stared at Nia's face down body.

"Turn her around," she then ordered.

"What?" Samuel said. Hoping everything was going according to plan, he glanced around.

Suzanne stepped toward Nia and kicked her foot. "Turn her around, I said. I want to make sure she's dead."

Nervously, Samuel glanced around, then complied with her wishes. Weak from all the alcohol he abused his body with, he struggled but did manage to turn Nia around. Her eyes were shut tight. Her chest didn't move.

Suzanne laughed. "It's finally over. I did it. I did it. She's out of my life. She took my Mikel's love and Kal's and Roland and *hers.*"

Samuel rubbed his hands together. "Now do I get my money? I stabbed her up like you wanted me to. Put the knife in her back over and over and over again."

Suzanne laughed again while taking out a bundle of money from her purse. She threw the stack at him. "Well deserved."

"You're under arrest, Ms. Greer."

A police officer pointing a gun was shouting at Suzanne, drawing her alarmed eyes toward him. He began rushing towards Suzanne.

Samuel backed away from her. A police car made a screeching halt in front of her. Two more patrol cars then surrounded her. Simultaneously, a van parked beside her. Roland, Kal and over a dozen officers jumped out. Suzanne didn't think the nightmare could get any worse. It did. Nia stood up.

CHAPTER TWENTY

"Why, Suzanne?" Nia ranted. "Just tell me why?"

She watched Suzanne struggling with the officers who were trying to handcuff her.

"You want to know why?" Suzanne wasn't listening as an officer read her her rights. She shouted over him. "Do you really want to hear it, Nia?"

Nia could hardly breathe she wanted to know so bad.

Suzanne was wildly resisting being forced into the squad car. "It won't be pretty."

Roland appeared at Nia's side, and began holding her. "Tell the truth for once in your life, Suzanne."

Her deep-set eyes shifting from one to the other, Suzanne laughed out, "Because of that slut!"

Nia's hand clung to her chest, her forehead tilted forward as she tried to get more clarity. "Who are you talking about? What are you talking about?"

"That slut, that's who."

"Who?" Nia was yelling.

Finally the officers had managed to shove Suzanne's bottom

in the car. They grappled with the rest of her. "My slut and yours."

Desperate to make sense of this, Nia approached the car. Suzanne's head was now sticking out of the back of the squad car window. "I'm talking about that slut—your mother!"

Roland pointed a finger. "How dare—"

"No, let her talk," Nia urged over the maddening pounding that suddenly jumpstarted her heart.

Suzanne smiled. "She was my mother too. Now how do you like that?"

The car drove off, beckoning a wind that swirled dust upward. It fogged the air just as Suzanne's words fogged the consciousness of Nia's mind.

"Baby, are you sure you want to put yourself through this?" Roland questioned.

In her old bedroom Nia was pulling the vanity chair close to the trunk that Roland had just pulled out of the closet.

Bending down near her shoulder, he caressed a light kiss on the back of her neck. "Don't you believe what that lunatic said. Your mother didn't have any other children. As close as you said you two were, she would have told you. Wouldn't she?"

Nia was listening, but not absorbing. What's more, she had been pondering about Suzanne's reason for such hatred more and more. There had to be more to it than met the eye. And ever since Suzanne had made such a statement about her mother, Nia had been hearing this voice inside her. A voice that now controlled her actions. Whether it was God's voice, an angel, her mother or just her own intuition speaking to her, it begged her to open the trunk.

One of her mother's most treasured belongings, Nia had brought it on the flight from New York to the island. It contained all that remained of her mother's things. The others she had gave to her siblings, other relatives and church charity drives.

Deciding she needed to be left alone for this moment, Roland headed to the study to read while Nia unpacked the trunk. She already knew what was in it. When her mother first died, she had packed everything in it possible: pictures, jewelry, gifts from her father, letters, her mother's bible, souvenirs from trips and some clothes. But there was one article she had packed last. It was her mother's diary. Temptation had always beckoned Nia to open it. Perhaps there was something about this woman she so dearly loved that would make Nia cherish her memory even more. Except she always convinced herself that she had no right to abandon her mother's privacy. No more. Nia had to know if what Suzanne spouted was true. If it was, she had to know the reasons why her mother kept such a secret and did such a thing. Had she given up her own child? Her own child, Suzanne?

Ever since Suzanne made the claim two days ago, Nia had been standing in front of the mirror, searching for some sort of resemblance between them. Outwardly there was none. Only her mother could solve the mystery through her words. Nia opened the diary.

Her mother had started writing the diary after her third child, Carrington was born. Her father died shortly after her brother's birth. The entries were very interesting and often sad. What she enjoyed reading though, was that her mother was very happy with her children. However, when Nia turned to a page where the writing was very sloppily written, she was compelled to read it.

Dear God:

Today is September 19th. Did you hear me? September 19th. Every year on this day I feel like dying inside. It was the day my baby was born—the beautiful baby girl I gave away.

Suddenly Nia laid the letter down, her heart pounding as if she'd been running a race. Her mother did have another child. Another child. Another child that she gave away. *Oh, God, it can't be true. Suzanne can't be . . .*

Anxious to know more, she looked up toward the ceiling, then looked back at the letter. She began reading again.

My Lord, I have asked you every day of my life to forgive

me. And I ask you today because I feel such agony inside. But at the time, I did the best I knew how to do. I was poor and having a hard time getting work. Family help was out because they were so poor they could barely take care of themselves. And the father of my child and I had broke up. I couldn't find him, and even if I could, he was also one who couldn't take care of himself.

There was a wealthy woman that a friend of mine worked for, a woman who was barren. Her and her husband were wonderful people and were desperate to adopt. My friend told me about them, and I also liked what they had. They could give my child everything, material comforts and most importantly love. When they met my baby, I could feel the love in the room. I knew it could only grow in time.

So I made the hardest decision I ever made in my life—I gave my baby girl away. I didn't sell her either. A proper, legal adoption was arranged. It was hard, even harder when they told me it was best if I didn't visit her. They said it would be too confusing to the child.

I didn't visit her. But years later after I was married and widowed, when I met a man who offered to take care of me, I found a house in the fancy neighborhood where she lived, and he paid the rent for me. I was a few blocks from her. And when that relationship broke up, I found another man who would keep me in that house near my child. I even put my other children in the same private schools that she went, too. And as fate would have it, my other daughter and her became friends. Several times I saw her as she and some other girls walked my daughter home on the way from school. I was so glad I was able to put my daughter in a school she went to. I was so glad to live in a home near hers.

I would have done anything for my child. I would have done anything for my child, Suzanne.

Roland heard a scream and piercing cries. He nearly tripped on a stray piece of carpet in his hurry to get to Nia.

He gently raised her shaking shoulders and held her up to his chest. Her cheek rested against it. "You found out something you didn't want to know," he concluded, stroking her hair. "It's all right, baby. I'm here. And I'll always be here no matter what it is."

Nia knew she shouldn't have been visiting Suzanne, but at the same time she had to see her. When the guard opened the door to her cell, Suzanne was sitting on a lower bunk, reading a magazine.

Smirking, she tossed the magazine aside and stood. "Come to gloat?"

Nia took a deep breath as the guard closed the cell door behind her, leaving them alone.

"I wanted to tell you that I know what you said was true," Nia announced.

Suzanne grinned. "How did you find out?"

Nia slid her bag higher on her shoulder. "Mama had a diary."

Suzanne rolled her eyes heavenward at that. "It figures."

"What is that supposed to mean?"

"That was her confession book. Sinners have them for their guilt."

"I'm not here to listen to you put down our mother."

"Your mother!" Suzanne corrected angrily.

"Look, I want you to see how bad she felt about it and why she did it." Nia reached down in her bag, fumbling through a few cosmetics before she reached the diary. Looking at Suzanne, she handed it to her.

Suzanne accepted it, then threw it on the floor.

"You're so wrong!" Nia raged, bending down picking up the diary. Standing up, she studied Suzanne. Beyond the stern facial expression, Nia could see inside her eyes. They held a sorrow Suzanne refused to reveal.

Suzanne folded her arms. "I don't want to read anything written by that woman! Accidentally seeing those adoption papers in my real mother's drawer one day with your mother's signature on it is all the writing I ever needed to read of hers."

"I'm sorry you found out that way. But if you would just

read this diary, then it would explain why she gave you away. She didn't want to give up her children.''

''And I guess I forced her to give me up. Maybe a little too much crying when her men were around.''

''I'm going to ignore that, Suzanne. I just wanted you to see that life made her give you up. Her life circumstances. Sometimes we do things not because we want to but because we have to.''

''Save it. I've heard all those I-was-so-poor-I-couldn't-care-for-my-child stories.''

''I'm not asking for sympathy for her. Just a little understanding.''

''Understand what!'' She swiped up the magazine she'd been reading, then flung it harshly across the room. ''How she abandoned me! How she didn't love me enough to raise me with her other children!''

''She always loved you. If you would read the diary you would know that.''

''I'm not reading anything! And if that's all you have to say, leave!''

''I'm sorry you felt unloved.''

''Leave!''

''Mama always needed to be near you. That's why we lived a few blocks away from you. She loved you so much.''

''Then why didn't she raise me, and show me that she loved me the way she loved you and those brats?''

''By the time we came along, she was better off. She was married.''

''No, she just didn't want me. I must have been in the way of her whoring around.''

''Stop talking about her like that!''

''I'll talk about her any way I want. She didn't love me. But she did love you. Everyone always loved you, didn't they? The man I married, Kal, Roland.''

''I'm not talking about them. I'm talking about Mama. She loved you with her whole heart and soul.''

''Well I can honestly say I don't love her back.''

"That's your right. And she's dead. But you and I can start anew. Despite what you tried to do, we are sisters. I can come visit you once in a while."

"Visit me? Visit me? Woman, do you think I plan to stay here and wait to see your mug come around?"

"You're going to be here a while. You tried to kill me, Suzanne."

"And I'll try again. Not physically though. But I'll get you back just the same."

"Get me for what?"

"For always taking the love that's supposed to be mine."

"Why can't you stop feeling that way?"

"You can't tell me how to feel. You always think you can get whatever you want, don't you, Nia? You have no control over me."

"Suzanne, you have two parents who adore you. They love you so much. You had a successful career, wealth. You should have been happy."

"And I'm going to keep on living the good life when I get out of here."

"You have to pay for what you did."

"I'll get out. I'm rich, remember? And when I do, you better look out."

"I'm not looking out for anything. I'm going to be enjoying my life with Roland."

Suzanne thought that was funny. "You think so, huh?"

"I know so."

"Like I said, when I get out, I'll get you back. I'll get you back where it hurts. And you know where that is—that man of yours! He'll be mine one day."

"Suzanne, why don't you stop this competitive game with me?"

"It's no game. One day—one day soon I'm getting out. And I'm going to claim that man. He'll see you for the bore you are. I used to get to him when we worked together. I did. I know I did. And I will again. And I can't wait to see the look on your face when it all happens. I can't wait to see you suffer."

With her lips parted with her amazement, Nia was shaking her head. "You know, what's wrong with you has nothing to do with my mother giving you away. It has nothing to do with anything you may assume someone did to you. It just has to do with your soul, Suzanne. Some people in this world are evil—evil to the bone. And you're one of them, Suzanne." Nia swung her back to Suzanne, stepping to the cell bars. "Guard, let me out of here."

CHAPTER
TWENTY ONE

"Aren't you the least bit nervous?" Roland asked. Smiling, he leaned against the wall with his arms folded, scrutinizing the sensuous curves of the creature before him.

Nia and he were in the dressing room of Destiny Resort's Paradise Cove Lounge.

Looking complacently at a front view of her pink chenille gown in the mirror, Nia then swiveled around to inspect the back of it. Shaking his head at her, Roland's eyes clung to her bottom and his grin grew bigger.

Pleased with what she saw, Nia stopped her examination and focused her attention on her fiance. Dressed in a light gray suit with a matching fedora, he was absolutely gorgeous to her.

"Why should I be nervous about anything anymore? I'm happy. I'm doing what I love—singing. And it doesn't matter that Kal isn't releasing my CD. As long as I have one person in the audience that I can make smile, I'm happy."

"Do you mean that?"

"Oh yes. But mostly I'm happy because of you. You make me so happy. When I'm singing about love and how good it feels, I'm singing straight to you. Straight to you, Roland."

* * *

Blue lighting bathed the Paradise Cove Lounge as Kal strode into it, and located a seat that faced a couple. They glanced at Kal, smiled and resumed looking at the stage. Swaying their heads to Nia performing Deborah Cox's hit song "Nobody Supposed To Be Here", they were thoroughly entertained by her outpouring of emotion.

Kal also looked at the stage, unable to help giving Nia a Lord-have-mercy-look, along with a shake of his head. If there was anything he was certain of in this world, that woman could sing. Hearing her live, he imagined even more awesome songs he could write for a voice with a range and quality like hers. What's more, Kal knew he could reach millions with all the feeling she poured into her performances. All of herself she put into a song.

When the song finished, Nia smiled and bowed to the audience. If she did catch sight of Kal in the audience, she pretended that she didn't. For nothing in her expression acknowledged his presence.

The host said she would return for another song. Kal chose not to hang around. He felt compelled to go home. There was much he had to think about.

Kal heard through the grapevine that Nia and Roland were having a pool party on Saturday night. When he walked into the crowded pool area with everyone clad in swimwear, he didn't feel out of place for wearing his sweat suit or for not being invited. He checked out a few ladies before spotting Nia doing laps across the pool. She was wearing a royal blue bikini.

"Can I help you?" Kal heard suddenly.

He switched his interest from Nia's blue suit and gazed into Roland's angry face.

"Yes, you can help me."

"Not if you keep salivating over my woman like that."

Kal laughed. "I could understand a man being protective of *all that.*" He glanced at Nia, then looked at Roland.

"No disrespect."

Now Roland laughed, cynicism coloring his expression. "No disrespect? How can you say that after what you did?"

"I'm here to make up for it."

"You're here to start trouble."

"No, really, man. I am here to make up for it. I have decided to release Nia's CD."

Steadying his gaze in Kal's, Roland reared his head back. "What's the deal? What's the cost? Why now?"

Kal rubbed his chin. "I've been thinking about it. A lot of money was spent on the project. I don't want to lose that much money when I can make such a profit."

Roland looked over at Nia. Unaware of them talking, or of Kal's presence, she continued doing laps across the pool. As much as she tried to pretend it didn't bother her, Roland knew she wanted that album to be released. She had worked so hard on it. He gazed back at Kal. "All right, we would like the album released, too. But we want a new contract—one that specifies a release date."

"You got it."

"And there is something else I want understood between you and I."

"Name it."

Again, Roland steadied his eyes in Kal's. "That you understand that your relationship with my fiancée is only business. That's all it will ever be."

"I'm with that."

"Good. Now if you will excuse me, Wade is waiting for me to take over the grill."

Nia lifted herself out of the water and went drenched into the empty house in search of a towel. Finding a large orange one in the linen closet, she was standing in the hallway drying off when she heard footsteps thumping on the carpet. Before long, she stared into Kal's face.

"What are you doing here?" she asked. Quickly, she wrapped the towel around her body.

"Don't worry. I won't try to touch you," he joked. "Though that doesn't mean I'm not wishing I could."

"I'm going to tell Roland you're here."

"He knows that I'm here."

"If he does, I'm sure he doesn't know that you followed me in the house."

"I have good news for you."

"What news?" Accidentally, her towel dropped.

Swiftly Kal picked it up and handed it to her. "You don't need to put it around you. I won't touch you."

Ignoring him, she covered herself anyway. "So what's the news?"

"I'm releasing the CD."

Her heart suddenly racing, Nia clutched her chest. "You are?"

"I am." His expression became very serious. "I'm even giving you a new contract that specifies the release date."

"This is great news!" She held in the scream she wanted to unleash. "It's wonderful news!"

"I'm glad you're happy."

Moments later, Kal drove off of Roland's estate and turned on the radio. The second song to be released from Torch's CD was playing. The disc jockey claimed that "If You Could Look In My Heart" was the number one requested song. Kal smiled a bit, but soon the glee faded as he thought of the meaning of the song. At the time, some time ago, when he wrote it, Kal couldn't identify with it. Loving someone who didn't know you loved them merely seemed like a good subject to base a ballad on. He didn't love anyone at the time. Still didn't, he told himself as he drove. He didn't love anyone. Not any woman. Not even Nia. No, he didn't love her. He merely thought of her all the time. That's all it was. "Not love," he whispered. "I'm not in love. I'm not!"

The swish of the ocean resounded like music in the soundless night air. Nia and Roland stopped to face each other during a stroll along the shore.

"I'm so happy," Nia told Roland, her arms wrapping around his waist. She felt his body tensing again. "I'm so happy because of this feeling you give me. I don't want it to ever go away."

"I'll make sure it never does." Gently, he held her face with each hand. "I'll always make love to you. Not just with my body, but with the way I treat you. From the time I get up in the morning until we go to bed at night, I'll always make sure you know that you are my queen. No matter what comes along in life, no matter who comes along, no matter who or what came before—no woman in this world makes me feel like you do. You're the only one I can feel like this with, Nia. I thank God for you."

Dear Reader,

Thank you for making this a special time in my life by sharing another love story with me. I feel that true love is one of the most beautiful, exciting and precious things about life. I love to see people fall in love. I love being in love. I love writing about love.

A reader expressed that one of the reasons she enjoyed romance novels was because she liked the fact that the hero feels something for the heroine that he has never felt for anyone else. I cherish romances for that reason too, and tried to portray that type of emotion in *A Taste Of Love*. I hope you enjoyed Nia and Roland, as well as the other characters in the story.

Please feel free to write me about A Taste Of Love at:

PO Box 020648, Brooklyn, New York 11202-0648
or
Email me at LoureBus@aol.com

If you would like to share your thoughts about my other novels, *Love So True, Twist Of Fate, Most Of All* and *Nightfall*, please feel free to write. Thank you for all the letters and emails. Each one always makes my day.

I wish you many blessings of love and success.

Until next time,

Louré Bussey

ABOUT THE AUTHOR

Louré Bussey is a graduate of Borough Of Manhattan Community College. She wrote 56 short stories for romance magazines such as *Bronze Thrills* and *Black Confessions,* before her best selling novel of *Nightfall* was published in 1996. Since that debut, she has wrote the novels *Most Of All, Twist Of Fate* and *Love So True,* all which have received wonderful reviews and garnered her many fans. A former secretary and administrative assistant, she is also pursuing a music career. Presently she is recording *Loure's Songbook,* a CD based on her novels.

COMING IN SEPTEMBER ...

REMEMBER ME   (1-58314-032-8, $4.99/$6.50)
by Margie Walker
DNA lab technician Layla Griffin made a discovery that could clear
a man awaiting lethal injection for one of Texas's most sensational
murder trials. She seeks out the detective assigned to case, Sergeant
Paul Diamond, but an assault leaves her with amnesia. In order to
uncover the real murderer, Paul helps Layla recover her memory—
and thus finds love.

INTIMATE SECRETS   (1-58314-033-6, $4.99/$6.50)
by Candice Poarch
Johanna Jones returns to her hometown of Nottoway, Virginia as the
owner of the town's only hotel, only to fall head over heels for the
town's most eligible bachelor and owner of an aerospace company,
Johnathan Blake. But there is a threat to both of their businesses.
Together they find solutions and strengthen a love they didn't know
existed.

FOR KEEPS   (1-58314-034-4, $4.99/$6.50)
by Janice Sims
Cheyenne Roberts is summoned back home to Montana to restore her
family's ranch. Her neighbor is Jackson Kincaid, whom she is still
attracted to. With an injured leg, he finds himself alone with Cheyenne
in a snowed-in cabin. He can only let her nurse him back to health.
Trapped, and in close contact, they must confront their undeniable
passion.

RETURN TO LOVE   (1-58314-035-2, $4.99/$6.50)
by Viveca Carlysle
Four years ago, Trisha Terrence left a perfect love for her career. But
her partner in the bed and breakfast she owns gambled away his
share to dangerous men. Seeking refuge, she can only think of Kaliq
Faulkner's Wyoming ranch. He has mixed emotions about Trisha
staying at his ranch, but spending time together once again, they
rediscover their love.

*Available wherever paperbacks are sold, or order direct from the
Publisher. Send cover price plus 50¢ per copy for mailing and han-
dling to BET Books, c/o Kensington Publishing Corp., Consumer
Orders, or call (toll free) 888-345-BOOK, to place your order using
Mastercard or Visa. Residents of New York, Washington D.C. and
Tennessee must include sales tax. DO NOT SEND CASH.*

BOOK YOUR PLACE ON OUR WEBSITE AND MAKE THE ARABESQUE ROMANCE CONNECTION!

We've created a customized website just for our very special Arabesque readers, where you can get the inside scoop on everything that's going on with Arabesque romance novels.

When you come online, you'll have the exciting opportunity to:

- View covers of upcoming books

- Learn about our future publishing schedule (listed by publication month and author)

- Find out when your favorite authors will be visiting a city near you

- Search for and order backlist books

- Check out author bios and background information

- Send e-mail to your favorite authors

- Join us in weekly chats with authors, readers and other guests

- Get writing guidelines

- AND MUCH MORE!

Visit our website at
http://www.arabesquebooks.com